THE OTHER END

Short Stories

THE OTHER END

Short Stories

R. ELLIS ROBERTS

Edited and with an introduction by
Gina R. Collia

NEZU PRESS

Published by Nezu Press
Queensgate House,
48 Queen Street,
Exeter, Devon,
EX4 3SR,
United Kingdom.

This edition published 2024
Editorial material and introduction © Gina R. Collia 2024
The Other End: Short Stories first published by
Cecil Palmer, 1923.

ISBN-13: 978-1-7393921-7-8

In the interest of preserving the original text, it has not been altered. For the same reason, the punctuation and spelling of the original text have been maintained, and the original formatting has been used wherever possible. Only minor publisher errors and spelling inconsistencies in the original text have been silently corrected.

CONTENTS

R. Ellis Roberts
Pall Mall Gazette, 11 March 1913

R. Ellis Roberts

The Critic Who Read for Pleasure

by Gina R. Collia

Richard Ellis Roberts was born on 26 February 1879 in Islington, London.[1] His mother, Anne Catherine Corbett (1850-1936), was of Irish descent. Her father, William Corbett (1804-1873), a Surveyor General of the Inland Revenue,[2] died before his grandchildren were born. Her mother, also named Anne (1814-1893), was 'a woman of strong personality' who had a profound influence upon Richard and his siblings during their young years.[3] The Corbetts were church people with profound religious beliefs; they were 'humorous and full of the zest of life', but they regarded theatre-going and card-playing as 'temptations of the Devil.'[4]

Richard's father, also named Richard (1848-1913), was a building contractor; he and his elder brother had inherited the family firm after the death of their father, Robert Ellis Roberts, who came from Aberystwyth.[5] Richard Snr. was extremely active in his local community; he was a Justice of the Peace, vice-president of the South Islington Liberal and Radical Association, chairman of the governing body of the North London Polytechnic, and representative for South Islington on the London County Council from 1889 to 1898.[6] Unlike his parents-in-law, he was a keen theatre-goer; he served as chairman on the London County Council's Theatres and Music Halls Committee. He was, nevertheless, a profoundly religious man; he was deacon of Islington Union Church, which his family's firm had built.[7] His uncle, also named Richard Roberts, was a Justice of the Peace, chairman of the Aberystwyth Liberal

Association, deacon of the Tabernacle Calvinistic Methodist Chapel, a councillor for twenty years, and twice Mayor of Aberystwyth.[8]

At the time of Richard's birth, the Robertses were living at 57 Canonbury Park North, Canonbury,[9] but shortly afterwards they moved less than half a mile away to 10 Willow Bridge Road, where they remained for the next thirty or so years.[10] The Robertses' house was one filled with books, and 'reading seemed to come as naturally as breathing' to the Roberts children.[11] Richard was the fourth of five children. The eldest, William Corbett Roberts (1873-1953), became a clergyman; he was also a pacifist, convinced socialist, and supporter of women's suffrage.[12] William served as principal of Dorchester Missionary College (1905-1909), rector of Crick (1909-1917), of St. George's in Bloomsbury (1917-1938), and of Sutton (1938-1946), and he was rural dean of Holborn, Finsbury, and Biggleswade; he was also the chaplain of a London County Council hospital for women and girls with venereal disease, a parish councillor, and the husband of Susan Miles (pen name of Ursula Wyllie, 1887-1975).[13] Both Robert Lewis Roberts (1875-1956), 'an alert highly intelligent man as upright as he was humane and kindly,'[14] and Arthur Noel Roberts (1883-1963), the youngest of the five children, followed in their father's footsteps and became building contractors.[15] Of the Robertses' only daughter, Margaret Annie (1877-1961), we know next to nothing.[16]

Richard was educated at Merchant Taylors' School, located in Charterhouse Square in Islington, as a day-boy, then St. John's College, Oxford (BA 1901).[17] He began his career as leader writer at the *Pall Mall Gazette* in 1902 and remained with the paper until 1904.[18] He was a contributor to various periodicals over the years that followed, including the *Bookman, Daily News, Observer, Empire Review, London Mercury,* and *Guardian.*[19] In 1905, his short story 'The

Ebony Box' appeared in *The Venture: An Annual of Art and Literature*.[20] In 1906, a slim volume of his poems was published.[21] This was followed by works of non-fiction: *The Church of England* (1908), *Samuel Rogers and His Circle* (1910), and *A Roman Pilgrimage* (1911).[22] His short story 'The Samaritan' appeared in the June edition of the *Open Window*.[23] In 1912, *Henrik Ibsen: A Critical Study* was published by Martin Secker, and it received 'hearty and sincere' approval from the critic at the *Pall Mall Gazette*, who wrote, 'it is the handbook par excellence for the student who would make the acquaintance of a great poet and a great mind.'[24] His translation of Ibsen's *Peer Gynt*, published during the same year, was the basis for a production of the play at the Old Vic Theatre in London in 1935 and a 1954 television adaptation.[25] A year after his Ibsen study was published, his short story 'The Hill' appeared for the first time in the January 1913 edition of the *English Review*.[26]

On 27 September 1913, tragedy struck. Richard, suffering from 'fatigue of the eyes', went on holiday to Florence with his father, who was then sixty-six years old.[27] The two men were staying at the Hôtel Métropole when Mr Roberts was killed in a terrible accident. Mr Roberts, who was in excellent health at the time—he had climbed 2,500 feet and gone on a long walking tour a few days before his death—was looking for his son when, having climbed the stairs to the floor he expected to find Richard on, he mistook the lift entrance for that of the writing room.[28] The door to the lift had been left open and he fell to the bottom of the lift-well. He died from a fractured skull before reaching a hospital.[29] His memorial service took place at the Union Church, Islington, on 4 October.[30]

On 4 August 1914, Britain entered the First World War. Richard continued to contribute reviews for the *Daily News* throughout the war years, though less frequently when he himself joined the war effort, and in 1915 his short story 'The Minotaur' was published in the June edition of the *English Review*; it was described by the *Westminster Gazette* as 'a very pleasant piece of fooling'.[31] In 1916, he became a First Division Clerk at the Admiralty, and he remained in that post until 1918.[32] Richard later claimed that it was thanks to him that British seamen could have their teeth filled at the British government's expense; prior to his time at the Admiralty, the government would only foot the bill if teeth were pulled out.[33]

In 1920, Richard married Philadelphia-born divorcée Harriet Ide Keen (1885-1971), daughter of Herbert Ide Keen (1858-1931) and Elizabeth Lyon Doebler (1863-1957). Harriet's father was the European manager of the Allis Chalmars Manufacturing Co., of Milwaukee—an American company that had offices in London and Paris—and in 1909, after visiting Italy and France,[34] the Keen family had moved to England.[35] In 1911, Harriet married Alfred Emil Wenner, and the couple lived in Manchester until in 1915, when the marriage broke down and Harriet returned to her parents' home in Hampstead, London.[36] The couple had one child, Herbert, who died in infancy.[37] In the spring of 1919, the Keens moved to Paris, to 9 Rue Bayard, and Harriet was granted a divorce later that year.[38] Richard and Harriet were married in Paris on 5 April the following year.[39] The couple returned to England and took up residence at Highcroft, The Edge, Stroud, in Gloucestershire.[40]

Richard had a liking for the unusual and uncanny. He wrote, in a review of books by B. M. Croker and Jack London for the *Daily News*, that the novelist who prides himself on 'transcribing life', the author who writes about etiquette and the such like, forgets mankind's desire for something different; 'If it were not for that itch for the unusual, we might still be groping on all fours and speaking the guttural esperanto employed by the great apes.'[41]

He was an admirer of Arthur Machen; in September 1922 he wrote an appreciative article about the author's work for the *Bookman* (see p. 217),[42] and five months later, in February 1923, he wrote a favourable review of *Things Near and Far* for the *Daily News* (see p. 223).[43] The following year, a long appreciation of Machen's work was published in the *Sewanee Review,* the American literary magazine (see p. 226), and in 1933 he reviewed *The Green Round* (see p. 231).[44]

In January 1923, Cecil Palmer published *The Other End,* Richard's only collection of short stories. It is made up of three sections, each containing three stories, and between each section is an 'interlude' or 'commentary', producing a total of twelve stories. It appears that only four of these had appeared previously in periodicals: 'The Ebony Box', 'The Samaritan', 'The Hill', and 'The Minotaur'. The collection received extremely good reviews, with Ethel Colburn Mayne describing the author's style as 'serene, yet glancing constantly with wit and humour; lucid, with the lucidity of deep, bright water, and the beauty of that water's living movement'.[45] The *Liverpool Daily Post* described Richard as 'a writer of quite unusual power and originality':

> 'Mr. Roberts is not content with the mere thrill of the strange and uncanny, though he gets that excellently, but rather rests his effect on the sense of the vital reality of these unrecognised powers, whose presence seems, indeed, less an intrusion upon our world than upon theirs.'[46]

The reviewer for the *Bookman* declared the author 'as well able to write stories of his own as to criticise those of others', having achieved a mastery of his subject that at times 'challenges comparison with Poe and Hawthorne'.[47]

> 'For all the uncanny air that enfolds these stories, the supernatural elements in them are so quietly taken for granted,

and are blended with so much of everyday circumstance that even their unrealities are made to seem curiously real.'[48] Gerald Gould, in the *Saturday Review*, wrote that 'Mr. Roberts is so good a scholar, so good a psychologist, and so good a writer, that he makes it all seem real', and that no nervous person should read the book when 'alone at night in a remote cottage on a lonely moor'.[49] Any attempt to summarise the stories, as the *Bookman*'s reviewer pointed out, would misrepresent them; 'they depend so much for their effectiveness on the atmosphere in which they are steeped, of little details of character and incident' that serve to convince the reader that all happening within them is utterly real. In addition to being disturbing, the tales are at times touching, ironic, funny, and often thought-provoking; 'there is a telling criticism of life as our culture has made it'.[50] The response to *The Other End* was so positive that it is a wonder—and a great shame—that Richard wrote no further uncanny tales.

On 8 October 1923, Richard gave a lecture, entitled 'The Other Side', to the Gloucester Literary Club, which took place at the Guildhall, Gloucester.[51] In it, he said it was to Edgar Allan Poe that we owe 'the transformation of modern fiction'; had it not been for Poe, he explained, we may never have found 'in greater artists that inner and mystic beauty which distinguishes their greatest works'.[52] It was Poe who had showed the way, and, as a result, Henry James, Joseph Conrad, Kipling, H. G. Wells, and May Sinclair had all attempted 'the literature of "the other side" '.[53]

In 1925, Richard and Harriet met and became firm friends with Max Bierbaum and his wife, Florence.[54] From that point on, whenever the Bierbaums were in London they spent a great deal of time with the Robertses; the two couples also met abroad, in Switzerland and Italy. And in August 1946, when Max and Florence were suffering some financial hardship and were in need of a place to live, Richard, who by that time was living in America, wrote offering them his house in Gloucestershire; the Bierbaums remained there until they left England at the end of September 1947.[55]

Richard was a literary columnist for the *Guardian* from 1924 to 1933.[56] In November 1926, he was involved in a libel action between the Guardian and James Evershed Agate, drama critic for the *Sunday Times* and the BBC. Agate sued Guardian Publications Ltd., Rev. F. A. Iremonger, and the Bucks Free Press—the newspaper's proprietor, editor, and printer—following the publication of a review of his book, *Agate's Folly*, in the *Guardian* on 20 November 1925. The review, Agate claimed, imputed that he had 'not wit, manners, or decency';[57] the reviewer, his counsel argued, accused him of being responsible for the deterioration and degradation of the British stage. The defendants pleaded that the words of the reviewer—Richard Ellis Roberts—had been 'fair and bona fide comment and criticism on a matter of public interest.'[58] Mr Justice Avory pointed out that it was the right of every person to comment upon a work that had been published to the world, and he objected to the idea of a critic suing another critic for criticising him. The jury found in favour of Mr Avery but awarded him damages of only one farthing, and he had to pay his own costs.[59]

Richard was an avid reader; he was rarely seen without a book in his hands. He loved to read poetry aloud and, according to his friend Robinson Jeffers, it seemed that 'there was not a book of any literary pretension, great book or small one, at least since the eighteenth century, that he had not read and digested, and more or less enjoyed.'[60] In 1928, Methuen & Co. published Richard's *Reading for Pleasure*, a collection of short essays, every page of which 'bristles with strongly-marked opinions, enthusiastic likes and dislikes' and is filled with 'good things'.[61] On the subject of making time to read—and proving that very little has changed over the past hundred years—he writes:

'To read well is to read at leisure; and modern life is losing leisure. There are, now, all over the world, groups of people, large and small, to whom leisure is a variety of boredom: people who never sit and watch, who see nothing of beauty because they never look long enough at anything, and hear nothing of the world's loveliness because they are deafened with their own din.'[62]

Richard was on the staff of the *Church Times* when, in 1930, Clifford Sharp appointed him to the role of literary editor at the *New Statesman* on a salary of £1,000 a year.[63] Unfortunately, he didn't hit it off with his new colleagues; he was a professional who could be relied upon to do his job without supervision, but he wore a cloak and a wide-brimmed hat and had too much 'character';[64] He was described by the *Liverpool Daily Post* as 'picturesque-looking';[65] T. S. Eliot referred to him as 'Chadband'.[66] A 'High Anglican man-of-letters', V. S. Pritchett described him as being 'like a soft fat cooing priest', and when Kingsley Martin, who hated religion, took over Sharp's job in 1931 he and Richard argued frequently.[67] Richard was the only writer whose contributions Martin could not stomach; he found his writing 'intolerable'.[68] Martin wanted rid of him, and he made his intentions so apparent that Harriet Roberts threatened him with legal action to deter him from sacking her husband.[69] In the end, Richard didn't survive in his post much past the 1931 merger of the *New Statesman* and the *Nation*, though he remained a contributor for well over a decade.[70]

In September 1932, a new feature, entitled 'Books and Men', was announced in the feminist weekly *Time and Tide*, to be contributed by one 'Richard Sunne', a pen name of Richard Ellis Roberts.[71] The following spring, Richard joined the periodical's staff as literary editor. But its founder, Lady Margaret Rhondda, felt that, despite his feminism, Richard would not find it easy to take orders from a woman, and he did prove difficult to manage. Also, his contributions were not regarded as being good enough 'for a literary number which all the high-brows read and criticise'.[72] A year later *Time and Tide* was looking for a new literary editor, and Richard was replaced in the summer of 1934.

In the spring of 1933, Richard joined Basil de Selincourt, the chief reviewer for the *Observer*, as a book critic for BBC Radio. Neither man's role was expected to last very long; the programmes were popular, but when it came to hiring reviewers the BBC appeared at the time to be engaged in 'a sort of literary musical chairs'.[73] 'Book News' aired every Monday and lasted about twenty minutes, and the following October Richard began presenting 'Some New Books on Religion', which was broadcast every Sunday until the autumn of 1939. In September 1934, Richard replaced Hamish Smile as editor of *Life and Letters*, which had just been bought by Constable and Company.[74] He remained editor until 1936, with some assistance from Desmond MacCarthy, the journal's founder.[75] In December 1935, he began writing 'A London Letter' for the *Saturday Review*,[76] to which, from 1941, he also contributed regular book reviews.

In the summer of 1939, while Richard was in France, Macmillan published his *Portrait of Stella Benson*. A few months later, as war broke out in Europe, Richard and Harriet moved to America. They travelled from Le Verdon, France, on 15 October 1939 on the *SS Manhattan*,[77] arriving in New York on the 22nd of that month.[78] The Robertses settled in Carmel, in California; their Arts & Crafts home,

Cypress House, situated on Valley View Road, was built in 1926 for Ralph Fletcher Seymour, the artist and author, and was one of the first houses to be built on Carmel Point.[79] To his new American neighbours, Richard had the appearance of 'a Victorian romantic poet exiled into a strange world'.[80] Elizabeth Paine, who interviewed him for the *Carmel Pine Cone* in 1941, as he sat before his bow window taking snuff from a silver box, described him as 'disarmingly folksy'.[81]

Following his arrival in America, despite the fact that his health by then was not the best,[82] Richard remained as active as ever. In the spring of 1941, while wintering at Wade Place House in Marshallville, Georgia, he lectured at the University of the South in Suwanee, Tennessee, and the University of Georgia.[83] On 9 March, he gave a lecture, 'Your England and My America', at the Piedmont Driving Club in Atlanta. At the time of his interview for the *Carmel Pine Cone*, he had just finished working on *H. R. L. Sheppard: Life and Letters*, which was published by John Murray the following year, and he was preparing to set out on a transcontinental lecture tour the following spring.[84]

On 28 November 1942, Richard gave his 'Your England and My America' talk at the Carmel Playhouse in aid of 'Bundles for Britain',[85] to an appreciative and unusually large audience; he appears to have been regarded as something of a celebrity by the residents of his new home. In referring to his qualifications for lecturing on the subject of England, Richard pointed out that he was of mixed ancestry—'Welsh, French, English, Scotch, and Norman'—and that he was very proud of the fact, because the 'best kind of human being is the mongrel, and there has never been any "pure blood" nonsense either in the island of England or the continent of America'.[86] When explaining his qualifications for speaking about

America, he said he could claim only that 'an American woman married me'.[87]

During the following years, Richard contributed articles, reviews, poems, and an obituary for Mary DeNeale Morgan, the plein air painter, to the *Carmel Pine Cone*. He gave lectures and readings at social gatherings and in schools and churches, and he and his wife became very much involved in the Women's Auxiliary of All Saints' Church in Carmel. He continued working right up until his final illness, about three months before his death; he died on 5 October 1953, at the age of seventy-four. In 1941 he had begun working on an autobiography, and he was still working on it when he died.[88] Sadly, it was never completed.

Many of Carmel's resident called Richard Ellis Roberts friend, and many wrote to the *Carmel Pine Cone* to pay tribute to him when he died; they had been deprived 'of a distinguished man of letters' whose presence 'gave dignity and purpose to any gathering and lifted it above the usual channels of concern'.[89] He stood for 'self-restraint in an age of self-indulgence, for patient study in a world of short cuts, for reality in an epoch of false values, plastic and pretence'.[90] A man who disliked show and falsehood, there was to be no funeral parlour and mortician's make-up for him; his sealed coffin was allowed to remain throughout the night before his funeral in the church where he worshipped during the last years of his life, St. James' Episcopal Church in Monterey.[91]

> 'Such a man dies yet he does not die. He leaves with us his inner stature and achievement. We who are conscious only of human presence feel deprived and grieved, but when the attainment of a life is in the realm of mind there is something beyond loss. The gifts remain in an undying form.'[92]

Notes

1   *England & Wales, Civil Registration Birth Index, 1837-1915* and *California, U.S. Death Index, 1940-1997.*

2   *1861 England Census.*

3   Susan Miles, *Portrait of a Parson.* London: George Allen and Unwin, Ltd., 1955, p. 10.

4   Ibid.

5   B. 1816, d. 1877. *1851 England Census.*

6   *South WalesDaily News*, 24 January 1889, p. 2, and *Islington Gazette*, 7 January 1898.

7   Miles, op. cit., p.11.

8   *South Wales Daily News*, 26 February 1876, p. 6.

9   *UK, Poll Books and Electoral Registers, 1538-1893* and *London, England, Freedom of the City Admission Papers, 1681-1930.*

10 *1881 England Census.*

11 Miles, op. cit., p.11.

12 *Biggleswade Chronicle*, 23 June 1950, p. 7.

13 *Northampton Mercury*, 6 February 1953, p. 2. *Biggleswade Chronicle*, 23 June 1950, p. 7. *Berks and Oxon Advertiser*, 8 March 1907, *Surrey Mirror*, 29 September 1908, p. 4.

14 Charles Orwell Brasch, *Indirections: A Memoir 1909-1947.* Wellington: Oxford Univerity Press, 1980, p. 152.

15 *1911 England Census.*

16 Margaret Annie Roberts was thirty-three years old, single, and living with her parents and brother Richard in 1911 (see *1911 England Census* and *England & Wales, Civil Registration Birth Index, 1837-1915*, Q3). She never married, and she died in Gloucester on 23 December 1956 (see *England & Wales, National Probate Calendar (Index of Wills and Administration), 1858-1995).*

17 'Richard Ellis Roberts', *The Canterbury Dictionary of Hymnology*. Canterbury Press, http://www.hymnology.co.uk/r/richard-ellis-roberts.

18 *Who's Who in Literature*. Liverpool: Literary Year Books Press, Ltd., 1933, p. 424.

19 Ibid.

20 Published by John Baillie, only two issues of the annual were produced: 1903 and 1905. 'The Ebony Box' appeared on p. 65 of the 1905 issue.

21 *Poems* was published by Brimley Johnson & Ince.

22 *The Church of England* was published by Francis Griffiths, *Samuel Rogers and His Circle* was published by Methuen & Company, and *A Roman Pilgrimage* was published by Frederick A. Stokes Company.

23 *Westminster Gazette*, 2 June 1911, p. 12.

24 *Pall Mall Gazette*, 24 June 1912, p. 9.

25 *Peer Gynt: A New Translation*. London: Martin Secker, 1912. *Western Mail*, 24 September 1935, p. 8, and the *Sketch*, 17 November 1954, p. 24.

26 *Scotsman*, 6 January 1913, p. 2.

27 *Pall Mall Gazette*, 1 October 1913, p. 4.

28 Ibid.

29 *Holloway Press*, 3 October 1913, p. 2.

30 *Westminster Gazette*, 3 October 1913, p. 6.

31 *Westminster Gazette*, 4 June 1915, p. 3.

32 Sabine Wichert, *From the United Irishmen to Twentieth-century Unionism*. Dublin: Four Courts Press, 2004, p. 126.

33 'Carmel Gets Real British Lion in Person of Ellis Roberts', *Carmel Pine Cone*, 28 August 1941, p. 10.

34 *U.S., Passport Applications, 1795-1925: Emergency Passport Applications*, Paris, France.

35 *U.S., Consular Registration Applications, 1916-1925*.

36 *U.S., Consular Registration Applications, 1916-1925*. The Keens lived at Canon Lodge, Canon Place, Hampstead, see 1911 England Census.

37 *England & Wales, FreeBMD Birth Index, 1837-1915*, and *England & Wales Civil Registration Death Index, 1937-1915*.

38 *U.S., Consular Registration Applications, 1916-1925.*

39 *California, U.S., Federal Naturalization Records, 1843-1999.*

40 *1921 England Census and England & Wales, National Probate Calendar (Index of wills and Administrations), 1858-1995.*

41 *Daily News*, 26 August 1919, p. 6.

42 *The Bookman*, September 1922, pp. 240-242.

43 *Daily News*, 22 February 1923, p. 7.

44 *Seawnee Review*, July 1924, pp. 353-356, and the *Daily News*, 13 July 1933.

45 *Daily News*, 30 January 1923, p. 7.

46 *Liverpool Daily Post*, 11 April 1923, p. 8.

47 *The Bookman*, September 1923, p. 290.

48 Ibid.

49 *Saturday Review*, 10 February 1923, p. 190.

50 *Liverpool Daily Post*, 11 April 1923, p. 8.

51 *Gloucester Journal*, 13 October 1923, p. 8.

52 Ibid.

53 Ibid.

54 David Cecil, *Max: A Biography*. Boston: Houghton Mifflin, 1965, p. 407.

55 Ibid., p. 461.

56 *World Biography: Fourth Edition of the Biographical Encyclopedia of the World*. New York: Institute for Research in Biography, Vol. 2, 1948, p. 4020.

57 *Stage*, 11 November 1926, p. 23.

58 Ibid.

59 Ibid.

60 Robinson Jeffers, 'In Tribute…', *Carmel Pine Cone*. Carmel, 9 October 1953, p. 1.

61 *Daily News*, 3 October 1928, p. 4.

62 R. Ellis Roberts, *Reading for Pleasure*. London: Metheun & Co., Ltd., 1928, p. 3.

63 Adrian Smith, *The New Statesman: Portrait of a Political Weekly, 1913-1931*. London: F. Cass & Co. Ltd., 1996. p. 187. Clifford Sharp (1883-1935) was the first editor of the *New Statesman*.

64 Edward Hyams, *The New Statesman: The History of the First Fifty Years 1913-1963*. London: Longmans Green and Co. Ltd., 1963, p. 161.

65 *Liverpool Daily Post*, 3 December 1932, p. 6.

66 Letter to Emily Hale, 16 June 1935 (The Estate of T. S. Eliot). Mr Chadband is a character from Charles Dickens's *Bleak House*; he is a self-serving, hypocritical sermoniser. Eliot also referred to Harriet Roberts as 'an American bore'—Letter to Geoffrey Faber (of Faber & Faber), 20 August 1934 (The Estate of T. S. Eliot).

67 Hyams, op. cit., p. 156, and V. S. Prithett, *Midnight Oil*. New York: Random House, 1972, p. 201. Kingsley Martin was editor of the *New Statesman* from 1931 to 1960.

68 Kingsley Martin, *Father Figures: The Evolution of an Editor, 1897-1931*. Chicago: Henry Regnery Company, 1970, p. 199.

69 Hyams, op. cit., p. 163.

70 Smith, op. cit., p. 187.

71 *The Calcutta Review*, University of Calcutta, 1937, pp. 340 and 345.

72 Catherine Clay, *Time and Tide: The Feminist and Cultural Politics of a Modern Magazine*. Edinburgh: Edinburgh University Press, p. 198.

73 *Publishers' Weekly*, 22 April 1933, p. 1334.

74 Marina Camboni, *Networking Women: Subjects, Places, Links, Europe-America. Towards a Rewriting of Cultural History, 1890-1939*. Rome: Edizioni di Storia e Letteratura, 2004, p. 376.

75 Andrew Thacker and Peter Brooker, *The Oxford Critical and Cultural History of Modernist Magazines, Volume I: Britain and Ireland 1880-1955*. Oxford: Oxford University Press, 2009, p. 429.

76 *Saturday Review*, 7 December 1935, p. 30.

77 *New York, U.S. Arriving Passenger and Crew Lists, 1820-1957*.

78 *California, U.S., Federal Naturalization Records, 1843-1999*.

79 Alissandra Dramov and Lynn A. Momboisse, *Historic Homes and Inns of Carmel-by-the-Sea*. Mount Pleasant: Arcadia Publishing, 2016, p. 33.

80 Bruno Adriani (the sculptor), *Carmel Pine Cone*. Carmel, 9 October 1953, p. 12.

81 Elizabeth Paine, 'Carmel Gets Real British Lion in Person of Ellis Roberts', *Carmel Pine Cone*, 28 August 1941, p. 10.

82 *Atlanta Constitution*, 9 March 1941, p. 11A.

83 *Atlanta Constitution*, 4 March 1941, p. 15.

84 *Atlanta Constitution*, 9 March 1941, p. 11A.

85 'Bundles for Britain' was an American voluntary organisation founded by Natalie Wales Latham in 1940 to send supplies to Britain during the Second World War. It began as a knitting circle, sending knitted socks to British sailors, but grew rapidly and eventually sent clothing, X-ray machines, bedding, ambulances, and medical supplies to Britain. Harriet became the vice-chairman of the Carmel branch (see the *Carmel Pine Cone*, 8 January 1943, p. 4).

86 *Carmel Pine Cone*, 4 December 1942, p. 1.

87 Ibid.

88 'R. Ellis Roberts', *Carmel Pine Cone*. 9 October 1953, p. 1.

89 Dora Hagemeyer, *Carmel Pine Cone*. 9 October 1953, p. 12.

90 Claude M. Kinnoull, *Carmel Pine Cone*. 16 October 1953, p. 7.

91 Ibid.

91 Hegemeyer, op. cit.

I

INVASION

We strain our eyes out yonder; where are powers
Who would fain break this fragile world of ours.

THE HILL

I T was one of those hard, precise evenings when, before sunset, everything seems to become flat: the fields that lay just in front of me were cut out of cardboard, the long road down to Broad Oak appeared to stretch, not to the country, but to a backcloth; and the trees that overarched the lane to Symondsbury were untouched by any breeze that might give them the illusion of reality. For, when the country takes the decorative note, it is reality which is the illusion: one almost imperceptibly flattens oneself along the hedgerows in order to avoid breaking the perfect truth of the theatre which Nature contrives so much more skilfully than man.

I was tired and walked a little listlessly. I had business to do in Bridport; but I knew I should be there long before seven, and I enjoyed sauntering down the road, while the decadent sun of early April made green tinsel out of the budding larches, while soft little puddles of brown glowed from the ruts and hoofmarks in the sandy soil. I was feeling well in a genially tired way, and quite ready for the walk home again; feeling, however, singularly un- sharp. I mean that my senses, after the exertions of the week, were rather sleep-haunted—I had caught Nature's lesson, and felt all the activity of limb and thought to be the substance of nothing but a rather beautiful dream. My mind was as casual as my walk, and was occupied, so far as I remember, with nothing more arresting than some vaguely pleasant remembrance of a youthful affection.

I dwell on all this because I want to insist that I was not in an observant mood, not at all in the state to make the adventure I had likely. Those to whom I have told this story have all insisted that my "imagination" or "fancy" has made more of the facts than they warrant; that I was deceived by shadows, or misled by reflections; that my eyes were tired and played me tricks, that my memory is false and ill-suited to exact accuracy. So I would insist that such imagination as I have was almost quiescent, that my mind was singularly unalert, and that nothing can explain the extreme vividness of my recollection of that night of April 3rd, except the truth of what I saw. Its very incongruity, not only with my mental condition, but with the actual character of the evening, with the verdant artificiality of that Dorset springtime, when the countryside is rather less actual than the contours on an ordnance map, is a witness to the reality of that experience.

I had indeed forgotten the Hill. I generally used to look out for the first sight of it, when the road begins to run under the shoulder of the wooded height, and to skirt the Hill of Sacrifice. I don't know who gave it that name: whether, indeed, it is more than a modern device of some local journalist; but it suits the Hill. Everyone who passes along the main road from Chideock to Bridport must see it; but its most characteristic aspect is only caught from the road between North Chideock and Symondsbury. It is a curious, conical hill, covered with green grass and generally delivered over to innumerable sheep. It reminds one instantly of those hight places on which the ancient Hebrews honoured other gods than Jehovah, the places where Solomon built temples for the family godlings of his heathen queens. Everyone felt this about the Hill, so it does not show any preoccupation of mine that I, too, always connected it with sacrifice, and the stone, square altars of the old faiths. I had never been up the Hill. I never met anyone who had. It was out of the way, and would be, though an easy, an unnecessary little climb for one whom Fleet Street had left without the wind of his youth. The sheep which grazed there belonged to a farm in the valley, and found their own way up and down.

Well, as I said, on that night I had forgotten the Hill; and when I caught my first glimpse of it, I had a shock. I thought at first the shock was due to the vision of a familiar but forgotten object. I think when one, so to speak, re-sees a perfectly familiar object, it has a more active and energizing effect on the nerves than contact with something entirely new. Certainly the Hill made me jump. I stood and stared at it. As I stared I realised that the shock I had received was not entirely due to the Hill's re-assertion of its presence to my forgetful mind.

The Hill was different.

I glanced hastily back along the road, and over to my left where the fields stretched idly away; they were the same as they had been a minute ago, comfortable, artificial, flat, with no more atmosphere than a landscape in a modern painting. Then I swerved back to the Hill. It was ominous, alive, clamant with some mystery that I had not guessed. I should explain that though it was the Hill of Sacrifice, no one had associated it with anything mysterious or unusual. It was obviously the servant of some settled, rather courtly, religion, where the priests of the second-century Roman, journeying from Dorchester, had made polite augury at dawn. This evening, all that was changed. The Hill threatened. It quarrelled vehemently with the rest of the landscape. It stood like something or somebody naked and hairy in the middle of a crowd of modish and courtly figures; it was like some primitive, pre-Gothic idol in a French classical temple; or as if you sundered a picture of Watteau's with one of those brown, watchful Tahitians of Gauguin's.

I stood and stared at the Hill. And as I stared I became aware of two things. First, there were no sheep on the Hill. Their absence aided the strange, nude look of the thing. And I began to think that perhaps, after all, the change in the Hill was my fancy. Then, as I looked, the Hill lurched: that, of course, is an exaggeration; but it was the effect made on me by the movement of something that was almost up on the round crown at the top. With that movement the power of the Hill became active: suddenly and as by antagonism, I, too, leapt into mental alertness. The Hill and I were there, enemies, but akin in this, that we were the players in the set scene; still the green fields spread away to the backcloth; still the road ran as a stage runs to the wings; still the sun, though now faintlier, flickered on green and brown, and turned them to paper and canvas—but now there were two lives on the stage, and the play was begun.

Before starting for the Hill—it is noteworthy that no other course but that of immediate access to my antagonist ever seemed possible—I looked at it once more, for I knew when I had scrambled through the hedge and across the first field, I should lose sight, for a while, of the top: I looked at the spot where the Hill had shuddered, and I saw that it was a figure, apparently human, and heavily burdened, which was now on the top and against the blue-black clouds which the sun was even now burning into angry gold. I was now much too far away—I have always suffered from short-sightedness—to make out clearly whether it was man or woman, or what it was that the figure carried; nor indeed did I greatly care, but I got through the hedge and started as quickly as I could for the summit of the Hill.

In the second field it was darker; and I felt that the atmosphere was a trifle oppressive; and there was a heavy, hot smell in the air, like musk. Of course, by now my imagination was at work; but I was not consciously inventing any explanation of what I saw or felt. I was simply bringing to bear on facts that were obtrusive all I had of perception and sensitiveness. I had not even then definitely decided whether what was abroad was evil or not. I knew it was an enemy—but it was inimical, at present, only in the sense of demanding effort and conflict. I could not proclaim that it was evil. As I climbed towards the lower slopes of the Hill, still hidden from view by a thick hedge, I was not conscious of any definite aim. I knew where I had to go; but I had no idea of what I should find, or what I should do. Just before I reached the final hedge something happened which removed all doubt as to the nature of that which I had to fight. Abruptly, and beginning on one long piercing note, a strange music clove the surrounding silence. After the first shrill rending of the evening's solitary quiet, the music went on with a wicked and luxuriant abandon that recalled to me all that I knew of the vague power of harmony for evil. It was not vulgarly lascivious or alluring; it had in it that higher note of defiance, that keener note of pride and power and of certain, though dishonourable, rule which distinguishes the ream of the devil from that of the world and the flesh. It had in it that perverse ascetic note, that strain of rapture and endeavour and adventure which the sons of Satan achieve no less than the sons of Christ. It gave out no single note of compromise or concession: it was music of the airless heights, of the wilderness, of the great wastes of sand, or the interminable vastness of evil waters where the greater devils meditate and morosely scheme.

When I heard it, all doubt dropped from me. There dropped, too, everything of the present. I knew the music: I knew, somehow, the player; and I knew his instrument. And as I went on up the Hill I knew what task lay before me, and with Whom I was to wrestle. I felt no fear and no confidence. No fear as to the terror or extent of the conflict, and no confidence as to the result. The whole incident, though still to come, seemed a part of my life, not something that I could do, or could not do, so much as something without which I would not be I.

When I was through the hedge the sun was set, but it was still quite light, and I hoped it would not be dark for almost another hour. I looked up to the top of the Hill, and there was the figure I had seen, kneeling and piling stones on one another. He—for it was a young lad—was half turned towards me; but he was stooping over his work, and evidently had no idea of my approach. The music, which was getting louder every moment, seemed to come from the top of the Hill; but I could see no signs of the player: nor, indeed, had I expected to.

I looked carefully to my stick, and wished it had been of some stouter wood than cherry; and then started rapidly up the Hill. As I went on the music altered in character: from defiance it passed to menace, and from menace to a curious thin anger that somehow seemed intended for other ears than mine. It was. The lad looked up, puzzled, and I saw him distinctly say something towards the sound of the music. Then he saw me, recognised me, I think, and started down the Hill. The music stopped.

I went on, and after a few minutes the lad and I met. We were both a little out of breath, and stood for a moment at gaze. He was a singularly beautiful boy, with one of those faces in which it is so hard to discover the lines which will afterwards coarsen and harden. He was about seventeen, and I remember that I had seen him working on some job between Allington and Eype. At the moment his beauty was almost unearthly: it had no intellectual qualities, and little of character, but just that even bloom which marks young animals. There was in his eyes, however, a look far from animal— a look of exultation, of absorption, and combined with it a hardness that showed me my task would not be easy. What he said was in curious contrast with his appearance, and in even odder discordance with what was in our hearts, and in the heart of the Hill, and in the heart of that old musician who this night, at least, was claiming the worship of his ancient altar.

"You be trespassing, Mr. O'Brien."

"I suppose I am," I answered. "It's so jolly to be in a country where trespassing doesn't do any harm. It's why I like Dorset, and these great grazing fields."

He looked at me as the country folk do when they don't quite catch what you say, and yet don't want to confess it.

"No one be allowed up here. I must ask you to go down again, Sir."

His tone was very polite; but his eyes were set, and I saw his fingers twitching, and noticed the tremor of his shirt above his scurrying heart.

"Nonsense," I said. "I'm going to the top. Good night to you," and I started to get past him, rather hurriedly and with little dignity, I am afraid.

With a sharp cry he stepped in front of me. Before he could say anything more, I spoke again, as sharply as I could—for I would have given anything just then to avoid the fight, and for the lad to go home—"What on earth are you doing, boy? You now perfectly well Mr. Goodere doesn't mind where I go on his land. Besides, you have no business here: you are not in his employ, and I don't know that he would allow you here. Get out of my way."

For the moment my tone of ordinary annoyance staggered him. He became—for a minute—an ordinary good-looking lad who, through clumsiness, had offended "one of the gentry," and made a fool of himself. I kept hold on myself and waited to see him go away, apologetic and abashed. If this was the fight, I had feared unnecessarily. He began to turn on his heel, muttering some excuse, and I went on upwards, when suddenly the music began again, insistent, defiant, challenging. In a second he rushed around; and with hot, hurried words, clung to my arm, impeding my way—"I was not to go—he was meeting his girl—he wouldn't let me—he would break me if I did—he would——" lies, and appeals, and foul threats followed each other as swift as sin; his face once more took on that strange look of unearthly beauty, of curious exultation, as he asked me not to go up the Hill.

And the music played faster and faster.

After a struggle that lasted, I suppose, but for a few minutes, I broke away from him and ran towards the summit. All pretence was now thrown aside. The lad knew that I was aware of his purpose: knew that I knew Who his companion would be, and what that awful music meant, as it broke the evening quiet of the spring fields with a challenge older and more hideous than any voice of cities or of civilisation.

I got to the top of the Hill, with the lad close on my heels: and when I was at the top I realised suddenly that it was night. Not, I think, that the ordinary world was yet dark, but a mist, acrid and pungent, hung over the top of the Hill, and seemed to settle on the rude altar which the boy had built.

I could not see him, but I heard his breathing close on my right. I thought I would try one last chance to avoid the conflict—for now fear had entered my very marrow. "Come down," I said, trying to make my voice as self-possessed as possible and as ordinary, "Come down and I'll go too."

There was no answer but his quick breathing; and then on a note of the music he began to sing. When he sang there was little trace of Dorset in his speech, and his voice was a beautiful treble, that of a boy whose voice is going to break later than usual. What he sang I cannot put down here. It soared up in unimaginable wickedness, clear and pure as crystal, full of thoughts and words that we believe to have forsaken our world. The music adapted itself to his song and grew subtly and insolently wicked. The psalm of Satan rose up, invitatory, clarion, ascending to heights of sin that I did not know had ever been expressed in human word. The air grew hotter, and the mist glowed with a strange blurred light. The keen, acrid smell grew more intense, and the music shrieked more and more riotously, as though preluding some monstrous apocalypse.

Then, with no warning, there was silence.

I could hear nothing, not even my own breathing; and I could see nothing but the blurred glow that was, I judged, just over the altar. Then I heard a sound. It was a voice, but of an accent not human, and the words it spoke were not English. I remember how, even then, it struck me as odd that one should hear a voice in a Dorset field speaking in tones that belonged neither to the place nor the age I lived in. It sounded very low, very sure, and very old; old not with any quavering, but with that sacerdotal certainty of age-long experience which people who are very old, or of a great tradition, so frequently possess. Yet any certainty I had caught in human voices seemed but a shadow beside the deep, awful solemnity of this utterance. The voice was magical, ecstatic, assured with an eternal assurance. I strained my ears to listen during the few seconds while the voice continued, but I could distinguish nothing except what I thought possibly was the syllable "Pai," and I wondered if the sentence was in Greek.

My senses by now were singularly acute: I had passed through fear into that strong, wine-glowing condition when one watches everything securely, oneself being external even to the dangers that are threatening one's body or soul. In this state, and in the boldness engendered by it, I took one step towards the glow that still shone over the altar. Long before I could approach, however, I was smitten—or rather not so much smitten as involved in a thick, palpable, and hideous atmosphere. Never have I been so submerged by anything external. The sensation was partly like that caused by a quicksand, which will wrestle with one's leg or arm as though the sand were endowed with life, and when one pulls out the endangered limb, it is as if one sprung out of some being's lively jaws. So with an automatic movement of repulsion, I leapt back and was released. Then the light glowed more brightly and I saw my companion. He was standing stark naked, with his arms outstretched like an Orante's on a Catacomb fresco. His lips were still moving, and his gaze fixed intently on the glow above the rude stones he had piled up. Every moment the glow increased; I was only just over three yards from the altar, but the glow gave no heat, neither was there any smoke. Then as the light grew, in the centre of it there appeared a figure, and yet not so much a figure as a face, not so much a face as a presence. It had the same beauty, that intolerable and sinful beauty which the boy had; or rather it seemed to *be* that beauty. It was, however, never still, but passed with incredible rapidity from the expression of one sensation to that of another; it had that most singular quality which can occasionally be seen on earthly faces, a complete lack of unity—there was no central and availing character in which the details might inhere, and it was this lack which gave the Presence its extraordinary sense of wrongness, of wickedness, of sin. It is vulgar comparison, but the mode of its loveliness, the mode of its very expression, reminded me of nothing so much as a cinematograph, that dreadful invention in which the mimicry of

Life treads breathlessly and continuously on the heels of Life itself, and yet neither attains it. The same absolute lack of peace, of joy, of truth, shone at me from the glow on the Hill of Symondsbury.

As I was looking, feeling numbed and rather sick from my effort to penetrate that infernal barrier which surrounded the altar, the boy stooped down and picked up something which had escaped my notice. When he stood up again I saw it was a spaniel which from the droop of its head was either drugged or dead—I guessed the former. Round its neck was a cord, and at the end of the cord a knife, whose blade glanced in the strange glow, gleaming uneasily in the shadow of the night. Carrying the spaniel the boy stepped forward. I waited anxiously. He, when he was within the circle of the light, not only appeared to feel no discomfort, but looked lighter, more at ease, supremely healthy. If it had not been for the look on his face, and the careless way he carried the dog, one would have judged him walking towards some celestial, instead of an infernal, revelation. As he approached the altar the Presence over it retreated, or rather ascended, and hovered, ominous, giving a sort of benison to what was going to be done.

For the strangest thing about that strange evening was not, perhaps, the events so much as my unhesitating acceptance of them. As I said, I was in no expectant mood when I first saw that movement on the Hill; yet I never doubted that what I saw on the Hill was an altar, never even questioned myself as to what the boy's purpose was, nor Whom it was he was going to worship; nor did he, in spite of the assumed ordinariness of our conversation, ever doubt that I was come to prevent his rites, if and how I could. Why this was I leave to others; I have only to record the facts.

As he stepped up to the altar, I felt once more that I must take some action, I knew not what. It seemed useless to approach any nearer to the circle of the sacrifice, and it was evident I could do nothing with the boy except by force; and he had on his side powers greater than I had on mine. . . . But, had he? Ashamed, I remembered my faith. Since this ghastly business had begun I had uttered no conscious prayer, taken no steps to set in motion that vast spiritual machinery which is on the side of beauty and holiness. I made quick, in my foolish flurry, to remedy my mistake. Hurriedly I scampered through an "Our Father" and "Hail Mary," and, making the Sign of the Cross, walked towards the altar. Once more I was sucked in—though this time with greater force—and it needed considerable effort, as well as natural revulsion, to pull myself out of the circle; and then I fell back on the clean, dark grass trembling with futile excitement.

As I stumbled out, the Presence laughed, and the boy echoed it. Anything more horrible in its perfection, more cruel in it note of absolute and casual conquest I never expect to hear. I felt not only beaten and baffled, but silly and childish; I felt as though some huge force had been not so much victorious, as possessive, over me. The boy knew, it seemed, that I could offer no resistance, let alone any active interference. Maddened by the laughter, I dashed once more towards the altar, and again was first absorbed and then, by the strong reaction of my body, flung out of the ring, weak and helpless. As I was thus beaten for a third time, the music began again.

This time it had lost its note of gay sinfulness, and was more ceremonial and evocative; but it still kept its undertone of essential vice; the grey of its formal progress was still marked by passages of scarlet and phrases of deep black. With the beginning of the music the boy stooped, laid the dog on the altar, untied the knife, and swiftly cut some string that bound its legs together. As he did so, either because the effect of the drug had passed off or because he touched the poor animal with the knife, the dog gave a little moan. I cannot hope to convey the effect on me of the dog's cry. Quite suddenly I felt that what I had to do was to save the dog. That possibly I should also have to struggle with the boy, and to fight that Presence which still hung over the altar and glowed in the darkness of the night; but that everything else was incidental to saving the dog.

The boy had now begun a new hymn, and this time he, too, used a language which was not English. Once again I stepped forward, and as I moved the dog shrieked loudly, horribly. I rushed forward, and in a moment was involved in the atmosphere of terror and power. This time, however, instead of fighting against it, I tried to ignore it, and simply kept in mind the fact that I must save the dog. I caught the boy's arm just as the knife was about to come down behind the animal's shoulder, and with a quick jerk twisted his wrist, so that the knife flew out of his hand. With a snarl of fury he turned on me—still ignoring him, I caught at the dog and rushed towards the darkness. Then something caught me: the glow buzzed like a million bees, the face of the Thing became altogether blurred with the rapidity of its changes, and loomed once more imminent and horrible. Hands that were not hands plucked at the spaniel, feet that were not feet tried to trip mine; whatever I caught changed and swelled and shrank and changed until I found myself again and again digging my fingers into my own palms, or clutching in foiled futility at the thick, obscene air. The smell was now rank and poisonous, and though there was no heat I felt the sweat running down my brow. The boy had fallen, apparently in a fit, but still clung tightly to my ankles; and as I pushed and heaved and struggled through the light I dragged his body with me. At first, as I say, the Thing which was there had seemed to attack me; but after a moment this stopped, and, instead of any active attack, I had to contend with what felt like a crushing, inchoate and slime-covered mass. I was near the end of my resources, and there was still more than a yard and a half of that atrocious glow to get through. As I fought on, the dog in my arms moved, gave a little bark and snapped furiously at the air. Strangely enough, the effort of the animal gave me extra strength. I burst out of the clutch that was holding me, and, the dog still barking excitedly, fell exhausted but outside the light. As I fell, my head truck something cold and sharp, and I fainted away.

*   *   *   *   *   *

I woke in the morning to find a small spaniel anxiously licking my hand.

I sat up, and saw some farm-hands approaching with a hurdle. I feebly waved my hand, and noticed that it was covered with blood. My head ached intolerably, and I put up my hand to it and found my hair was caked with dried blood. Then on the ground I saw a knife, with blood on the blade. The men came up. "Are you better, Mr. O'Brien?" "Yes, I'm all right," and I tried to struggle to my feet, but my head swam and I had to sit down again, rather ignominiously, on the ground.

"I shan't need that hurdle, I don't think—but thanks very much. How on earth did I——" then I recollected what my last conscious experience had been, and I could still smell that acrid stench.

"How did'ee get here? Why, we don't know. Farmer Goodere's spaniel bitch brought us up here. She were in a terr'ble to do. Don't 'ee remember aught?"

I did: but nothing I could tell these men. I muttered something about having fallen against a stone; and they looked puzzled.

I got up again, and found I could stand.

Yes; there was the altar, or rather its ruins, for the stones had fallen. I began to walk along with the men, when I noticed some pebbles arranged rather curiously round the altar. I looked more closely at them—and spelled out in Greek letters the words ΠΑΝ, ΠΡΙΑΠΟΣ, ΑΠΟΛΛΩ;[1] and then I knew under what titles the boy had come to sacrifice to Evil, and with Whom I had fought that night. I stooped and caressed the dog, who was frisking at my side in extravagant pleasure.

" 'Ee must have a pup of hers, Mr. O'Brien—she won't be long now," said one of the men.

*   *   *   *   *   *

That afternoon there was a caller—or rather two—at my cottage. My little maid came and told me that Mrs. Toogood would like to see me, and a woman entered whom I knew well by sight. She was evidently in great distress. When she was a little calmer she told me how her boy—who had just begun work as a railway porter—had been rather odd lately, humming to himself, and looking, as she expressed it, "all overish." This morning she had gone to wake him, and found him looking dead white; no effort of hers could rouse him from a slumber that seemed deeper than natural. She made up her mind to send some excuse to the station, and ran round for the doctor. When he came the boy was awake. "He seemed, Mr. O'Brien, to be a child again. He just put his arms round me and kissed me—which he hasn't done for three weeks—but he can't speak."

"Can't speak," I echoed.

"Not a word," she sobbed. "The doctor says he's had a shock." Here she broke down again and wept.

---

[1] Pan, Priapus, Apollo.

I sat wondering. "I suppose, Mrs. Toogood, you don't know whether he was out last night?"

"Out? No, sir. I still go up and see him after he's in bed—and he was in at half past nine. He was very curious, though, and didn't say a word to me, though I knew he was awake."

"Ah! but earlier in the evening—about sunset?"

"No, sir. He was home to supper, though he didn't eat a bit and wouldn't speak a word. But it's this morning, sir. Though he's so kind and nice and happy, he has such odd ideas. He got a slate and wrote on it, 'I belong to Mr. O'Brien'——"

"What," I said—"I belong——!"

"Yes, sir; that's what I'm telling you. And the doctor said we mustn't excite him, though he doesn't get annoyed like he used; and so I've brought him up here. I thought you might help me, sir."

"Where is he?"

"Outside, sir." She rose eagerly. "May I have him in?"

"Yes," I answered.

In a minute she was back with her son. There was no doubt about it. It was the same boy. He was not less beautiful than I had thought; but this morning there was nothing sinister or evil about his beauty. He saw me and then, with a grace very rare in an English boy, knelt and kissed my hand. I hastily drew it away, and asked him—

"What do you want?"

With a smile that was quite jolly and boylike, he darted into a corner, where there was a pair of old boots of mine, and went through the motions of polishing them. Then looked, first at me, then at his mother, with an air of plaintive request.

Well, after some discussion that lasted longer than it needed, the boy became my servant. He was perfectly sane, though more childlike than most country boys. He has never recovered his voice, but is so quick that one hardly realises his dumbness. I can give no explanation of how he was on the Hill of Sacrifice at the same time that he was at home eating his supper; but would suggest that there is more than modern incredulity will admit in those old stories of the Sabbath when demons assumed the places of men and women who were temporarily absent from their homes, entangled in the lures of the Devil.

Farmer Goodere had to give me, not a puppy, but Jessie herself: for she ran to my cottage that evening, and has lived with me ever since.

THE RABBIT ROAD

KITTY Trefusis was sitting in Toole's front room looking at the local paper, which had just arrived from Bridport by the carrier. Toole was glancing, with pishes and pshaws, at a London weekly, and Terence Brandon, to whom Kitty was engaged, was gazing at the *Daily Herald*, rather ruffled at Dyson's caricature.

"He's cruel," said Brandon suddenly, throwing his paper down. "I hate capitalism and wage-slaving: but after all we are all brothers, and I loathe this Cain and Abel business. At least, it's worse than Cain and Abel. For when Cain murdered Abel, Abel was all right— all right—but Cain! why, the world is full of his descendants, marked and unmarked——"

"Well, now," interposed Kitty, "Terence, my dear, who's being cruel now—Dyson doesn't call them all murderers."

"No—no—Kitty," answered Terence eagerly—"I'm *not* cruel. Cain was branded so that we could pity him. A murderer, or a financier, or a great landowner is something to be pitied. You know it's the only way to humanise them And—and—" he ended with a characteristic kind of glee—"it annoys them even more, and breaks them up. This kind of thing that Dyson draws simply stiffens their backs: and makes people like Mrs. Webb get up and say, 'Doesn't Mr. Dyson *know* that capitalists have not got small heads and large stomachs?' She's right, of course: and so's Dyson. But each of them is irrelevant. We want the truth told. And this"—he held up the obnoxious paper—"Isn't the truth. It's just a brief."

"But, my dear Terence"—Toole was beginning, when he was interrupted by a little squeal from Kitty.

"Sorry, Terence," she said, "but hark:

'Little Milton. Sale at, of modern and antique furniture. Bedding, etc. Fire irons and bellows. Several pewter plates and hot water dishes. A skillet, etc., etc.'

We must go, Terence, mustn't we."

"I expect we must, Kitty. Where is Little Milton, Toole?"

"Oh, you go out to the Four Roads, where is the turning to Broad Oak, and then go down through Dottery and away over; or else you can go to Bridport and out through Bradpole. The first road is difficult—a bit stony and uncared for; but passable, with a little energy."

By this time Kitty was sitting on the arm of Brandon's chair, and talking eagerly about the bargains they could pick up—not of things useful, but of quaint things, and of good pewter and brass; and of course they must have a skillet.

The way to the Four Roads was beautiful. Kitty thought the surface might have been better for bicycles; and was a little scared when the road, trodden once by King Alfred and his followers, took them through fields in which the Big Bull of Bufferlands was grazing quietly, proprietor of ten or eleven cows. In those fields they had to walk; and after them, when they had crossed the Chid, they cycled on till they came to the Great Gulley which led to the Four Roads. The Great Gulley is hard to describe. It is a road, a gr-reat r-red r-road, with a deep red loam for soil, in which the flints threaten and stub like the first growth of a harder civilisation pushing through the sane, unhindered life of the fields. On either side the Gulley rise the cliffs—sheer and over-hanging, red as the soil, and tangled with trees and ferns and roots which droop from the fields above; and in summer make a roof of broken green and silver through which you can just catch the turquoise blue of the sky.

You never seem to meet any one in the Gulley; yet people come there—though now Terence Brandon thinks they may not be human people. I cannot decide. The truth is that the walls of the Gulley from the ground to the height where the foliage hangs, are covered with symbols, initials, hearts, dates, grotesque heads, occasionally a feebly obscene scrawl, sometimes a carved idol, huge and impressive, and in one place a Latin cross, cut, with a simple faith, about thrice as deep as anything else.

Terence and Kitty as they walked their bicycles down the Gulley (for the riding bumped too much) gazed at these quaint, inept and at times pathetic marks. Where the walls overhung considerably there were old markings—1879 was the oldest and the initials against it were K and T, interlocked. 1879 was the year of Terence's birth, and he felt that the chance was a happy one. Kitty thought that was simply silly.

At the top they paused, and looked at the map, peering for Dottery. As they stood there, arguing, they saw a countryman approaching the Cross. He was burdened with a yoke; from each end swung a pail full of water.

Terence hailed him. He was an ill-looking fellow, with a glint of malicious humour in the kink of his mouth, and a set, wicked eye: but he answered courteously enough to Terence's question "Is this the way to Dottery?"

"It es; but 'ee cannot go with *them*," pointing to the bicycles.

"Oh, but," intervened Kitty, "we can cycle over very bad roads; we've just come———"

The man interrupted.

"There bean't no road to Dottery."

"But I thought you said—"

"Wait a bit, master. That be a *way* to Dottery; but half a mile on it ends in a field, and then it be nowt but fields."

"How would you advise us to go? We want to get to Little Milton."

"You must go back to Chideock, and then 'long the main road to Bridport; Little Milton be a mile beyond Bradpole."

And the man took up his yoke again and strode down towards Broad Oak.

Afterwards Terence thought it was odd that any one should be there, so far from any houses, and so far from the water. But at the time he had forgotten how lonely a place the Cross was.

He and Kitty, as they did not know the road on to Symondsbury, past the Hill, followed the man's advice and went back down the Gulley. As they approached the middle, they heard a rush, then a sharp yelp of excitement: there followed a pitiful tearing and falling, and a little rabbit fell over, and, with one quick struggle, died. As it moved convulsively, they heard the voice of their countryman saying, "Good dog—that's one less, bean't it?"

Kitty and Terence looked at the poor little body, and Terence stooped to make sure that the animal was quite dead. As he did so the face of the man above pushed through the trees, and he called out to them, "Better take 'n home and cook 'n—just the meat for sweethearts," and after this he disappeared, leaving the green whispering above them.

"What a brute," cried Kitty—"what a low nasty brute. I hope he'll fall down the Gulley one day."

"Eh, lass—when that come, happen others will fall with me!" and before Terence could answer, he heard the man call to his dog and his feet breaking through the bracken.

"It's quite dead, Kitty, and we had better go on." So, oddly disheartened by so small an incident, the two went on, and came soon, under the walls of the old Manor House, to the road that runs between Chideock and North Chideock.

Little Milton was reached without further adventure: and they found the sale going on in the garden of a low, thatch-roofed cottage. The auctioneer, who was a little deaf, was trying to get rid of bedding, which always goes well in a country sale. The cottagers never seem content until they have a bed heightened by two or three huge flock or feather mattresses. Kitty and Terence were disappointed when the sale reached the brass and copper work: it was only at rather an exorbitant price that they bought their skillet, and they got home tired and barely reconciled to their journey by the amusement of the sale.

That evening was very hot. It was about full moon in June, and for long there had been no breeze blowing in the Marshwood vale. If you climbed to Hardown Height, you could get a cold, light river of air that just cooled the surface of you—and under you, towards Lyme and Lambert's Castle, flocked great, casual bundles of mist that never formed into cloud, nor moistened into rain—vague, driven stuff that had little substance to anything but the eye, and yet was enough to block from the vale the land wind that was blowing in Chard and Crewkerne or even, perhaps, in Axminster. Down in the village itself the little party had gone to bed early. Toole had listened with some amusement to his friends' stories of the day, and had assured them there was a road to Dottery and on to Little Milton—and shewed it them on the map. It was rough, he admitted, but no worse than parts of the road to Chideock: and he also admitted that they might have gone quicker by taking to the high road. Kitty went to bed first, and shortly afterwards Brandon and Toole went. Toole vexed Brandon a little by insisting that there were many supernatural powers of evil. Brandon was as firmly convinced as his friend that the world was full of creatures not human, of spirits and powers; but he had been led away by the skimmed metaphysic of modern days, that seeks to ignore or to deny evil. It had not helped matters when Toole answered one of his arguments (taken from some foolish text-book) with the brief comment "Clotted bosh": and on being further pressed he could only say with a reticent jerk of his pipe—"Look at my man, the blind boy—why do you think he's blind?"

Instead of asking Toole for his reason, Brandon had started on one of those urgent disquisitions that serve youth as mental exercise, and serve no other purpose. To this Toole had listened politely, answered "Ah! I daresay!" and then suggested they ought to go to bed.

*   *   *   *   *   *

It was just after midnight. The moon shone full into the bedroom where Kitty was asleep. She was tossing uneasily, and a troubled, childlike frown disturbed her brows. Quite suddenly she sat bolt upright and said, "I'll go." In a minute she was out of bed, half awake and half asleep, and scurrying into her clothes. She went across the passage and knocked at Terence's door. "Are you awake, Terry?"

"Yes—what on earth's the matter?"

"You must get up and dress. I must go to Dottery."

"To Dottery?"

"Yes, don't make a noise—or we will disturb Toole. Come quickly. I'll get the bicycles out and wait by the shed."

"But——"

"Ah! now . . . ." a note of fear crossed with anger was in her voice. "Come quickly, or we shall be too late."

When Terence got down, he found Kitty standing by the bicycles.

"Now, please don't ask questions—or I shall go by myself, Terence. I'll tell you what it is as we go along."

She was obviously extremely excited, and controlled herself with a violent effort. She was breathing quickly, and Terence noticed that her hand, which she had given him as he approached, was hot and dry. Her eyes were calm, but oddly intent and far-looking; and about her mouth there were lines of suffering and also, in some strange way, of hardness and defiance.

Terence was frankly puzzled. He knew Kitty was capricious and irresponsible, but always, to his remembrance, in a gay, light-hearted way, not in this exacting, almost ill-humoured manner.

However, it was plain that argument would be no good, so he wheeled the bicycles out into the road; and they started off on the familiar way to North Chideock.

When they were walking up the steep hill to Ryall, Kitty turned to Terence.

"Terry, you're a dear to come like this. I don't know why, but I just had to go. It was a dream, yet not altogether a dream. Quite suddenly I found myself awake. I heard just as sometimes one overhears a remark of one's own, 'You will start now and go to Little Milton by Dottery, won't you?' and then I was answering, wide awake, 'I'll go.' As I was dressing I noticed a strange sound in the room like the murmur of leaves, and a low, heavy scent like the scent of hay——"

Well, dear, considering how much cut grass there is in the garden, and how the trees——"

"Ah! don't, Terry. I thought of all that: but it was different. The scent was not the scent of our hay, nor were the leaves that whispered our leaves. They were further and lonelier trees, and more distant scents. And—and—Terence, there was something, too, which I could not understand, though I smelt it definitely; it smelt like the smell of blood."

Kitty shuddered as she spoke.

Terence saw that her impression was too vivid to be dismissed by argument; and yet he was anxious she should not stay in this morbid, difficult mood.

"Darling, you may have had some unpleasant dream-experience; but I do not understand why we are going to Dottery, and then, by a rough bridle-path through heavy fields, to Little Milton."

"Ah! but the road will be all right—if we turn off before the Cross. It's no use going to the Cross. We must turn off sooner. I heard that—in the dream."

"But you can't go———"

"I *must* go by a dream, when other guides fail. What is it if truth comes to us only in sleep, and waking life is the dream sent through the gate of horn?"

Terence was going to take this speech lightly and chaff Kitty for her reference to Virgil, but a look at her face, blanched and almost haggard, and at the strange set, looking-outness of her eyes, as of one striving to see something long unseen, or waiting to meet someone dreamt of, but never known save in dream, kept him silent for a while.

Then he said:

"Very well, Kitty, we will go on, but don't be disappointed if we have to walk."

"Walk! I wonder if we will have the luck!" And with this Kitty mounted her bicycle and started off under the slanting moonbeams past the white railings on the road to North Chideock.

It was an odd ride under the moon, but Terence soon began to enjoy it, and looking at Kitty was relieved to see how the set look was leaving her face, and that she was taking a natural pleasure in the beauty of the night. They soon, by silent consent dropping the subject of why they rode—chatted about things indifferent, and when they got off to cross the Chid, Terence felt, and Kitty behaved, as if nothing was more normal than to have started for a bicycle ride a little after midnight.

Just before the road to Chdeock church, Kitty turned with a warning cry to the left up a slight grass-covered track which Terence failed to remember. This soon bore away to the right, and certainly, as Terence said to himself, in the direction of Dottery. After about half a mile, the road ascended abruptly, and they hurried to get over the incline. At the top, labouring slightly in breath, Terence pedalled slowly—gazing at the wide moor which stretched before them. Then with a whoop to Kitty he sprang forward, and the two dashed along a perfect road.

"Well, Kitty—you dream some more. This is the best road in Dorset or in England, I believe. It's like riding on rubber."

Kitty gave him a curious, half-furtive look.

"Isn't it splendid? Do you know, Terence, I'll tell you now—now that it's all right. I don't understand it a bit. But it was that man told me of this in my dream."

"What man?"

"The man with the water. The man with the dog. He said, 'You'll have a good road—a road like silver—but you mustn't mind the rabbits.' "

"Funny things, dreams. The road certainly is silver-coloured; but that, I fancy is the moon. But it *is* a good road."

Terence turned round to look behind them, where the road swept back and down over the dark moor. He shivered slightly with physical enjoyment of his surroundings. And as he did so, he heard a slight chuckle. It seemed to come from Kitty, but Kitty had made no sound. She was pedalling rather faster than her wont, and Terence was obliged to make an effort to keep up with her. Again he heard the chuckle—and then Kitty turned to him.

"Terence, did you hear that?"

"I did, and before; and I was wondering what it was. It was like——"

"Yes——"

"It was like that damned old fellow whom we met this afternoon."

"It was—wasn't it? What can it mean, Terry? I'm getting frightened."

"Now, Kitty, don't be silly. If it was like the old devil, it probably was him. He's somewhere——"

"Oh! Terence, do think. Is there a spot of dirt for a man to hide himself behind, and us going at fourteen miles an hour, and we've heard two chuckles within two minutes. Is the man two men, or a hundred, maybe?"

In uncanny answer, the chuckle sounded again.

Terence turned sharply in its direction—he had been peering, rather ashamedly, for the spot of dirt that could hide a man—and what he saw nearly sent him off his bicycle. He almost screamed out——

"Kitty——"

"What is it now?"

But Terence had recovered himself.

"Oh! nothing, darling—I was going to say something even more foolish than my other remarks."

"Oh!"

Terence gazed in silence. He saw, plainly enough, on Kitty's shoulder, a little figure of a man, about six inches high. He was clothed in rabbit-skin and wore the skin of a rabbit's head over his head. Out from the skin peered a young boy's face, infinitely mischievous—but the creature's hands—one was on Kitty's neck almost—were old and skinny. Instinctively Terence felt sure that the creature did not know that he was seen—and also that it would be wiser not to call Kitty's attention to the presence.

Suddenly another chuckle gave Terence his opportunity.

"Kitty, let's get off and look for that noise."

"Oh! yes, let's."

As Kitty made as if to stop her machine, Terence to his horror saw the thing on her shoulder stretch out an arm, until it reached the handle-bar—and then clasping Kitty's fingers, compelled her forward.

"Terence," she gasped. "I can't stop. Something's making me go on. And oh! oh! what are we riding on?"

The bicycles were going faster and faster, Kitty's urged not by herself, but somehow by the atomy on her shoulder, who leaned forward in vile mimicry of her actions, while Terence whirred along in his effort to keep up with Kitty in the frantic race. Then Terence peered at the road.

He had noticed before that its surface was odd. Apart from its colour and resilience, its amazing freedom from stones or wheelmarks, it seemed to differ oddly in texture from any road he had ridden on. But they were going too fast for him to see at all clearly what it was, and what had evoked Kitty's cry. But as he looked, straining his eyes in vain, his quick ears caught something. It was not a cry, nor any definite sound; it held pain, and helplessness, and a thin surprise. He listened more intently. Then he remembered the scene in the Gully that afternoon, the little tumbled rabbit, and its scarcely audible moan. He called out to Kitty, who with a white face and terrified eyes, and yet a hint of dreadful pleasure in the line of her lips, was still pedalling furiously, while the imp on her shoulder still governed and guided her movements.

"Kitty, I must get off, we can't go on riding like this. It's foul, Kitty. Kitty! Kitty! can't you stop?"

Kitty answered nothing. She did not even look round; but the imp turned and grinned vilely at Terence, and chuckled.

Terence made a desperate effort and caught her up. He seized her arm roughly.

"Kitty, I must get off. I'm going to."

At this she turned, with pain and longing in her eyes.

"Terence, don't leave me. I don't know what will happen—ah!" the cry sprang from her as the thing on her shoulder gripped more hardly.

Terence saw that it was time for desperate measures. Holding Kitty firmly by the arm, he succeeded in lessening a little the furious pace at which they were riding. Then he jammed on his back-break, and still grasping Kitty's arm, he managed to slow the bicycles sufficiently to make dismounting a possibility. He leapt from his machine, and then with a furious effort dragged Kitty from hers—and they tumbled together at the side of the road.

As he fell Terence saw the Imp leap from Kitty's shoulder, and vanish. Then the road seemed to rise, slowly, painfully, and to thrust asunder and divide . . . then he supposed he swooned.

Anyway the next thing he knew was that Kitty was bathing his head with water, and that he was lying propped up on the bank beside the Chid. Their bicycles, looking rather damaged, were still lying in the road, and Kitty was anxiously gay.

"Well, Terence, of all the silly things!—to grip my arm just as I was struggling up this little hill—and without a word too! Did you mean to help me up the hill? It wasn't the best of ways, was it?"

"But Kitty, how did we get here?"

"Ah, then that nasty blow has upset you. Don't you remember

31

I thought we'd try to get to Dottery, because it was a fine night, and I had a dream?"

"Oh! that was true!"

"True, of course it was—but I don't think we'll go on now, thank you."

Terence looked at Kitty. She seemed absolutely care-free, and undistressed. There was no sign at all of the worry she had when they started, and none of the dreadful pain when they went along on that silver road.

He felt his head. It was sore to the touch. But he did not think he was ill—and his recollection of the devil's ride was still perfectly vivid. He stood up uneasily, and looked down in Kitty's troubled, affectionate eyes.

"I'm all right, dearest. We'll go back, shall we?"

He moved across and picked up her bicycle: and as he lifted it he noticed something on the tyres—something that clung in blotches and patches. He looked at it closer. Little bits of rabbit fur were there, silver looking in the moonlight. He glanced at Kitty—she was busy brushing her skirt, and gazing at the great field which spreads to the farm by the river. He decided quickly to say nothing, but just stooped and twirled the wheels around. Then he looked again and the fur was gone.

"Is it still rideable, Terence?"

"Oh! I think so—only the handle bar a bit bent."

*   *   *   *   *   *

"You don't think it was a dream, then, Toole?"

"No—not exactly a dream. At least not for Kitty."

"But Kitty didn't remember it a bit. At least I've never mentioned it. It is too filthy somehow. But I'm sure she doesn't"

"No—you remember it, because you dreamt it. Kitty forgets

it, because she experienced it. It is not uncommon that, in these things of witchcraft—of the evil spirit. One suffers, and another sees. Sometimes the one who suffers, sees too—and you may get a great tragedy: but this is rare, unless indeed a man sell himself to evil.

"As to what you saw—it was certainly the harrying of the rabbits. The imp—you have never read of him——?"

"Never a word. I didn't know there was any folklore about rabbits. They seem too pitiful somehow."

"Yes, don't they? But the weakest of the evil imps is allowed to harry the rabbits at the full moon in June—if he can get a human being to help. He thought Kitty would do, when he met you yesterday afternoon—and the rest you know."

"You're not going to tell me, Toole, you think the old brute with the water——"

"Oh! I won't argue about it. But look here—you can look up the rabbit story in Hutchins. You'll find that the imp's favourite methods of torturing are by taking away all water, and by crushing. It's in the third volume, I think."

THE WIND

I

MARY had been at the rectory for three months; and Hugh Randall had been there only two days, but Mrs. Summerlease saw that it would not *do*. She emphasized, characteristically, the "do" rather than the "not." She had no real anxiety about her nephew: he was not the type, in spite of his easy eccentricities, to become seriously intrigued by a governess. Nor was Mrs. Summerlease worried about Mary. If a governess knew her place, well and good. If she did not know her place—well, no one could accuse Mrs. Summerlease of ruling with too strict a hand. She allowed Mary liberty, and it was the girl's business how she used it. Flirtation with governesses is a recognised form of social pleasantry in the country—and Mary ought to know that. She *must* know it. So Mrs. Summerlease silenced a conscience that never, except, perhaps, when Templeton, the charming curate with the baritone voice, intoned the Litany, was encouraged or even allowed to do more than whisper admonition or advice. Yet, not through the intervention of conscience, but by the promptings of that instinct, half social and half personal, which women such as she cherish so firmly, she had decided "it would not do."

Her reasons, unexpressed, were nevertheless ever so definite.

To begin with, Hugh was wanted elsewhere. So long as his eyes were caught by Mary's, and his feet insistent on following hers, he was unavailable for all those pleasurable duties for which Mrs. Summerlease chiefly valued him.

Then Mary, too—well, the girl was a *good* governess. And that is not a thing to be lightly said: and Hugh, if he gave her so much attention, might distract her from her business—nay, might himself prove so much of an attraction that Mary, when the unescapable disappointment came, might feel unable to stay on at the Rectory.

That, mused Mrs. Summerlease, as she gave a final pat to the roses she was arranging, would be terrible.

As she turned to the door, she heard Gladys' voice crying out "Hughie! Hughie!"—She sighed, not without the suspicion of a smile after: of course, there was Gladys.

Gladys was really the principal reason against this flirtation of Hugh's. Not that Mrs. Summerlease was a match-maker; still, she was too sensible not to know that the hero of *Amours du Voyage* was right in putting "juxtaposition" in the forefront of incentives to love, or at least to matrimony. "Juxtaposition, in short, and what is juxtaposition?" That question Mrs. Summerlease found it easy to answer. It was precisely what Hugh and Mary were having too much of: and even more precisely what she desired to encourage in Hugh and Gladys.

But how?

Gladys panted for it: a little too eagerly, perhaps, for she was a modern maiden, and, if she wanted a young man's company asked for it as she asked for tangerine marmalade at breakfast, oblivious of the fact that the modern young man, if demanded in that way, might say "Damn" and hurry off.

"Hughie! You slacker! Come and give me a single before dinner."

Silence.

Yes, certainly, Gladys was eager; but Hugh was provokingly indifferent to Gladys. So how was the desired juxtaposition to be achieved? Even if Mary was eliminated by being given that much-needed holiday—Hugh had come to D'Abernon to work; and, at a pinch might do some. No: if elimination were the method, Mary ought to have been sent away before Hugh's arrival. To ask her to go now, would be to give to natural charm the added attraction of enforced separation. Nor could Mrs. Summerlease get her object by hinting that Mary was neglecting her work. *That* would only serve to heighten her appeal by adding to it the old cliché of the down-trodden governess. It might precipitate a crisis.

"Hughie, where the devil are you?"

And Mrs. Summerlease, as she went out to remind Gladys that, though the rector's daughter, she was not entitled to shout language of that kind, determined on using her last weapon. She would tell Hugh about that curious episode in Mary's life. It might not be fair; but then are good tactics—really sound tactics, ever anything but grossly unfair? And after all, was it so certain that Mary had—reformed? Mrs. Summerlease smiled at the over-emphatic verb, but somehow felt that it suited.

II

Perhaps if Mrs. Summerlease had seen Hugh and Mary, she would not have been so positive that "nothing would come of it": she would certainly have felt even more positively that "it would not do." She and Hugh both belonged by temperament and training to that class which loves the limits of life—that believes you can only know the real range of the world if you yourself are enjoying the confinement of a cage.

But Mrs. Summerlease was just under fifty, while her nephew was only twenty-five: and, at that age, however definite one's temperament and careful one's training, there is always a danger of the desire for freedom. Mary Macleod had never thought much about freedom. It was her air: her ready feeling for it enabled her to be contented as a governess. It is only girls with narrow and

36

conventional minds who yearn to be gypsies or vivandières.[2] Still, Mary, besides being an exceptionally "engaging" girl, had really that temperament which sets no limits to thought, and few to action: and her companionship was dangerous enough to Hugh.

At the moment they were talking about squirrels. Hugh knew rather less about animals than he did about girls, but he loved watching Mary's eager eyes as she told him about the habits and the haunts of creatures she loved. In the two days of their acquaintanceship Hugh had got on quicker with the girls' governess than had any previous guest. It was not that he had attracted her: she had, in an odd way, fascinated him. Good looking, full of those mild accomplishments that compel popularity, Hugh was accustomed to admiration, taking in a good deal of praise. Mary had, from the first, been perfectly indifferent to him: at first he was piqued, and then, when he found—for he was observant enough— that her attitude was perfectly genuine, and connected, vaguely enough, with a certain mental pre-occupation, he set himself to take an interest in her. Men of his type, the static, diligent persons who succeed in the professions or in the Civil Service, always think of women as their audience; but in youth their self-conceit, not yet case-hardened, compels them not to disregard a beautiful woman even if she is interested in something else more than in them.

So in the course of his second morning—as he teased his cousins, and successfully begged them off their day's work—Hugh discovered that Mary Macleod was her own mistress; or seemed to be—for even then, in his first effort to treat a woman as an equal, he could but search for some explanation of her independence, her singular completeness, her rather desolating self-reliance.

---

2 Women attached to military regiments who sell provisions to soldiers.

This search for an explanation had involved his seeing as much as he could of Mary; and her willingness to be with him teased him almost as much as her apparent indifference to his charm. Still, he seized the opportunity to show her that he was capable of giving his attention to another's character and concerns; again her calm reception of what he regarded as an important concession teased him still more. Mary talked eagerly as well; but it was plain even to Hugh's considerable vanity that she was more interested in her subject than in her auditor: and that struck him as unnatural to the verge of impropriety. So he had spent Tuesday and Wednesday, and now was busily spending Thursday afternoon, in efforts to rouse in this cool Scots girl some attention to his own claims as a person and as a subject.

She could not, he thought, meet so many people at D'Abernon Rectory, as to make the arrival of Hugh Randall a small thing: yet she talked to his uncle, his aunt, the children, nay, even to Gladys with as much vivacity and feeling as to him. Such behaviour was a kind of social capacity entirely new to him—and he was as determined to find out its cause as he was convinced that some cause must exist.

So, had Mrs. Summerlease known her nephew's determination, and known, too, how Mary was unconsciously encouraging him, she would have been more decisive in her pronouncement that it would not do. That nothing would come of it rested not with her, but with quite other forces.

And among them poor Gladys, with her petulant anger at being cut out by the governess, was destined to play no part at all.

III

D'Abernon Rectory stands not far from the sea, in that part of the Hampshire coast where the traveller sensitive to atmosphere always begins to feel the pull of the West. Unlike as it is to Dorset proper, still more unlike the wonderful West Dorset, the Christchurch valley yet has something of the charm that the West of England exercises. D'Abernon, whose post town is Ringwood, lies a good deal nearer the sea than that often flooded district; the Rectory, built shortly after the time of Queen Anne had surrendered a little of the church's stolen property to its original owners, was plain, huge and comfortable; while the gardens, stretching down to the river, and with a view over fields and hedgerows towards the sea, had all that distinctive mixture of comfort and dignity which atone, in not a few eyes, for many evils of the Establishment.

It was at the end of the garden—or rather in the outskirts of a copse that stretched beyond the garden, that Mary was talking to Hugh Randall. She was a girl who had never, one could see, had that somewhat too much arranged prettiness that passes into insipidity; and now, at twenty-four, she held enough of the real charm of beauty to attract finer men than Hugh. Her severe, yet soft, outlines; the singular poise of her body, and the fine thrust of her perfect neck combined to give an air of power that only beauty, physical or spiritual, can entirely secure. It is a beauty perhaps more often found in men than in women, but has in it nothing distinctively masculine—nothing indeed distinctively sexual at all. And it was this which held Hugh captive—the most casual might feel that this girl had her values right, that she was balanced not by training, but by nature; and calm, not through indolence, but through control.

She was quite unmoved, Hugh noticed gladly, when Gladys with a loud whoop burst in on the pair.

"There you are, Hugh, you devil—I want a game before dinner."

The pretty, rather sulky, face glowered at Mary.

Hugh was outwardly undisturbed.

"Oh, it's too hot, Glad! I really can't move. Sit still and listen to Miss Macleod's stories about the squirrels. I believe you're fonder of animals than of anything else, Miss Macleod?"

"I wonder. Sometimes I think I am, and sometimes——" she looked at Hugh and saw that he was obviously more interested in annoying Gladys than in anything else, and stopped abruptly. "Ah! well, I must go and put the children to bed."

"I say—it's early yet. Oh! well—if you must"—as Mary showed no signs of yielding—"You're dining with us to-night, aren't you?"

"Yes, Mrs. Summerlease wants me to to-night."

She went, and left Hugh to the difficult and unpalatable task of soothing Gladys' susceptibilities.

IV

"But my dear aunt, it's nonsense. I never heard such utter bosh. Why there's no one within miles——"

"Really, Hugh, we can't say that, can we? Bournemouth is only seven or eight, and there are bicycles. Mary is a good cyclist."

Mrs. Summerlease was angered at Hugh, or she would not have spoken that last sentence.

She was not a cattish woman, but she was annoyed at Hugh's refusal to take her disclosure about Mary at all seriously. Hugh was such a domestic fellow, in a way so feminine, that his aunt had almost forgotten that he was a young man, and that what appeared to her rather odd behaviour in a girl might strike him as delightful. She was a little frightened too at the energy of Hugh's most unnecessary defence of Mary. Of course she didn't think anything was wrong with the girl, but the habit was curious. It was in keeping perhaps with Mary's withdrawn character—but there!

"And she refused to tell you anything, or to promise not to

repeat—her offence?" said Hugh, in an ironic and rather shrill tone.

"Quite. I pointed out that it would not do if she was seen out at that hour of the night. It was nearly two in the morning, and such a terrible night. A great west wind blowing—that was why I happened to be awake and up. The window on the landing went on bang, bang—and I had to get up to shut it."

"Oh! you don't understand Miss Macleod, auntie. She adores nature and she only went out to look at—oh! at the trees and things!"

Hugh's efforts to put Mary's taste for nature in a sympathetic way made Mrs. Summerlease smile; but she was anxious to suppress her mirth.

"Well, you may be right, Hugh. But I think it is very off for a girl of Mary's age to go out on a wild night just to look at 'trees and things.' "

"You think it's odd—but then you're old——"

Mrs. Summerlease winced: she was still under fifty.

"Oh! I don't mean really old; but you don't like wind, do you? And any way it was not the sort of night a chap would have cycled from Bournemouth, was it, however keen he was? But perhaps you think Miss Macleod is being courted by a duke in a Napier. She deserves one, by gad."

"Oh! very well, Hugh. If you are going to make a joke of it— you may. I only told you because I saw you were interested in Mary; and this funny wild habit must throw some light on her character—I don't say it's an unfavourable one. But night expeditions in high winds are scarcely your form of enjoyment, Hugh dear."

V

Dinner that evening was an uncomfortable meal. Only the rector, a quiet, elderly man who was absorbed in the prospect of the publication of the seventh part of his "Exact Relations between the Gilgamesh story and the Adventures of Beniah," and Mary Macleod seemed at all at their ease. Gladys was still sulky and cross, and tried to "get back" on Hugh by attempting to flirt with the new curate, who was so embarrassed by the attention that he was very ill at ease. Mrs. Summerlease's graciousness was a trifle heavy and premeditated. She was over-aware of herself. Hugh, while not precisely disturbed, was still restive from the slight strain of the conversation with his aunt.

Since the sunset the wind had gradually risen; and now it was blowing with a steady, purposeful persistence. The great elms were creaking, and the oaks and pines caught and struggled with the blast, but did not hinder its passage to the house, where it shook the windows, and rattled the panes.

Mrs. Summerlease shuddered. She had a genuine dislike for wind.

"I do hope this gale will drop again before the morning."

"There's little chance now, Mrs. Summerlease. It will blow till the morning, I think," said Mary, and there was a curious, almost gleeful lust in her eyes.

"Then we shall have a devil of a night," said Gladys.

The curate, horrified, was wondering if he dared venture on a rebuke, when the quiet voice of the rector intervened.

"Now that expression of yours, Gladys—I do not think girls used it in my day, by the way—has an extremely interesting history. If we accept, as I think we must, the identification of Gilgamesh with the Satan and ultimately with Judas, who is of course a mere double of the Satan, we then find that there is a very intimate connection between bad weather and the betrayer. No doubt in the East—I beg your pardon, Fanny."

Mrs. Summerlease, despairing of stopping her husband by any

less definite means, had risen and was preparing to lead the way to the drawing-room.

"I will tell you afterwards, Gladys, if you remind me, the precise point which was in my mind. I think it may be worth an excursus in Part Eight—" the rector added as, with an old man's courtesy, he anticipated Hugh's youth, and held the door open for his wife.

Hugh was anxious to get to Mary, and the rector never knew what to talk about to his young nephew. He knew that Hugh was not in the least interested in Biblical criticism, or in the Babylonian myths which were his own passion; and Hugh had never been sufficiently sympathetic to create any common interest between them. So the stay in the dining-room was not long—for the curate had no taste in wines, and had not the courage to tackle his rector on anything more abstruse than flannel and soup: and the rector, to do him justice, had too much ordinary sense to attempt to talk criticism with his curate. That young man was pertinacious in his efforts to make small talk with Hugh—but found the other's dim interest and vapid answers too dulling even for his persistence, and no one was sorry when the rector suggested a departure.

But Hugh was not to be contented that evening. He found Mary there in the drawing-room—he half feared Mrs. Summerlease would have sent her away—but very unready for conversation. She seemed preoccupied—not nervous, but tense and, as it were, expectant. Hugh, against his will, recollected his aunt's stories and he found himself angrily wondering whether there could be anything in them. His anger was against himself, but he could not prevent or dismiss his suspicions. There must be some reason for Mary's extraordinary aloofness—for it was not as if she were at all odd otherwise: she had health, and youthful interests, and youthful kindness (Hugh had noticed that she was the only person in the house who even tried to follow his uncle's fantastic mind), yet here she was sitting careless of him or of Gladys, heeding nothing, it appeared, but the great wind that still blew hard from the west and beat against the house.

"It sounds as if he wanted to come in, Miss Macleaod, doesn't it?"

"I beg your pardon, Mr. Randall: I'm afraid I'm frightfully inattentive—I didn't catch who you were speaking of."

"Oh! only the fellow who seems to absorb you and your thoughts—this great, blustering bully of a west wind!"

To Hugh's surprise, almost to his consternation—a deep blush spread over Mary's face. She was moved to an extent he had hardly thought possible. Her words almost stumbled in answer.

"Oh! no—why do you think I'm heeding the wind? It seems curious"—and she tried to laugh—"to speak of the wind as though he were—were a person."

"Of course it is stupid. I wasn't in earnest, Miss Macleod."

Hugh was convinced now that there was something in his aunt's tale, something in his own indefinite but abiding suspicions. What it was he could not guess. Mary had not seemed embarrassed before she heard that he was speaking only of the wind. She might have been taken aback by his sudden reference to "him"—but that left her unmoved.

Hugh was still youthful and he actually found himself wondering if Mary were a member of some secret society. Hadn't he heard of a colony of Nihilists at Christchurch—possibly she was involved with them; perhaps they had some code in which the word "wind" figured. He did not pursue this line of thought long, but he abandoned it only because he had made up his mind to watch during the night. If Mary did go out in this howling gale, he would go with her— or after her.

VI

Hugh felt ashamed and rather silly as he sat, fully clothed under his dressing gown, by his bedroom fire. The bright blaze, the comfortable chair, the table with his bottle of whisky and its soda, the general gaiety of his room made his suspicions seem childish. It was long after one, and he had not heard anything significant since they had all separated for the night. The wind still blew—it occasionally caught the smoke of his fire, and sent a little vagrant curl down and up over the mantel-piece; but he could not hear it as plainly as he could in the big drawing-room. He could, however, hear every sound in the long corridor on to which all the occupied bedrooms gave. Mary's was separated from his by his aunt's, and except for the occasional creaking of a board, or the rattle of an obstinate window-frame, the corridor and its rooms had been silent for the last two hours. He had made up his mind to sit and smoke, listening, until the dawn—and he was some time from the end of his vigil yet.

"What a damned fool I am!" he muttered: "as if anyone would go out on a night like this. My aunt must have dreamt her story—or Mary has got more sensible."

He filled himself a fresh glass of whisky, and took up Anatole France's "Ile des Penguins" again.

Then he heard a sound. It was faint but unmistakable. It was followed by the faint noise of a woman's footfall, dancing rather than walking along the corridor. Hugh threw off his dressing gown, and stepped, as quietly as he could, out into the passage. He was just in time to see Mary's figure at the foot of the great staircase; he went down, but slowly and quietly. A glance at her had altered all his suspicions. The light, almost passive progress, the high carriage of the head, the curious sense of a forgotten purpose, made him almost certain that she was sleep-walking: and he was anxious not to awaken her suddenly.

She did not attempt the big bolts of the hall-door, but turned down the passage which led to the kitchen. There was a little side-door, secured only by a key; this Mary turned, and vanished into the garden. Hugh, following, was nearly beaten back again by the force of the wind. It was blowing furiously right against the side of the house, and he could scarcely close the door. He did not notice then, though afterwards he remembered it, how it had shut apparently with no difficulty, for Mary. He noticed immediately, when he had at last secured the door, and started forward to follow, with what amazing ease Mary danced against the wind. Himself, he could only just manage to walk at a decent pace. Every step was contested. The wind beat in his ears and his eyes, pushed with a steady unceasing thrust against his body, grudged him every inch of the ground he was covering. He set his teeth, bent his head, and staggered on.

Mary was making for the copse where he had sat with her that afternoon. As she glanced on ahead, speeding as though with the wind, she seemed taller than her wont. Hugh managed to keep her in sight, until she reached the copse, where she plunged in and for the moment was lost. In the copse Hugh found his going easier; but it was, in a way, more alarming. The trees and bushes were all maliciously alive, full of quick, crepitant sounds; and the wind, which outside had one note, here was broken up into a hundred different challenges and cries. In the garden, too, and down the drive, the big oaks and beeches seemed to keep the wind at bay. Although these little trees were more of a shelter, Hugh felt that their shelter was sinister: that acceptance of it put him in their power—and he tried to hurry out of this protection of thorn and bramble.

Emergence form the copse was not unlike his first exit from the house. He stood at the edge and looked for Mary. She was about one hundred yards off, and had stopped running. As Hugh looked at her in the moonlight, he had for the first time a natural, immediate sense of her desirability; her astonishing vitality, her splendid balance appealed to him without any veil. She was standing with her head thrown back, and her hair was hanging loose and magnificent. Her arms were at her sides, but were bent at the elbow, and her open hands seemed to reach for something—or someone.

Huge gazed, crouching so as to escape the blast. Suddenly he was aware of something slight, but so uncanny that it nearly made him dizzy: he felt the wind pouring through his hair, and some association made him look again at Mary's. Its great length, black in the moonlight, hung perfectly straight and still down her back. Then Hugh realised that neither were her clothes disturbed by the gale, and he noticed that Mary's pose had an ease which seemed incredible.

He began to try and cross the clearing, when he heard her voice. The words were difficult to catch, and for a moment Hugh could make nothing of them. Then he heard—tossed on the wind, the syllables *Magister . . . iuvenis . . . venio.*[3] Mary was speaking in Latin. Hugh once more stood upright and struggled towards her. But now he found progress almost impossible. Twice the wind, bursting into a fury that seemed personal, flung him over on to the bracken—and each time he lost the foot or so he had gained. The roar of the wind rose higher and higher and yet he could still hear—

---

[3] Trans.: Master . . . young . . . come.

separate and distinct—Mary's voice speaking in the full-mouthed syllables of Latin hexameters

> *Maxime tu divum* . . . .
> *Ah! venio* . . . .
> . . . . . *ventorum princeps et maxime* . . . . .[4]

Mary seemed perfectly oblivious of anything but what she was doing. Her attitude was that of absorbed ceremonial prayer; and yet there was something not satisfied, something more expectant than certain in the quality of her voice. Hugh, prone on the ground, listened and dragged himself nearer. He abandoned any idea of walking and crawled through the gorse and heather, over the sandy soil, angry, passionate, and determined.

He was within ten yards of Mary: he had come round slightly and so could see her face. She looked rapt, almost dreamy, astonishingly calm, the strangest contrast with the uproar that surged round and over her, and seemed to touch her mind as little as it affected her body. Hugh, leaning on his elbow, shouted her name; but his voce, cracked and crumpled, was tossed away by the wind, and was scarcely audible to himself. The gale increased, not in fury, but in persistence and in purpose, and suddenly there was a change. Hugh was first aware of it by a change in Mary's face. She lost something of her calm. Her lips parted slightly, and the slack easy pose of the neck became a little strained. And he heard

> *Mi, domine, indignæ* . . .[5]

Then the world came to an end.

That, at least, was the feel of it. There was a huge, exultant crash of wind, like to a burst of thunder—a crash through which

---

[4] Trans.: Greatest God . . . Ah! come . . . prince and greatest of winds.

[5] Trans.: My, lord, unworthy . . .

there sounded something of a cry, and Mary seemed enveloped by a kind of whirlwind. It was not a whirlwind. It had not either the colour or shape. Dark red, it had the vague semblance of something not human, nor animal, but yet indubitably organic. Like some great mantle which retained the wearer's form in dubious, uncomfortable outline, this red mass hung over and about Mary. Something like blunted hands stretched behind her and a great heavy head hung above, and down form it flowed the vague outline of a body. And in the centre of it there was an eddy—an eddy that now glowed the same dark brick red as the rest of the mass, and that now shone with a livelier, quicker glow. As Hugh watched he saw that the edge of the mass changed colour. The blunt hands seemed to become blue, the huge head blue, and ever the eddying, whirling centre changed to a ruddier and ruddier red. Its movement was as the movement of innumerable leaves, but moving infinitely faster than those blown upon by any autumn breeze.

And through the leaves something danced and darted, something whose form remained indistinguishable, but yet was determinate, something that gave a sense of life and reality to the enormous fantasy of this shadowy, potent mass.

Then Hugh heard a cry, and turned his eyes away from that great shadow to Mary's face. Again the cry rang out, and Mary's face changed horribly. It seemed to distend—the eyes started with agony, the mouth forced open in terror, the hair flung back in a great stream behind her. Then as she gazed in frantic fear, her whole figure seemed to alter. With incredible and ghastly swiftness the great red shadow pressed and pressed——

Hugh turned, and stumbled, shrieking, back to the Rectory.

When the old rector, and his coachman and half a dozen farm hands started out half an hour later, the storm had completely subsided. They found Mary lying, as if asleep, on her side. She looked quite peaceful: the doctor said she had been dead for about twenty-five minutes; and that she must have died without any pain.

THE EBONY BOX

T HERE was nothing, to the glance of a casual observer, of the extraordinary in Colonel Hicks' drawing-room. Furnished with that absence of discrimination or of elective taste which is the recognized indication of a sober position in the country, it was a room in which anything of the centre, anything of essential art or manifest beauty would have struck as false a note as anything of exuberant vulgarity. People who are given to self-expression at all speak as plainly by these accidents of personal temperament, furniture, pictures, books, as by the conventional symbols of thought; and the drawing-room of the Hicks' was as insignificant and common-place as their language. Just, however, as a man, whose ordinary speech is the fumbled accidence of childhood, will at times, with something of the inevitability of chance, break out with a passionately coloured expletive, so the drab monotony of the drawing-room at Fairholt was interrupted, with a suddenness that stung, by the ebony box. The box itself, while beautiful in a fantastic way, was not so remarkable as its apparent effect on the room and the occupants; it seemed, in all circumstances, to be at once both the point of rest and the centre of conflict. In any large gathering of people, which is not merely the disunited clutter of ordinary gossips, the unity of the crowd gains expression in some one central person; a man of great reputation, or of great ability, serves as a lightning-conductor for whatever of capacity there is in the company; he attracts and emanates, elicits and bestows with a potency as definite if not so incurious as that of the sun. At Fairholt the position thus usually taken by a person, was the inalienable privilege of the ebony box. This was experienced by the most unimaginative of callers. Their feelings in the matter were summed up by Miss Jenkins, whose life was a breathless game of character making and character taking, when she circulated Tommy Forbes' *mot* that 'If the devil was not in Colonel Hicks' ebony box he ought to be."

The presumed immanence of the devil may have accounted for Mrs. Hicks' sentiments towards the box, sentiments that had that mixture of fascination and repulsion which arrests the reader of mediæval witch-trials, as the most distinct mark of feminine diabolists. Mrs. Hicks was a woman who had married first for curiosity, secondly for comfort. Domestic by temperament, she had but an undeveloped sense of the art of housekeeping, that clear-headed capacity for selection without which domesticity dribbles away in a passion for fidgety alteration. Mrs. Hicks would change the position of a chair not because she thought it would be better elsewhere, nor even because she was dissatisfied with its first place, but simply because with her a distrust of permanence was the only sign of the capable housewife. In appearance, she was pretty without being attractive, and in her frocks she affected that shade of blue which has an unwholesome affinity for pink. It would not be true to say that she had captured Hicks as a husband; but certainly when he fell into the water of possible matrimony she held his head under, a fact that Hicks took care she should remember and regret. Hicks himself was a man whose marriage had caused a real surprise to his acquaintances. He was not a sufferer from misogyny, but a man who could be cordial to women without committing himself, and might treat a girl whom he liked very much as he would a favourite retriever. His marriage with a woman like May Buchanan was bound to end in some kind of grotesque tragedy.

That Ralph Hick's treatment of May was deliberate it would not be just to affirm. It sprang naturally from the contact between the two temperaments; the conflict between the curiosity which a woman calls loving interest and the conceited reserve which is the basis of the masculine idea of honour. Their honeymoon was uneventful enough. A honeymoon is not, as the cheap satirists would have us believe, a time of disillusion; it is not a period in which the lover and the beloved are stripped of singular qualities, the gift of earlier and less intimate affection. It is rather the time in which new delusions, equal in force though different in character, are superadded to the old. Their honeymoon was a time in which two comparative strangers, with no kinship of blood or of association, constructed masks with a facial resemblance to the reality, which they agreed, validly enough, were to be the conventional symbols of Ralph and May. At the end of his two months' trip on the Continent, Ralph Hicks knew his wife by rote, not by heart; and embittered by knowledge he led her down the way of agony and doubt.

One afternoon, when they had not been a month settled at Fairholt, the family estate in Somerset, to which Hicks had come back after his return from India, Ralph interrupted some of his wife's purring questions with "One moment, dear, I want to show you something." He went to his library and returned with an ebony box about the size of an ordinary writing desk. It was elaborately and beautifully carved; in the centre of the top an enamel was inset, with the figure of an Indian god, and around it was scroll and leaf-work. There was no key-hole to the box, nor any obvious method of opening it; but where the key-hole should have been was the word Taman in English letters, and the same word was repeated on the bottom of the box, which was otherwise perfectly plain.

"What a sweet box!" said May. "We must keep it here in the drawing-room. Where did you get it, Ralph?"

Her husband hesitated for a moment, and then began in that style which is the invariable prelude, made by the human man, to something exceptionally mean.

"May, I have always been perfectly frank with you; I have, and desire to have, no secrets from you, except the secret of that ebony box. I can tell you nothing as to where I got it, what it contains or what its possession implies. It is my one secret, and I must ask you to respect it as you trust me." Without waiting for curious and pathetic expostulation, Ralph then left the room, putting the box on the table.

The passion for knowledge is difficult to analyse; but the normal person, one may pretty safely suppose, finds his chief pleasure in the chase, not in the capture; most of us value our experience in proportion to the difficulty of acquisition. With May it was otherwise; she collected facts just as some people collect stamps, and would feel it a serious grievance to be deprived of a piece of information, however unimportant, whose existence was matter of knowledge to her. Her husband's abrupt disclosure of so startling a fact as this mysterious secret left her for the moment in a condition of huddled and impotent amazement; her next instincts, as is always the case with the weak, were towards immediate and practical action; it is only those who are afraid to be alone with an idea who seek aid in force, physical or moral. May flew after Ralph, and mercilessly besieged him with indignant question and protest. To all her expostulation he replied with repeated requests for her confidence, requests the more maddening because she was totally unable to explain, what she nevertheless felt was true, why the appeal, in this case, was entirely unjustified.

From that afternoon the ebony box began to assume at Fairholt position and a sinister importance. If one has the unhappy experience of calling at a house just after some family bereavement or domestic quarrel one feels something hidden in the atmosphere. A husband and wife may sit together dry-eyed and self-controlled, talking common politeness to some casual visitor, who nevertheless can see, after five minutes' intercourse, that the only thing in their minds is a subject whose interest and importance can be measured by their avoidance of it. At first Mr. Hicks' friends were puzzled at the new atmosphere in the house. They all felt, as Miss Jenkins said, that "Ralph and May talk to you as if they were away and wished that you were anywhere except with them"; but it was some months before the curious influence, immanent in the room like some strong scent, was tracked to its undoubted origin, the ebony box. The method of discovery was accidental enough. At a dinner party, when the Hicks still gave dinner parties, one of the guests, a Dr. Innes, picked up the box and said to Hicks, "This is a very beautiful piece of work; where—." Then he stopped suddenly in his question, feeling that Mrs. Hicks was looking at him. He turned and saw her, oblivious of the company, her face fixed in a hungry appeal for knowledge, pleasurably apprehensive of the keen pain she hoped was coming. With strained eyes, parted lips and short convulsive gasps, she leaned forward, anticipant of the arrival of some potent passion. So might the Sibyl have looked as she neared the acme of her ecstasy, or so, the doctor thought, the half-cured victim of some degrading drug or bestial indulgence, in painful expectation of a dreaded yet desired fall. Dr. Innes was only saved from anxious and indiscreet inquiries by the swift action of Ralph Hicks, who went over to his wife and, under the pretence of conjugal attentions, changed the look on her face into one of sheer and submissive terror. In similar circumstances, other events conspired to help Hicks in the game of torture that he had now definitely, however indeliberately, entered upon. He could no more help reacting upon his wife's nervous and terrified curiosity than the wall can help returning the fives' ball; and the hand of fate was apparently very hard upon Mrs. Hicks. For years they lived together, a strange man with a strange woman, their only bond to be found in the fear which the husband encouraged, the wife indulged and the box inspired. At times, in moments of optimism, Mrs. Hicks would once again definitely ask her husband to tell her about the box, and so give his devil's pride one more opportunity of irritating the wounds, to the nursing of which she now abandoned all the shallow intensity of which her nature was capable. More often, however, the box was as it were the conscious background against which they played the drama of life. If a man could be imagined carefully conscious of the process of breathing or motion, it would be a slight analogy to the manner in which the ebony box entered into the lives of May and her husband. Every remark he uttered, still more, every sentence that he checked half-way, was connected immediately with the secret enclosed in the box, by his wife's desperate attempts for initiation into the mystery. In his sleep he uttered disjointed sentences, of sufficient coherence to spur on May's anxiety; and the apogee of tragi-comedy was reached when she wrote to *Notes and Queries* to inquire after Indian secret societies. They practically gave up seeing any of their neighbours, who were, in truth, not a little scared by the unnatural atmosphere of the house; and it is small wonder that the visit of Gillingham, an old friend of Ralph's, who had not seen him since his marriage, should have aggravated the severe strain under which the two had lived so long.

When Gillingham arrived, one afternoon in September, there

was an armistice of mere weariness between Ralph and his wife. His friend noticed some change in Hicks since his marriage, changes that he put down, conventionally enough, to the influences of matrimony, even accounting in that way for the furtive ingenuity with which Ralph invested the most ordinary remarks as though they were fraught with interior meanings. For when two people live alone, their minds unnaturally intent on one object of thought, the one gradually learns to put into his conversation some hint of that mystery which the other is always suspecting. So, quite apart from direct references to the horror of his life's secret as contained in the ebony box, all Ralph's spoken words seemed to arranged as to be centripetal, so many radii that had only meaning and importance as they were related to the centre. Of what that centre was Roger Gillingham was of course entirely ignorant at first; but his ignorance was soon to be dissipated.

On the second evening of his visit, Gillingham and Mrs. Hicks were waiting in the drawing-room for her husband, who had not finished dressing for dinner. Gillingham, to pass the time, went round the room admiring commonplace pictures in a commonplace, genial manner, and discoursing occasionally on one in particular with that elaborate carefulness of language of a man more anxious to air his artistic vocabulary than to express his appreciation. Finally his eye fell on the ebony box, and, recognizing India in its make, he took it up to pass some local and suitable remark on it to Mrs. Hicks. When he turned to her, however, he saw she was looking not at him but at the door; her face, a mask of gaping terror, was fixed on her husband, who stood in the doorway, on his countenance that calculated and lustful cruelty that you may mark in the debased boy who will torture a cat. The three stood there for a moment, Hicks making no pretence of hiding the joy he felt, any more than Gillingham attempted to disguise his amazement or May her terror; the advent of a servant, with his formula, seemed to restore things to a more ordinary state, and Mrs. Hicks fluttered out of the dining-room, followed by her guest.

Lack of imagination is a great source of worry. Gillingham spent a good few hours of the night trying to solve the mystery of the scene before dinner and of the heavy gloom that shrouded the rest of the evening. At first—for he was one of those men who are egotists, not through conviction of their own ability, but merely through intellectual laziness, which makes them base things on the personality that comes first to their minds—he thought Hicks must be jealous of his wife. He soon dismissed the idea; characteristically enough, not because of his long friendship with Hicks, but because of May's unattractiveness; then he worried through most of the causes of matrimonial differences that had impinged on his brain from the perusal of third-rate novels. After a troubled sleep, in which he eloped with May Hicks, and her husband with the ebony box, he awoke with a cry: "Gad! it's to do with that black box." He lay in bed pondering for some time. It was getting towards half-past six, and Gillingham, full of his clue, did not attempt to resist the temptation to get up and inspect for himself this box which had so mysterious an effect on his old friend and his wife. It is needless to say that when Gillingham arrived in the drawing-room and picked up the ebony box he did not gain much from its inspection. He had just turned it upside down and was going to carry it to the window to investigate more carefully, when a footstep made him turn hastily, to see Ralph Hicks coming towards him. Gillingham dropped the box with a bang on the floor, looking and feeling, he could not explain why, like a school-boy caught at the jam-cupboard.

"Morning," began Gillingham; "interesting box that; hope I haven't——"

But Hicks interrupted with a gesture and tone that was almost melodramatic.

"Don't be a damned fool, Roger. You came down to look at that box?—("It is the box, then," thought Gillingham)—Well, that box contains the secret of my life; that part of my life which no one shall share, neither you nor May."

He spoke almost as if for an audience, and Gillingham, turning from the window, saw in the doorway Mrs. Hicks, with the same look of terror as on the night before, gazing not at her husband or at his friend, but at the ebony box which lay on the floor, the cold sunlight picking out the fantastic limbs of the god on the lid.

After that morning, Gillingham vamped up some conventional excuse, and returned to his rooms in town, leaving Fairholt to its strange monotony of perplexing horror.

*   *   *   *   *   *

Ralph dying. Come at once. He wants you.—May Hicks.

That was the telegram which, some three years afterwards, Gillingham found lying in his rooms. Not altogether unwilling to hear a death-bed confession, he put up a few things and started off that afternoon for Fairholt.

He was met at the door by Mrs. Hicks. "Ralph wants to see you about the box," she said, her passion for knowledge cheering the sorrow she felt at her husband's illness, for she recovered, now he was ill, some affection for the man she had married. Gillingham unconsciously drew himself up, proud at his prospective rôle of confidant, and followed Mrs. Hicks to the door of the bedroom, where Hicks lay dying of pneumonia.

"The box, Roger," gasped Ralph.

"Yes?" queried Gillingham, anxious and important.

"Get it me—you, no one else; not May."

A sick man must be humoured; and so Gillingham went down to the drawing-room, murmuring his errand to Mrs. Hicks on the way, as she stood, expectant, on the landing. He returned to the bedroom with the box, and put it into the invalid's hands, which let it fall on the bed-clothes. Gillingham, with that irrelevant logic that attacks us at moments of emotion, thought of the bang the box had made when he dropped it on the floor.

"Do you want to tell me anything, old chap?" said he to Hicks.

"Tell, tell? No, no," murmured the sick man. "Where are my keys?"

Gillingham, who had noticed the absence of any key-hole in the box, was startled at the request, but fetched the keys from where they hung and gave them to his friend.

"Thanks," said Hicks; "now go."

"But—," began Gillingham.

"Don't chatter, but go; and you too," he cried, turning to the nurse. She nodded to Gillingham, and they left the sick man to his secret in the sick air of the room.

Outside the door Mrs. Hick was standing; she did not attempt to disguise the fact that she had listened to all that passed in the room. For minutes, that dragged like hours, she and Gillingham stood side by side, waiting. On the staircase was a cuckoo clock, and the bird came out five minutes before the hour. As it sounded its absurd note, Mrs. Hicks said to Gillingham: "The clock went wrong three weeks ago."

Just then came a cry from the room, baffled; then a loud shout, "Not my wife, not my wife"; and then silence. Gillingham fumbled for a few moments nervously, and then, full of his responsibility, went into the room. Ralph Hicks lay dead, with the ebony box clasped in his arms.

The next morning Mrs. Hicks babbled to Gillingham the story of her married life. It left him as unenlightened as before; and his practical sense propounded the immediate solution.

"Mrs. Hicks, the box must be opened."

That afternoon, in the presence of the doctor, the vicar and Hicks' solicitor, the ebony box was solemnly smashed open.

It was perfectly empty.

II

WAYS OF ESCAPE

Out of the world of men and things,
Comes that uttermost wind which brings
Freedom and respite and danger—there
We escape from the burdens we will not bear.
But whoso travels uncharted roads,
Must stoop his back to alien loads.
You may pass if you will the ring and the pit
But always you have to pay for it.

UNDER THE SUN

I

A GIRL of passionate temperament, Helen Ainslie had developed in a way which is only possible in the country. Like all really intense natures she was aware—in her nerves, as it were—of her passionateness, and so was incapable of that light approach to subjects of sex by which gay and frivolous women so frequently mislead men, for whom gaiety has one source and one end. Helen lived in Little Oak, just beyond Broadwindsor, with her father whose one interest in life had been for Fuller, who had written his "Worthies of England," while vicar of the little Dorset parish.

She had her dreams; but never had the least temptation to carry them into the small social world whose fringe her father occasionally touched. The vicarage garden-party; the Squire's annual dance, and the County Ball at Dorchester were never awaited by her with the flutter of preparative excitement which stirred most of the girls she knew. Nor was Helen, in spite of her father's interests, at all literary. She had indeed a real difficulty about self-expression. Words seemed to her troublesome; and so much conversation was phrase-making that she had unconsciously adopted a manner that older people thought sullen, and younger folk conceited.

In Broadwindsor itself she had no friends—and at Little Oak lived none to be friends with. She was glad to go occasionally and talk with the cottage people; she could be conversationally intimate with farmers' wives and daughters about pigs and cows and the different ways of making money; but there was no one who elicited anything of her character, no one who gave her any opportunity for development. Her father had never troubled to be polite to those "of the Country," who had called, and he was too negligent of the growth of his daughter to realise anything except that sometimes her likeness to her mother gave him an agony too keen for his peace. His projected life of Fuller, his minute collation of the different editions of the old historian's books, kept him fully occupied. At least it occupied the surface of his brain, and the rest slept, buried with his youth and his wife, in the dreary cemetery at Abney Park.

Helen did not feel his selfishness at all. She would have denied that he was selfish, and he was sincere in his incapacity to imagine a different or pleasanter existence for his daughter. Once the vicar's wife had protested to him that Little Oak was not the place for a girl of Helen's temperament—that she was apt to be moody, and that the remote life of the country was too empty for her. But Paul Ainslie refused to listen. "There are at least peace and time here: in the towns if there is peace you have no time to enjoy, and when you find the leisure you are too weary to enjoy anything. Town-life is a habit, a bad, character-destroying custom: a far worse drug than tobacco or drink—for it affects a man on all sides at once, and attacks not only his senses, but his reason. Helen is not happy here? Of course she is not. But she would not be happy in London—and she might think she was. And then one day she would know—and that is what breaks the spirit. No, Mrs. Porter, it is just because she is moody I feel she may stay here without hurt. If she were light-hearted, London might not harm her."

So Paul applied to his daughter's case the excuses he had long ago made for himself, and forgot one thing which the old often forget, that the young may find new experience everywhere, alarming, disturbing experience, for adventure will seek them, scenting some response, long after it has abandoned the mature or the elderly.

II

When the gorse is once lit on a Dorset hill, there's no knowing what will happen. They burn it so that it shall grow fresh and young again and be better food for the beasts and sheep; but sometimes they burn it carelessly, and a strong wind may light a bigger fire than ever was expected. Some three years ago there had been a huge blaze about a mile from Little Oak. A west wind had risen suddenly, and blown sparks down on to the thatched roofs of a couple of cottages. Water was scant, and helpers came late; and in the end the cottages were burned out. The outside walls remained in ruins, and pitiful bits of fence and gates led into a wilderness of tossed brick and crumbling stone. The people who lived there owned the cottages, and they had, only just before the fire, moved our their furniture in preparation for a departure to Canada. So when they went, the ruined houses were left for the bats and the birds; and the ivy soon began to creep up the calcined walls. You can see many houses like this in Dorset. They get abandoned, and fall to pieces, and after twenty years or so become fairly decently clothed in ivy and thorn. Wisteria Lodge—that was the name George Diment had given his four-bedroom house—was, however, still deplorably naked; one room had half a ceiling and three grey walls; an oven leered out at you, rusted and bulging, and docks clustered at the sickly-looking blue railings.

One May morning, Helen Ainslie was out walking. She had always disliked the desolate look of the burned houses, and was hurrying past them, when she thought she heard a moan. She stopped and listened again. A faint cry came, its syllables oddly at variance with its pathetic sound. "Hallo." She turned and peered into the ruin. Leaning against the far wall of the old kitchen, with his feet against the oven, was a young man. He was startlingly fair—almost bleached hair, steady, round blue eyes, and a dead-white face.

Helen stepped over the gate and went to him.

"Are you in trouble?"

To her surprise, he answered with a briskness that contrasted not only with his previous moan, but with his appearance.

"Not a bit, thank you. But I had just woken up, or just got here—I'm not sure which—and you were going past. That wouldn't have done, would it?"

"I suppose not," answered Helen, scarcely aware of what she was saying, or what his question had been—"at least—really, if I can do nothing for you, I must be going. Good-morning."

"But of course you can do something for me. For one thing you can display a little ordinary human curiosity. It can't be usual, even here, under the foot of Pilsdon Pen where Coleridge tramped, for a young man to appear and moan out his morning greetings to the vicar's daughter. Come, ask me who I am, and where I came from, and how I got here. Please! I'm most frightfully hungry. Miss———?"

"I'm not the vicar's daughter. My name is Miss Ainslie. If you are really hungry, they will give you milk at Peace—or at Plenty."

"Peace—and how can I find it? Plenty—ah! you're laughing at me. There are no such places, and in a moment you will vanish, and I shall be unhappy again. I am unhappy, you know, as well as hungry, Miss Ainslie. Don't you want to know my name? Are you happy?"

"Really I ought not to stay here, Mr.———"

"Trenchard—ah! you don't like it? Well, let us say Penhaligon; that was my mother's name. John Penhaligon, of Cornwall, at your service."

The odd stranger at this rose, and tried to stand up, but he had no sooner got to his feet than with a little sob of pain he sank down in a dead faint.

When Helen, by bathing his head with water, had brought him to again, she could not suppress a slight reproach.

"You *were* in trouble, Mr. Penhaligon."

"But I told you I was hungry and unhappy—there aren't any other troubles, are there? I believe I've sprained my ankle too: but that's only a mood of unhappiness—just a discomfort. How do *you* get unhappy? Sit down and tell me about it."

He patted a large dock invitingly.

"Mr. Penhaligon, it's no wonder your unhappiness expressed itself, if you are always as careless as you seem to be now. What you want is some food and some milk, and I'm going to Peace to get them."

She went, and John Penhaligon Trenchard fainted again twice in the ten minutes she was away.

She brought him back some milk in a blue quart jug, a large loaf of bread and a good piece of cold bacon on a quaint old fashioned plate.

After he had drunk some of the milk, Penhaligon turned the plate hastily upside down, and looked at the mark.

"Ah! it's a bit of old Beaminster pottery. You know they used to make pottery at Beaminster—oh! years ago! when they made carpets at Axminster. And now—this *is* good milk!"

"When did you last eat?"

"When did I—what is it now?"

"This is Tuesday, May 9th."

"Is it? Tuesday is an odd day always. I should rather like Tuesdays to be left out. Monday is a day of recovery, and Wednesday a day of disturbance—and on Thursday you work, and on Friday you are sorry for it, and on Saturday you take a holiday. Sunday is just Sunday, but I never knew what to do on Tuesday. I expect I was keeping Tuesday for you."

"You talk a great deal of nonsense, Mr. Penhaligon. I believe you are light-headed with hunger." And Helen smiled at him kindly. It was impossible to be angry with any one quite so irresponsible and gay.

"But of course I am light-headed. Look at it. I am the lightest man in England. I was too light for Cornwall. So I left Buryan and I walked and walked. I began unhappy and I ended hungry, and now here is Tuesday and you. I believe I shall like Tuesday. I say, is your father Paul Ainslie?"

"Yes—do you know him?"

"No—but I know about him—and the life of old Fuller. You must be bored to death with that old proser?"

Helen considered. It was the first time she had wondered whether she was bored: and she could not immediately decide.

"No—I don't think I am. There are bits of the church history I like.

"You *read* him?—you shouldn't do that. It's dreadful to read 17th century folios: you might get satisfied. And if you lost both hunger and unhappiness, where should I be?" Tuesday would never come back again. No: I don't think you ought to read at all. You should be sung to. Do you know this:

> "Man was walking merrily
> Down the lanes of Devon——"

"Mr. Penhaligon—I'm sure you oughtn't to talk so much. If you have finished—and I think you've had enough for a beginning, you must get up and take my arm, and see if you can walk as far as Peace. I asked Mrs. Barnes to get the trap out, and I'll drive you to Father's."

"Now I shall never finish my immortal poem about Man in the garden of Devon. For I've lost my hunger, and I'm not as unhappy as I was. And now you are going to drive me home. Come, let us see if I can walk."

Helen, free as she was from self-consciousness, was just a little surprised at the calm way the stranger took her invitation. But she said nothing, but "Come then," and offered her firm young arm for him to lean on.

III

Paul Ainslie received Penhaligon quite naturally. Rather to Helen's relief the stranger did not attempt to speak to her father in the inconsequent manner he had adopted with her. He apologised ordinarily for his intrusion, and for the trouble he had given Helen: and then after their dinner that evening, displayed considerable knowledge not only about Fuller but about books in general. The result was that Paul asked him whether, if he had no immediate reason for leaving the neighbourhood, he would care to stay at Little Oak and help with the collation of the church history. To this Penhaligon agreed, and before a week was out he was perfectly at home in the house.

Helen hardly knew herself in these days. She had too much general sense not to know that she was falling in love with Penhaligon; but she was distressed at her uncertainty as to his feeling for her, and still more at her doubts about his character. Often enough he kept up with her the gay spirit of nonsense—but at times he would drop into an unaccustomed moodiness, refuse to speak at all, or only in tones of anger or depression. He had not told her or her father anything more about his history. He never spoke again of Buryan, though he often spoke of Cornwall in general. Once he and Mr. Ainslie had a long discussion on the supposed connection between Cornwall and Phœnicia. Ainslie was sceptical about this, whereas Penhaligon was a firm believer. He quoted the case of the saffron and the clotted cream; he said there were resemblances between the language of Carthage and that of Cornwall. He insisted that names such as Kneebone were but corruptions of the old Nebo, and that Marazion was what it seemed to be, a Phœnician word.

"But what does it mean, Penhaligon? Bitterness—Zion—?"

"I believe it is the record of one of the greatest triumphs ever held over those accursed Jews. You know the story that Dido and Jezebel were sisters? Well, that I believe to be true. Now when Jezebel went to marry Ahab, the King of Israel, she went as an emissary of Moloch. She, like her sister, was a priestess of Moloch, and she deliberately entered on an alliance with Ahab in order to spread the Empire of the Sun. Shortly after the arrangement of the marriage, one of the royal family was exiled from Carthage. There is no need to enter into the circumstances. He came to Cornwall, and there, as a record of the triumph of their religion over the dark superstition of the Jews, he called his castle Marazion—Bitterness for Zion. The City of Jahveh had become the City of Moloch. And even in the Western Isles the servants of the Sun rejoiced. That is the origin, too, of the absurd Christian legend about Michael driving the Devil from the Mount. It simply signifies the uprooting of sun-worship, and the growth of Christianity. But the Sun-God must get back his own."

"My dear Penhaligon, surely your identifications are just a little wild. Quite apart from the evidences for all this private history of the royal Carthaginian families, what makes you so sure that the Devil of Christian legend is one with Moloch, and he again with the Sun?"

"Always the champion against the Jews and the Christians is the Sun. Their own legends witness it. Do they not pretend that the death of their God only occurred when he had blotted out the Sun? Does not Jesus himself speak of Satan falling from heaven—like the Sun setting? Always the Sun is the enemy—whether he be called Moloch, or Satan, or Apollo."

Conversations of this sort made Helen uneasy. She had always ignored her father's vague dislike to orthodoxy: but Penhaligon's extravagances, she could see, made him a little uneasy. He did not pursue the more startling subjects which Penhaligon broached; and once at least he definitely rebuked his guest for venturing on a discussion of the details of human sacrifice in Carthage and Mexico. But it was not his talk only which made Helen feel so unhappy about Penhaligon. It was happenings, too, and yet the grimmest of them somehow served to bring them together. One afternoon they were walking in the woods that cover the slopes of Lewesdon Hill. It was a bright sunny day: and quite suddenly they came to one of those sights which disfigure the English country—a row of beautiful birds, pinned through the brain, hung up as a warning to others not to interfere with pheasants' eggs.

She turned to Penhaligon, intending to say something expressive of her disgust for the barbarity of gamekeepers; but his face kept her silent. He, too, was gazing at the pitiful little row, their feathers looking dead in spite of the sunlight, their poor, opened eyes, and the limp despair of claw and beak. But Penhaligon had nothing of disgust or pity in his look. His eyes shone, hard, but glittering, like blue stones, and there was a twitch of nervous pleasure at the corner of his mouth: his nostrils were distended, and Helen, in a moment of frantic wickedness, caught herself thinking that he was actually sniffing for the scent of decay.

While Helen hesitated, Penhaligon spoke.

"It's beautiful, isn't it?"

Helen shuddered, but said nothing.

"Fools think it is ugly, this gracious, dispelling power of the sun. They prefer life dull and steady, or slow-moving and otiose. Here you have it quick and glittering: not a moment but a change occurs, not a moment but some wonderful step to the unknown is taken—beautiful decay, beautiful dissolution! Don't you think so, Helen?"

"No: it seems cruel and wasteful to me. These wonderful little birds——"

"Ah! but you must not think of the birds. You must not think of the individuals. They are only food for the sun, food for the great light, modes of manifestation. The power that killed them was the sun's; the power that makes them decay is the sun's; the power that will make them vermin is the sun's. You ought to love decay, Helen, if you love me. You do love me, don't you?"

This was the first time Penhaligon had spoken of love to her: and the untoward circumstance of his question, the odd savagery in his tone, made her flinch.

"I don't know. You are so different. I thought I did. I still think I do—but I hate you sometimes when you seem cruel, or bitter. I like you as I first met you—and I love you as I first dreamt of you."

"Well, then, you must learn. I am cruel—as the sun is. I have no scruples and no regrets. But, Helen, I am hungry and unhappy. Hungry for love, and unhappy till I get it—and unhappier still when I get it. Darling—would you rather be without love and unhappy, or with love and unhappy? No way is happiness to be found. They who tell you otherwise—those damned Christians and their priests—they lie——"

"John, you must not say that. I do not believe that—but certainly happiness seems far off."

"Dearest, believe me there is no such thing. Unless indeed they have it—" and he pointed to the row of birds—"They may have, but I don't know. I can give creatures decay, but I can't suffer it. I can't suffer it."

He had caught Helen in his arms—and as he pressed her mouth to his, she had a sensation that his wonderful lightness of complexion threw off a light, was dazzling her. She closed her eyes, and murmured:

"Not here, come in under the trees."

They went a little further into the wood. The sun came gentler through the green leaves of larch, and the silver leaves of birch, and was caught by the broad branches of the oaks. And there Helen held her head up to be kissed.

"So you want me under the trees? I wonder why? Why not in the hot, beautiful, naked sun? I'm not half so real, you know, under the trees. I haven't the same power, have I?"

In an odd way Helen felt he was right. His grasp was less firm, his kiss not so fervent. He seemed more like the boy she had found in the ruin, more like himself, as she phrased it.

"John, I love you better so. Out there you were too—too flaming, somehow. And I can't bear it. You must remember how new all this is to me. You see you are a man—but still you are very young. How old are you, John?"

"Old? I'm not old at all, except when I'm hungry. I'm young. I'm young as you, and younger. I'm as young as your father, and younger. But, Helen, really, I'm just young. I shall sign the certificate—or whatever it is you sign—just 'John Penhaligon' Young. And you— you will be of full age—or over age. That's a jolly expression, isn't it? While we are children we are so old—five years, or ten, or fifteen. But always 'years old': and then, when we are grown up, we are just 'over age.' Past age, past all the countings, and dates and calculations. Just young—or old. You must be young, Helen."

She was glad to hear him talking nonsense again, and told him so in the happy moments of love first expressed. Though she still found it difficult to get words to speak properly in—she was sure that Penhaligon understood her. She had never felt understood before. Her father loved her, and looked on her now as a copy of himself, now as a painful portrait of her mother. The other people she knew frightened and distracted her. Penhaligon sometimes frightened her, but she knew he understood her. And though that did not quite bring peace, it gave a certain security, which is the foundation of peace.

IV

For a week or so after that day on Lewesdon Hill, Helen seemed perfectly happy. She and John said nothing to her father; but they regarded themselves as affianced, and Helen did not seek to disguise her affection. John, too, altered. He became more gracious somehow— more ordinarily kindly, more attentive in little things. Helen began to dismiss her old fears as silly and wicked. John was just rather a creature of moods, and said more than he meant; but his love for her was certain and no one could be really cruel who loved.

It was in the first week of June that the accident to the aviators happened. Helen and Penhaligon had gone for a long walk. They had taken the road to Four Ashes, and then on to Shave Cross, right across the end of the great vale of Marshwood, with its hidden farms, and long fields and damp mists, then across fields to Ryall and up to the top of Hardown. It was a gorgeous afternoon. The air was still, and shimmering with slow heat. The sun. although strong, was veiled in a mist that broke its rays a little, and a deep haze was settled over the sea. The lovers sat on the top for an hour or so, playing with the stones and the gorse, and watching a peewit circling, in great rounds, about her nest. Then they moved on and had tea at Morecombelake; and, at Helen's suggestion, crossed the high road and went up to the cliff between St. Gabriel's and Charmouth. When they had reached the highest point they flung themselves on the grass and watched the slow life of the valley, varied by the busy, ridiculous hum of an occasional motor-car on the road, or the faint tapping of a horse's hoofs.

Suddenly Helen heard the buzz of an engine which seemed far nearer than could be, unless the motor-car was coming up the broken lane that led to their cliff.

"What a frightfully noisy car that is, John!"

Penhaligon was lying almost on his face, his head at her knee, humming some quaint tune.

"It is, isn't it? I wish the beastly thing would burst."

"I believe it is going to. It's getting extraordinarily loud."

Something made Helen look away from the road, and upwards. Then she saw that the great burr came from an aeroplane which was already over Morecombelake and rapidly approaching their hill. It was flying at a good height, but she could just see two little dots—the aviator and his passenger.

"Oh! look, John—it's an aeroplane!"

Penhaligon pushed Helen's hand away, and leapt to his feet. He was transfigured with fury. He stood there, the sun shining in his long bleached hair, his hands held above his head, ablaze with anger. Helen was dismayed and terrified.

"John—John."

"Hold your tongue, Helen! The devil, the presumptuous, defiling devils! But they shall rue it."

He stopped, and clenched his hands with a hideous effort at complete concentration. Then he seemed to Helen's eyes as if he leapt towards the monoplane which was now lying nearly over their heads. With a horrible abruptness, the noise of the engines stopped: then followed a sickening silence, and then, one field away, a thud. And then silence again.

Penhaligon turned to her, once again all gaiety.

"Two more fools dead. Why don't they understand that it can't be done? That it never shall be done? They are insolent brutes, aren't they, darling?"

Helen shrank away from him. She was speechless, and afraid of her own thoughts. It was absurd to connect John's anger with this dreadful accident. And yet—the coincidence. His evident desire for an accident. His alarming concentrated effort. She looked at him as if he were something inhuman. When her voice came, it was husky and strained.

"John—you must fetch some one. You must get help."

"Ah! I'd forgotten. Of course we must. Come along," and he offered his hand so that they might run down the hill together.

"No—John. I can't move yet. But go quickly." Then, in a lower voice, "Quickly, for God's sake. They may be alive."

Penhaligon shrugged his shoulders and started towards the farm, whistling.

But before he had reached there, men were coming out. They had heard the aeroplane and noticed the abrupt silence. The next half hour was occupied in the dreadful necessary business. A doctor was sent for. Men pulled and pushed at the scrapped machinery, and tried to smother the scurrying flames. Penhaligon went to help them; and this lightened Helen's heart for the moment. But afterwards she lost that consolation. When all was done that could be done, and she moved towards the farm to join her lover, she heard one labourer say to another:

"There's summat unnatural about that bleached-looking fellow. He looked at those poor twisted corpses like a dog do look at a rat, or a hawk at a bird. Rare pleased, he seemed."

And Helen remembered the scene on Lewesdon Hill, and felt ill and unhappy.

Two days afterwards Helen, who had gradually yielded again to Penhaligon's charm, and was feeling not happy but joyful in a strange poignant way, left him and her father while she went to pay a visit at Broadwindsor. As she came back she was a victim to that uneasiness which is so often an accompaniment of gaiety. She remembered how strange she had once thought the confession of a girl acquaintance, who told her that the afternoon of the day on which she was engaged she had sat in her room and cried for an hour or more. It seemed natural now. Helen felt herself varying between sudden melancholy and extreme joyfulness: and yet she knew she was neither hysterical nor ill. It was towards dusk, and the dim little slip of a new moon was already visible in the sky— looking like a bit of cloud. As Helen passed the big field by Peace she heard a voice. She stood and listened. It was John's voice, but it was different from that she usually heard. Its tone was not, however, quite unfamiliar. Helen had heard it, but less assured, when Penhaligon had discussed some old religion with her father. What puzzled her more was the identity of John's companion. Then she heard another voice—a woman's. It was curiously like John's in quality, but sterner and less flexible.

Without a thought of untrustfulness, Helen crossed the stile and went along by the hedge. The field was a huge Dorset pasture-field: a great hill of a field, that dipped down sheer between two accommodation roads, one of which was a good fifty feet higher above sea level than the other. Helen was above the speakers, and as she got to the edge of the slope she saw them. They were standing with their backs to her, and the woman was talking. She had on a curiously made white dress, and on one shoulder gleamed the yellow of gold. Her head was bare, and she had a bow in her hand. Helen recognised this with relief. It was evidently one of the members of the Beaminster Archery Club—though who she could not make out in the dusk. Nor could she recognise her voice.

"It was well done, brother."

Helen gave a little gasp of surprise. How odd of John to have a sister in the neighbourhood and say nothing about her. Or had she newly come?

"It was well done. And this girl. You are playing with her, as you have so often done. It is always your weakness. Why cannot you be swift and smite?"

"Ah! sister, yet rumour says that even you in your dreams—"

"In my dreams! If it were only in your dreams you loved the daughters of men, it would matter little. But we high ones should not condescend to mortals, as you do. It is time, brother, that you made an end."

"Well, my sister, I can deny you nothing. It shall end to-night. She is a silly girl and afraid. Let us forget her now, and practise."

Helen, ashamed, puzzled, weeping, lay under the hedge and watched the most amazing archery those fields had ever seen. John and his sister shot at things; they divided daisy stalks; they cleft the tails of martens; they shattered the bodies of shadowy bats. Finally John bent his bow, and his sister hers—almost together: but John was first by a little, and his sister's arrow sped after his and split the end of it. The two, looking strangely foreign, Helen thought, laughed with glee at this last feat.

Then Helen heard John speak again.

"Farewell, sister."

"Farewell, and remember—away from here to-morrow."

Helen's anguish was not accompanied by healthy rage. She loved Penhaligon devotedly; but the shock she had received from different things was intensified by the callous tone she had now heard him use. She stood up, still by the hedge, and giving a last glance down the hill, saw that John's sister had gone, and that he had turned and was coming up towards her. For a moment she was doubtful if he had seen her. Then he hurried his steps, and called out "Helen!"

"Well, this is luck, darling. I was wondering where you were. Shall we go to Cornwall to-night? Just straight away—Get a boat at West Bay, and I'll row, row to Lyonesse—we'll not stop at Cornwall. We'll drive down and ring the bells of those buried churches. We'll bring the sun back to them."

Characteristically, Penhaligon had ignored the obvious signs of weeping on Helen's face. But she was not to be put off.

"John, I heard all you said to your sister."

He stopped abruptly.

"Ah! I was afraid so. It is a pity. Still, it hastens things."

He seemed to speak more to himself than to her.

"John, have you nothing to say to me? I thought you'd *say* you were sorry."

But Penhaligon remained stern; he seemed entirely uninterested in her distress.

"Sorry? I told you I had no scruples and no regrets. And you heard my sister say I was at my old play. I don't change much. Come, Helen, kiss me; and we will part."

He stood, not so much inviting as commanding: the sun, not yet set, looked redly at them, and Helen was seized with an unnameable fear. She gave a little shriek, and ran, ran up the hill. . . . .

She stumbled. Twice she fell and tore her dress. But always she picked herself up and went on running. And behind her she heard the even breathing, and the quick feet of Penhaligon. She could not understand why he did not catch her sooner. That he was bound to catch her she felt sure. Yet on she ran, ran round the great field, and then down, then over the hedge and into the copse. On she went, her breath labouring, her feet heavy, her eyes frightened. Then by the laurel he caught her.

"Ah! Maiden, not lightly can you escape."

Then he kissed her, and she knew no more.

V

"A curious case, my dear Mr. Ainslie, a very curious case. Undoubtedly sunstroke—oh! undoubtedly. Probably accelerated by strain and anxiety. Ah! but fathers don't know everything, not everything. No. Subsequent treatment? Oh! no worry, no trouble, no cares—and society, plenty of congenial society—young women and young men, Mr. Ainslie, young men! Good day, *good* day."

THE GREAT MOTHER

I

Extract from a letter of John Prideaux Scott, one time fellow of the College of Our Blessed Lady, Oxford. The letter was addressed to his friend Geoffrey FitzMaurice, and given to him by Scott's executors.

"MY Dear Fitzmaurice,
"You have asked me rather frequently in the last few months to give you some information about Hugh Flinders. As his biographer, you've naturally been anxious to discover when his astonishing talent as an artist showed itself, what were his interests and his bent while he was at Oxford, and whether the rest of us prosy fellows guessed what a genius we had among us. I'm afraid you've thought me both stupid and ungracious; you've known me to be uncommunicative. Others have told you that I was Flinders' best friend and constant companion; and you've not unnaturally resented my silence and my evasions. When you have read the enclosed story, you will, I hope, understand. I knew I had not long to live; and to discuss the story, as I should have been forced to, had I told you in conversation, would have been unbearable. Even now I am not sure whether I am right in putting it on paper. But I promised Flinders before he died, that a record of his strange experience should be made; and entrusted to you, his biographer. It was his expressed wish that you should make what use of the story you thought fit. You may either publish it, or suppress it—tho' if you do this my manuscript is to be kept in the British Museum—or you may simply draw your own deductions as to the significance of this story, and use them in writing the life. I am not going to advise

you. I cannot, if I would, decide on the value of Flinders' experience; I can only vouch for its reality. Now as to his later career . . . ."

The rest of Scott's letter is not relevant to this story. I have used the information his letter gives me n my large biography of Flinders; but I could not decide to do anything about this document except publish it as he wrote it.

II

I had always been friendly with Flinders. He was a quiet man. Not retiring, but never anxious for acquaintance. He played no games, except lawn tennis and cricket. And he did not work at all hard, except at subjects and periods not touched on in the average man's work. He was a well-made man, big in bone, but with very small hands and feet, and a head which, in its heavy droop, seemed almost to be quarrelling with his body. He had no parents, and felt his loneliness acutely. He used to say that an orphan was a new Adam, and could not be expected to remember his ancestry.

When I first got to know him—somewhere in our second term— he was a very keen Catholic. He generally used to go to High Mass at Barney's; but occasionally he went to the Cowley Fathers. But he definitely liked the popular Orgiastic music, and almost rollicking services of S. Barnabas, and he liked its mob of undergraduates. Although he was an ardent classical scholar, he was very impatient of the false Hellenism which still marked Oxford in our undergraduate days. He loathed that tired statue of Antinous which decadent men would have in their rooms; and he was still more intolerant of the vague ardour which balanced the Lady of Chartres or Nürnberg by a Chinese Buddha or a little group of the Bull-killer. His Christianity was by no means simple, or easy. It was a savage effort. An effort after experience, in which he appeared to demand rather more than those emotional and spiritual experiences which for most of us are the results of religion. Yet he was not, as I could see later on, a mystic. What he really wanted was magic. And I have often wondered whether official Christianity, especially in this country, is not too hard on those who need magic. No doubt their claim is difficult to satisfy: but ought we not boldly to admit the fact that many people do not belong, religiously, to our period at all? Just as some are medieval, others Renascence, others Puritan—so some are primitive, and can understand nothing but the swift cruelty of the knife, or the harsh discipline of the blood-stained stone.

However, for a long time (as Oxford time goes) Flinders remained orthodox in his practice. When he first found other avenues of approach, I don't know. He would never speak afterwards about his first adventures into other paths, except to insist that they were accidental. For myself I have little doubt that he was attracted from the other side. I don't think he was the aggressor; but that the powers which he ultimately found had sought him out. After all, we believe that in our religion God seeks the soul, and may it not be so in others?

Flinders, like most young men who think at all, and talk at all, at Oxford, thought and spoke about sex. Rather too much: but then so long as we deliberately feed our adolescents on the two literatures that are fullest of sex-atmosphere, what can we expect? The callous are not, perhaps, much harmed. The sensitive either win through, or are broken. I don't quite know which fate overtook Flinders.

He, at this time, somewhere about the autumn of 1898, had got to the period, or to the mood rather, when the things of the flesh seem intolerable. He was determined on celibacy, on virginity, on that agonised purity which so often overtopples into lust. He was not (he had too keen a sense of ordinary decency) that most despicable of objects, a woman-hater; but his interest in women was very small. He had been brought up in the ordinary way, and had not, in spite of his public school, lost all delicacy of feeling: but he had been sufficiently revolted by what he learnt at school to give him a bias against women. He found it difficult to remember that they were individuals, and he had no women friends.

The assault must have begun in the Lent term of 1899, when he was in for mods. I found him one day poring over Grant Allen's edition of "Attis." I read a little anthropology in those days; and I asked him what he thought of Allen's theory which, as you will remember, reduces the idea of God to manure. He muttered something about "Mucky nonsense," and then went on excitedly—"Scott, it's not Allen I've been reading, it's Catullus. I'd never read the 'Attis' before. It's fine. Listen."

And he chanted out that amazing passage:

Simul hæc comitibus Attis cecinit notha mulier,
Thiasus repente linguis trepidantibus ululat,
Leve tympanum remugit, cava cymbala recrepant,
Viridem citus adit Idam properante pede chorus.
Furibunda simul anhelans vaga vadit, animam agens
Comitata tympano Attis per opaca nemora dux,
Veluti iuvenca vitans onus indomita iugi:
Rapidæ ducem sequuntur Gallæ properipedem.
Itaque ut domum Cybelles tetigere lassulæ,
Nimio e labore somnum capiunt sine Cerere.
Pigu his labante langore oculos sopor operit:
Abit in quiete molli rabidus furor animi.[6]

---

[6] Poem 63 from the Carmina of Gaius Valerius Catullus. It tells the story of Attis, who castrates himself with a stone as an offering to the goddess Cybele.

"Yes; very like the Salvation Army," I said.

"Oh, don't be flippant, Scotty. Yet—perhaps it is. I'm sure we want more of it. More of this self-sacrifice. More of this ardour. More of this reckless desire for service. It's more gorgeous, this, than the organ at Barney's." And he read again:

Mora tarda mente cedat: simul ite, sequimini

Phrygiam ad domum Cybelles, Phrygia ad nemora deæ,

Ubi cymbalum sonet vox, ubi tympana reboant,

Tibicen ubi canit Phryx curvo grave calamo,

Ubi capita Mænades vi iaciunt hederigeræ,

Ubi sacra sancta acutis ululatibus agitant,

Ubi suevit illa divæ volitare vaga cohors:

Quo nos decet citatis celerare tripudiis.[7]

"Well, I think I prefer 'Berenice'—and I'm certain I do the 'Epithalamion.' But I daresay it will be useful for you to know the 'Attis.'"

"Useful," he asked sharply. "Useful? What do you mean, Scott? Useful for what?"

I stared at him.

"Why, you old owl, for the schools of course. There's only three weeks, you know———"

"Oh! the schools. I'd forgotten all about them. Come along and play a game of squash-fives in the Wuggins Courts. Old Prothero promised to keep us places."

III

It was about a fortnight later that I saw Flinders again. I don't mean that we had not meet in the interval. But that on this occasion I should have guessed something of the real Flinders and of what

---

[7] Also from Catallus 63.

he was suffering, even had the day not ended in the catastrophe it did. I had been to confession on a Friday afternoon, to the Cowley Fathers' church. As I was making my thanksgiving, I heard a groan from somewhere near. I saw Flinders kneeling about three chairs away. His face was contorted with trouble, and the tears were falling from his tight shut eyes. A lay-brother, a funny little man like a tortoise in spectacles, gazed at him professionally as he trotted past. Then something roused Flinders, for he opened his eyes, got up and went to Father Terence's confessional.

One does not as a rule wait for a fellow undergraduate, if one happens to discover him at his religious duties; but something made me stay until Flinders should come out. I knelt there, looking at the image of Our Lady, and trying to pray. Flinders' appearance had driven me to think about him. I somehow had a presage that he was, not merely in trouble, but at some crisis in which I was to bear a part. I had not then any kind of idea what it was, nor how it would effect me. I think now it is possible that the same power which had been impelling him, had, out of caprice, begun to control my mind, and so procure for itself a witness and a tribute to its potency.

Flinders was not long at his confession. When he came out, he came—I had anticipated it somehow—straight to me.

"Come along, Scott. I want to talk. No—" as I hesitated—"I've no penance. I've not had absolution. Come along."

We came out of the odd little door—it was before the days of the present west end, and its big tower—and when we were in the Iffley Road, we turned and walked away from Oxford. At first we tramped along in silence. I could see Hugh was trying to make a beginning; and that it was no little thing he had to talk about. I didn't like to begin myself; and it would have been futile to make conversation.

I wish I could give you some idea of the force and character of Hugh Flinders. He was quite the ablest man, not of our year, but of our times: for sheer brain power, for æsthetic sensibility and for a general sense of values he was incomparably bigger than the ordinary able undergraduate. I remember conversations of his in which he anticipated much of modern thought; and his insight into the past was almost uncanny in its power of realizing not only the mental, but the physical and moral atmosphere, of the classical period.

Gilbert Murray has a little of that power now, and so has poor Benecke; but Murray at his best cannot avoid bringing the Gods of Olympus into the barrier of Temple Fortune; and Benecke, with all his brilliant diagnosis of the Greek temperament, had too loose a hold on the essential human character. That was where Flinders excelled. He knew humanity in a way that would be surprising in any one, and was staggering in so young a man. It was that which made him so intolerant of the æsthete. He loved Lang's "In the Wrong Paradise," and was never tired of insisting on the falsity of the Renascence idea of Hellenism. It would be difficult to say whether he hated Pater or Wilde more. Both had, in his eyes, presented the English public with a picture of Greek life and ideals that was false even to the decadent Hellenism of Alexandria.

I tell you this that you may not mistake his tragedy for that of a man obsessed by the fancy picture of Greek civilisation. What he did, or suffered, he did or suffered from a firm belief in the reality, the primitive truth of that intense nature-worship which Greek religion shared with other faiths.

He did not speak until we had turned the corner where the Iffley 'bus used to stop, and were climbing the hill to the "King of Prussia." Then he began:

"Scott, do you believe in classical mythology?"

"How do you mean, Hugh?"

"How—well, would it surprise you to know that the old worship goes on? That hills near here are still sacred to Apollo? That groves are still dedicated to Diana, and woods to Pan? I don't mean stupid revivals like old Taylor's: I mean survivals of the old faith among the old people—people to whom Christ and the saints are less direct of access than earth-stained Pan, gross Priapus, or even Jupiter of the storm.

"For months now I have resisted and I can resist no longer. I'm going to the grove to-night; and I should like you to come too, if you will. Will you?"

I was not much enlightened by Hugh's revelation. I could see he was serious, and I did not doubt he was sane. But I found it difficult—as you must in reading, to actualise what I heard. It seemed like a poor game; and its vagueness left me a little annoyed.

"What grove, Flinders? And what's the point of going now? I don't see what you are at."

"You will if you come," he replied. "Anyway, I must go."

"But do explain more, Hugh. Whose devotee are you?"

He looked at me in an odd way, and replied as oddly.

"I *have* found the 'Attis' useful, Scott. I go to worship the Great Mother. I go to get strength. It is not there for me, I am sure"—and he waved his hand at the country behind us—"nor in the church at Cowley, though they, too, know something. But they don't go far enough."

He refused to speak any more. I did not dare leave him. Apart from my feeling that it was only decent to see him through whatever he was going to experience, I felt an odd power impelling me on. It didn't seem possible to evade or to refuse. We walked on steadily in the growing dusk; and by the time we reached Nuneham

Courtenay it was quite dark. We went down the hill through the village, and Hugh turned abruptly into the road which leads to March Baldon—or to one of the Baldons. I have never been there since. After following the road about half a mile, he cut through into a field. It was one of those sinister fields, which, one knows, have at some time harboured the suicide or the abandoned. I have been told since that I am "psychic"—to use the jargon of theosophy—and on that night I first felt the advantages of that power. There were other presences in the field, curious, thin, meagre little things. I turned to Hugh.

"This field is strange, Hugh, isn't it? Somehow one feels there are things—things deserted—helpless little things. Bah—*I'm getting stupid.*"

"Ah! you feel it—" said Flinders exultantly—"I wondered if you would. Yes, this is the field of renunciation. Or one of them. I don't like coming through here—" he seemed suddenly to be asking for sympathy.

"Well, for God's sake, Hugh, let's go back. I'm ready to talk this over—but I don't like—"

"No—I have turned back too often. After all, if I can't persist in my Christianity, there are other ploughs to hold, and other fields to sow. And I believe this is the way."

We went on in silence.

At the end of the field there was a stile which led into a wood. As I crossed it I noticed that it did not seem much darker in the wood than it was outside. I missed that descending cap of darkness which usually overtakes one on the first entry. It was a dark night. The moon was small and young, and the stars did not avail much against the Lenten gloom which preludes Easter. Yet in the wood it actually seemed lighter than it had been in the field. We were walking along a little path heavy with damp grass and trodden straw. Hugh was more rapt than he had been, and he seemed more careless of his way. Once or twice he stumbled against a root, and righted himself with a sharp laugh. I was by now thoroughly nervous. I am not an imaginative man, but the odd matter-of-factness of our proceedings, contrasted with Hugh's vague promise of something mysterious, produced its result. I was strung up, and ready to start at a shadow. As I walked on, uneasy, Hugh spoke again.

"I have never been in the wood before. It is here they meet. Here——"

Suddenly I felt irritable.

"What 'they'—who are 'they'?"

"They—those who worship the Great Mother—she who is called Cybele. Those who get into contact with her; who know how to sacrifice nature, and by sacrifice win strength, and self-control. This faith, too, knows the new truth 'He who would save his life must lose it'—aye, and"—here he muttered something which I could not hear.

I did not then guess what he meant. Classics are so taught in this country that few boys realise the essential significance of the classical myths. Things like the story of Leda, or of the Bull, horrors like the tale of Io have not the reality of our native fairy stories. Why, boys can read about Marsyas and still admire Apollo.

I had lost the end of Hugh's last sentence. He was walking ahead of me, and then that happened which I cannot explain. I suppose it makes my story useless as evidence. Hugh vanished. It was a moon-lit night, and I was within reach of him; we were clear of any trees, and the ground was flat, yet Hugh, with whom I had been talking and whom I had seen a moment before, had completely disappeared. I was frightened with that complete, stark fear which you can explain as you please. It may be only the unconscious memory of our cells, those damnable, blessed cells which keep some secular knowledge of the days, æons ago, when that which was to become man, was spawned upon the waters or crept in the ancient lime, and knew its one chance was never, never to be overcome by the insensate and unspeakably strong powers of Chaos. Whether it was fear of that old disorder moved in my blood, or— but it does not matter. I was sweating with fear. I cried aloud, "Hugh! Hugh!" And all the response I had was an echo which turned his name into a cry of woe and loss. I then, in spite of my fear and a strong instinct against my action, pressed forward— but I could not move. A mist—oh! not unlike the valley mists we have near the Thames, and yet so unlike, which blew heavily at my feet and before my face seemed to solidify if I tried to pass it. I could go back, but terrified as I was, this I would not do. I leaned desperately against that cold and clammy wall, and strove to find Hugh's figure in the little patch of green which showed faintly in the moonlight.

Then I heard the song. It was high and shrill, and as I strained to catch the syllables I recognized phrases in Latin—"*Procul oh! procul este profani!*"[8] The chant seemed to come from very far off; and even more faintly I heard a low, continuous shuffling, and then a quick, sharp stamping and then, in incredible rapidity, the pad, pad, pad, of what must have been hundreds of bare feet on the hard ground. All the time there was the far-off chanting. I was nearly swooning with terror, and with the dreadful baffled effort as I pushed against the mist which wavered so slightly and lightly, and yet barred my progress as if it had been a wall of mesh-steel. It

---

[8] Trans.: "Keep away oh! Keep away profane ones!"

was like one of those nightmares in which you cannot wake, cannot rid your mind or your body from some weight, something unknown which obstructs for a moment all the freedom of your life. It was complete suffocation without loss of consciousness. And all the time, faster and faster the bare, invisible feet of the frantic, invisible dancers raced and beat, pad, pad, pad . . . and I could feel nothing but the horror of cold and damp behind which was my friend. The dread of it was frightfully increased by the fact that while, to my ears and my touch nothing was present that was not incredible and awful, nothing which did not disgust and dismay me—all the time I could see, thro' the floating wraiths of mist only the moon shining very calmly on a four-acre field of grass, a field with a stone in the centre, against which Farmer Morrell's cows were used to rub themselves. There were no cows in the field that night.

That, I say, was all I could see. Suddenly, though, as I gazed—trying to reduce the deadly effect of what I heard and felt by what I could see—I realised that the strangest thing was to be shown to my eyes. The grass in the field was tall and rank. As I looked at the field, I saw that the grass was being beaten down, beaten as if by some storm of tremendous hailstones. It was going even as I gazed—though nothing fell upon it but the light of the moon and the quick sound made by those invisible feet—the grass was disappearing, broken and crushed and trodden to the earth. I made a final desperate effort to break through the wall of mist, feeling I should be nearer reality if I could handle that smashed grass; as I thrust, suddenly, as suddenly as the chanting and the dancing had come, came complete silence. Then a long, high shriek, a shriek of agony and triumph, in a voice I knew so well.

*   *   *   *   *   *

94

Hugh's life was saved; he left Oxford and, after a time in a nursing home, started work in London and succeeded. It was Farmer Morrell found him and me—I had fainted on hearing his cry— and he fetched Dr. Whitman, and was kind and efficient. He was singularly uninquisitive about the whole affair, except as to how his good field of hay had been turned in a few hours, to a hard clay without a vestige of grass upon it.

THE OTHER END

I

I HAVE been accused, very unjustly, of culpable neglect in the affair of Terence Burke. Those who have brought the accusation are persons, I gather, with little or no sense of the ordinary decencies of society, and the limits of tutorial interference. One of the greatest difficulties of the mixed state of modern society is that one is constantly meeting individuals who are really practically anarchic in their view of human intercourse, and who have no sense of those comely gradations which alone make possible the true structure of English life.

My dear mother, who is a Conyng of Conyng, always impressed on me that nothing, except imminent danger to one's faith or one's wife, could every justify a breach of the recognised social rules: fortunately the Established religion, of which I am of course an adherent, is never in danger of an extreme kind, and as a bachelor I lack the other incentive to overstep those canons which govern our intercourse with our fellow creatures.

Still, I can see that even well conditioned people, persons of birth and breeding, might look askance on my share in the Burke tragedy, and so I have thought right to set down the precise course of the incidents from the time I entered Sir Humphrey Burke's house. Indeed, seeing that the Duke of Munster, whom Sir Humphrey always claimed as a cadet of his house, has said frequently that "if it had not been for that little snipe of a tutor, poor Terry would never have suffered," I must insist upon putting before the Duke and the public a clear statement of the whole business.

II

My mother always admitted she had made a mistake in marrying William Smith. It alienated the Conyngs, and when Mr. Smijth (my mother insisted of course on his reverting to the old spelling) died the year after their marriage, my mother was left very badly off. I do not think that she had more than four thousand a year, and it was with difficulty that she sent me to a decent school and to Oxford. Herbert Conyng, her brother, who lived in wicked ease at Albany, refused to help her: and it is to her self denial that I owe the education I gained at Eton and Christ Church. After I had left the house, I was rather at a loss for a living. My mother had hoped I would take Holy Orders: but two things deterred me. I am a man of exceptional intellect and great critical ability, and I could not quite make the Articles of the Church tally with what I saw was reasonable. Then, while I might have accepted Orders in the Church of the earlier part of the century, I was naturally revolted at the growth of degrading superstition and idolatry, fostered by the distressing *intransigeants* of the Oxford Movement and the Ritualistic conspiracy.

So I determined to find, if I could, a suitable tutorship and use that perhaps as a stepping-stone to the foundation of a decent private school, a thing which England sadly lacks. Owing to my independence of mind my actual career at Oxford was not academically noteworthy. Indeed I only secured a pass in my Honours Moderations, and a fourth class in History finals: but, as my tutor said in a testimonial he was good enough to write, "my classes in the schools in no way represented my real ability." (It is true he was heard, in explaining this testimonial, to say that "he had spoken the strict truth, as Conyng-Smijth's ability could not fairly be represented by Omega"—but this injudicious pleasantry I attribute to his habitual over-indulgence in sherry.)

So I gave my name—about this time I dropped the Smijth—to the Appointments Committee, and went to my mother's exiguous but comfortable Brighton cottage, until I should hear of any position which a gentleman would with propriety accept.

While I was in Brighton I earned a little pocket money by acting as a witness for the Spy Association, and provided a good deal of the more pungent evidence for the Royal Commission on Ecclesiastical Disorders which was then sitting.

It was indeed just after I had been present at Exposition—a piece of disgusting and childish idolatry—at the notorious church of St. Bartholomew, that I found the first communication I had had from the Appointments Committee. The letter of the Secretary was, I thought, oddly abrupt.

"Dear Mr. Conyng,

"I don't know if this post will suit you. Sir Humphrey Burke does not seem to be particular in his requirements. Will you write to him if you care about the post.

"Yours truly,

"A. B. NIXON."

He enclosed a small type-written sheet which ran as follows:

"Sir Humphrey Burke requires a tutor for his nephew, a boy of twelve. Terence Burke is difficult, sulky and backward. He needs a firm hand. Sir Humphrey requires a gentleman, Eton and Christ Church, if possible. Academical distinction is not necessary. Applicant must be a convinced Protestant. Please apply to Sir Humphrey Burke, Oakridge House, Beaminster, Dorset."

On the whole I liked the tone of this advertisement; and after looking up Burke in Debrett, I wrote to Sr Humphrey, and stated that I might be willing to accept the position, if the remuneration was sufficient, and if I thought the post likely to do justice to my powers. Sir Humphrey's answer was extremely courteous: I keep all papers of importance and am able to quote it in full:

"Dear Sir,

"Of the many applicants I have had, yours strikes me most favourably. My nephew is to enter at Harrow, if possible, next year. He is already far overdue. I will be frank with you. He is a fanciful, idle boy, and, I fear, has tendencies to vice. I have had four tutors for him in the last year: the first left because, he said, Terence was stupid: the others because they differed from me on the necessity for discipline. The salary I offer is at a rate of £200 a year. You will live in the house, and yourself be responsible for the hours of work, etc. I am a widower, and live alone here, save for Terence. If you think the post suitable, can you kindly be here in a week from to-day?

"Yours faithfully,

"HUMPHREY BURKE."

After consultation with my mother, I decided to accept the post. I had no doubt as to my capacity to manage the boy, and I could not but recognise that the terms offered were far above the average.

So on Thursday, September 21st, 190—, I took the train for Bridport.

There are people who profess to admire the country in the West of England. Dorset, it is true, has not the offensive bleakness of character which makes Cornwall impossible for civilized beings; but as I drove out from Bridport, I was not at all favourably impressed with my surroundings. The immense fields given over to a few cattle, the irregular formation of the hills, the staccato aspect (as Miles of Trinity once put it) of a few solitary trees on the horizon, all struck me as extremely displeasing. Still, I admit there was a gentle warmth in the air, and when the conveyance entered the drive of Oakridge House, I was prepared to be pleasantly moved. The drive, which was short, led up to a small Georgian house. There were, I afterwards found, only ten bedrooms and four or five attics. Two of the four reception rooms were of a fair size, but the study in which I had to work with Terence could not have been much more than thirty feet by twenty-five. Still, though there was no billiard room, the general appearance of the house was one of comfort and decent gentility.

I was received at the door, not as I had hoped, by Sir Humphrey, but by a large person who supposed I was the new tutor. Having satisfied her on this point she condescended to explain that Sir Humphrey was at a magistrate's meeting, but would be in before long, and that meanwhile, after I had been to my room, tea would be served in the study—the small room I have already mentioned— and that Master Terence would be available for inspection.

The windows of my bedroom, to which I was conducted by a maid-servant of unnecessary plainness, looked out over an undulating and considerable stretch of parkland. It was kept, I noticed, rather poorly—but that of course might be due to the fad of some eccentric gardener. There are people who profess to admire wildness instead of the more gracious lines of classical and Italian landscape. For myself, Protestant as I am, I have always felt that the more spacious and severe styles are better suited to a civilised and rational people than the gloomy Gothic of the barbarous middle ages. I made a leisurely toilette, and came down to the study. There I found Terence Burke waiting for me.

Since the unfortunate incident which has compelled me to commence authorship, many people, including some of the ruder sort of journalist, have examined me as to my "first impressions" of

Terence. They seem to think that his unusual history must enshroud a peculiar personality, or at the least, a striking appearance. They picture him as a kind of innocent Byron, a less experienced Shelley. He was, as it happens, a perfectly ordinary boy in appearance: and what was not ordinary in his character was only to be deprecated by persons of sound judgment. (May we not say this of all deviations from the ordinary? And would not its general admission preserve us from much foolish adventure and heady admirations?) Terence was short for his age; he was good looking in an Irish way. There was not enough determination about the jaw, and there was too much weakness—miscalled sensitiveness by the Duke of Munster—about the mouth. He had curly fair hair, bright blue eyes, and his face, near the nose, was slightly freckled. He was well built, but had the legs of a boy who rides over much; and he combined a superficial politeness with, as I was afterwards to discover, an astonishing capacity for being deaf to what displeased or fatigued him.

Sir Humphrey told me that his nephew took after his mother, who was a Smith O'Brien, a family notorious for its disloyalty and Popish proclivities, but otherwise distinguished enough: and this may explain Sir Humphrey's animosity towards his nephew. Terence was an orphan: his father was killed in the South African War, and his mother died—she was an over-emotional woman—not very long afterwards. Up till then, I subsequently discovered, Terence had been nominally a Catholic. His mother of course was a Papist: and his father belonged to that malicious party in the Church of England which is indistinguishable in its devices and devotions from the Roman Catholic heresy. By a providential dispensation, neither Mr. nor Mrs. Burke left any will or appointed any guardians or trustees: so Sir Humphrey, in taking the child to his house, felt at complete liberty to ignore the parents' superstition, and brought Terence up as a sound Protestant. That he was not more successful must be taken as evidence of the terrible, undermining power of the Romish faith: for though Terence sat through morning prayer at the chapel which Sir Humphrey had built in his grounds—the parish church at Beaminster, though not actually Romish, was far too advanced—he was admittedly "bored" with the gospel-service, and retained loving recollections of Rosary, and Benediction, and Mass.

I had no vaticinations as to my position as I shook hands with my pupil in the study and told him to sit down, and tell me about himself. I anticipated a dull time, but I could see no signs of the disorder or unruliness which the advertisement in the paper had led me to expect. Terence was polite, even a little formal, in address. He had no tendency to chatter, and I felt justified in congratulating myself on my perspicacity in selecting the position. I found out, during tea, that Terence was not at all backward in his studies. He had an almost unaccountable enthusiasm for the Latin poets, and I did not always find it easy—having of course not looked at the Classics since Moderations—to remember his exact allusions. He seemed to have read nearly the whole of Walker's "Corpus," except Lucan, Silvius Italicus and Juvenal. In discussing the last named— certain of whose satires I took as a special book—he became almost voluble.

"Please, Mr. Conyng" (I was glad to notice he gave the "o" its right value) "Don't you think Juvenal is horrid? I don't see why he should have written in such a rage: I gave him up after the first satire. I can't stand people being furious with other chaps. It doesn't seem to help somehow."

"Ah, but you must remember, Terence, that Juvenal had a very sad state of society to cope with. The unmentionable vices of the Roman Empire needed the poet's rhetoric to quell them——"

"Oh, were people better then after Juvenal, Mr. Conyng?"

This question unfortunately found me unprepared. Roman History is a Greats, not a Mods subject; and I really did not know quite what improvements the satirist effected. So I took refuge in the undoubted fact that we don't quite know when Juvenal wrote, and that therefore it is difficult to ascertain positively if his satire improved society. Terence seemed unwilling to drop the subject, and so I deftly turned the conversation by asking him how far he had got on with Horace.

"I've read most of him, Mr. Conyng. I hate a lot of the odes; but his satires are rather jolly, and so are the epistles."

So far as I can remember, these sentences accurately represent Terence's manner of talking: so it will be seen he did not greatly differ from the normal boy, except by the avoidance of the more distressing vulgarisms such as "top-hole," "hot-stuff" and "the limit"—an avoidance attributable, I fancy, to the fact that he had not yet been to a school.

I attempted to question him about his previous tutors, and their reasons for leaving. Here he was curiously uncommunicative. His answers became abrupt, and his manner not so much uneasy as absurdly dignified, almost as if he thought I was being unduly inquisitive.

Finally "I think you had better ask my uncle, Mr. Conyng," he replied: and made it inconvenient to continue the conversation. A little later I dismissed him to his play.

Sir Humphrey came in shortly afterwards. This unfortunate gentleman has met with a great deal of obloquy. I grant that he was unwise and hasty; but I have no reason for supposing that he did not believe himself to be swayed by the best of motives. Certainly no one could have been a more considerate host. He was full of apologies for his absence on my arrival, but trusted I would excuse an apparent discourtesy committed on the grounds of public duty. He seemed to have a very sound view of the position of the Conyngs, while professing a humorous preference for the Celtic families with which he was connected. He begged me to excuse any seeming incivility in the servants. "I know," he said, "that Mrs. Hansford has an odd manner. But she's an honest housekeeper, and looks after the other servants. And she's a good Protestant." We chatted then a little about affairs at Brighton, and about the degraded type of person, with neither birth nor breeding, now too frequently raised to the Episcopal bench. It is true that some people more suspicious than I might have thought that Sir Humphrey was rather long in coming to the subject of his nephew; but I thought his delay showed a real delicacy and a genuine wish to treat me as a guest rather than as a tutor. I did, however, at last mention Terence myself; and I was, I confess, a little surprised when Sir Humphrey replied, quite casually and shortly:

"Ah! yes. So you've seen him. Odd boy, very; wants discipline, wants good discipline."

I find on re-reading this that I have given no idea of Sir Humphrey's appearance. It is no use pretending that it is prepossessing. Apart from his extremely short stature, and the tendency to an obesity greater than is usual among gentlepeople, his actual features cannot be regarded as other than displeasing. I noticed immediately the large mouth, the rather cold and uneasy eye; an eye which I have heard Mrs. Hansford unfairly describe as shifty, and the oddly undeveloped eyebrows. Even so, had Sir Humphrey only conformed with the style his appearance suggested, and worn the ample beard of our grandfathers, he could have posed quite well as a representative of the honest, plain, rough English country gentleman. But his unfortunate trick of shaving the upper lip clean, and leaving a fringe of hair round the cheek and under the chin seemed to be a wanton insistence on the original defects of his countenance. Still, I think it absurd to lay so much stress, as is now the fashion, on personal appearance. Sir Humphrey's manner was excellent; his table was exceptionally good, and his cellar stocked with real taste— though I could not agree with his overvaluation of the Burgundy of 1900 against that of 1904: and when I retired that evening I congratulated myself on my unerring sense in finding a house where the work promised to be light, the society that of gentlefolk, and the remuneration more than the pittance so often given to men in my position.

III

Extract from Terence Burke's Diary.

"The new Tutor came today. He's not use, except that he has some books. He sucks up to Uncle Humphrey like anything, and I don't believe he's got any pluck at all. Still, I got off last night and went to sleep pretty soon. She came just about three o'clock, and this time we got out of the side-door. It seemed longer than usual; but it was like heaven when we got there. She insists that there are still difficulties in the way; but promises that I shall see the Other End in a week. And that will mean no more horribleness. She told me last night that most of them do believe in Jesus and Mary: that those who didn't have gone. I asked her 'where'—but she didn't seem to understand. 'Just gone, Terence, you know—?' 'You mean they aren't anywhere—they're nowhere.' 'Oh—no! That's quite different, that happened to the Greek things, Pan and Apollo and things like that. They're nowhere: and they can come out. But those of us who couldn't believe just went. They're quite safe: and they wouldn't hurt anything. But of course it has made a lot of difference to the trees.' 'It must have,' I said. I put this down, because if I ever do meet someone clever and decent, I'll ask him about everything. I could have asked old Fellowes, if he hadn't drank so much. I'm sure I can never tell Mr. Conyng anything about anything, or ask anything except information and things."

IV

Mr. Conyng's Story.

I had been at Oakridge for two days and, except for two slight incidents requiring the prayerful consideration of a Christian and the discretion of a Conyng, nothing untoward had occurred. I always make it a rule to familiarise myself, in so far as it is possible and convenient, with the habits of those I am living with. To know how much an after dinner nap is valued, to remember whether your host really dislikes offering you his newspaper first, to be certain about the hour of meals, and the appetite of one's fellow-diners are all matters which only the reckless or the ill-bred will neglect. For proper consideration, however, one needs a fair amount of what some people call inquisitiveness: and though by temperament averse from meddling in others' affairs, I refuse to neglect any opportunities which a little patience enables me to seize. So, when on the second evening I heard a strange noise while I was dressing, I felt bound to investigate.

I slipped into my dressing gown—a really handsome article of red silk, made from some vestments very properly taken from an Italian monastery—and went into the passage. The noise here was more distinct. It was a kind of thud, as of wood falling on some softer material, and it seemed to come from one of the rooms. I knocked lightly at Sir Humphrey's door, but there was no response.

I was just going to walk on and knock at Terence's, who had already retired for the night, when his door opened, and Sir Humphrey came out, looking rather flushed. He had a smile on his face, and his eyes were not quite as cold as usual. (My capacity to observe minute details is, I believe, the only trait I inherit from my father. Mr. Smijth was high up in the Toast and Tape Department, where the duties involve a very close attention to detail.) He seemed a little surprised to see me, so I stepped forward and said:

"Oh! Sir Humphrey, I thought I heard an unusual noise; I was about to investigate its source. Possibly it was Terence at some prank?"

"I'm glad you noticed it, Conyng (Sir Humphrey had asked me to drop the formal Mr.). You remember I asked you not to whip Terence at any time?"

"Yes, indeed. I shouldn't dream of going against your wishes."

"No. Well, now I'll tell you my reasons. I flog him myself— when he needs it. And he needs it most nights. He's a deceitful, and I'm afraid, lecherous young cub."

"Surely, Sir Humphrey: that is—is—a little strong. A boy so young can hardly—well—scarcely be susceptible to the charges you hint at."

"I didn't hint, Conyng, I know. And I daresay we can work together to cure him."

With that he ended our conversation by going into his room.

I returned to mine, to ponder over this strange information, and to make a note of how early the worst effects of Romanist superstition can show themselves, and how difficult it is for any one to eradicate them.

The next incident occurred the following morning after luncheon. Sir Humphrey asked me to come with him to his smoking room, as he wished to discuss something of importance. When I joined him there, I found him ready with an account of Terence's general character and temperament. As a rule, as I may have indicated. Sir Humphrey was a man of blunt language and quick expression; but on the subject of Terence he was strangely vague. Indeed, had he been of a different class, I should say he was guilty of something approaching verbiage. So I shall make no attempt to reproduce the exact form of his communication; but will give the substance in as few words as possible.

The root of the trouble was that Terence was at heart a Papist ("a bloody Papisher" was Sir Humphrey's expression. His family is a Belfast one.) His conformity with Protestant forms of worship was purely superficial: and though Sir Humphrey had broken an idol of the boy's—an image of the Virgin Mary; and had smashed his crucifix, and taken away his rosary, it does not seem that he had managed to wean the boy's affections from his early superstition. That these superstitions had bred their inevitable crop of sensuality Sir Humphrey believed with a conviction I was unable to share. I had no doubt, of course—no Protestant with the history of Rome writ in lustful letters for him to read could have any doubt—that the boy would, unless cured, fall a victim to evil practices; but I could not think that Terence, who was an honest, plain-spoken youth, had yet acquired any disgraceful habits or formed any dishonourable connection. This I told to Sir Humphrey with a firmness which I think impressed him. And I hope my accusers will take notice that on the matter principally under discussion, I from the first defended Terrence. My subsequent action was directed not from doubt of the boy, but a desire to satisfy my employer, and, if possible, to rid his mind of an ungenerous suspicion.

Did I then agree to the floggings? On this matter I refused to be cross-examined. Here I will state plainly that I acted for the best.

Had I known the severity of the floggings I might have protested; but Terence did not complain, and I have no personal experience to guide me. To say, a the Duke did, that any man, except one with the skin of a rhinoceros, the brain of a bullfinch, and the heart of a snake, would know a cat o' nine tails hurt like the devil, is to assume a knowledge of penal instruments which is no part of a decent education. Sir Humphrey was a gentleman: he used a stick to which nine small cords were attached. Therefore such an instrument was one which could properly be used by a gentleman in correcting his nephew. I know it is the fashion now to sneer at the syllogism, but I can see no flaw in that. I did hint to Sir Humphrey that his floggings were rather frequent; but he assured me that Terence was a hot-blooded, lustful young devil and needed cooling. And he did, after all, know the boy far better than I did, or any of his critics. For if years of close intercourse do not constitute personal knowledge, what, I may ask, does?

I have still to disclose the request Sir Humphrey made me: compliance with which has brought me so much blame.

To support his suspicion of Terence's character, he informed me that once he had met the boy walking in his sleep. That he had stopped him without waking him, and that Terence tried to get past, saying "He must go and meet her." I pointed out that this was scarcely evidence of any sound kind. Terence might have been dreaming of his mother, or even of the Virgin Mary. Sir Humphrey then said:

"Well, Conyng, there may be something in what you say. So I'll ask you this. Will you help me to find out? We can make certain: but you must help me. Terence keeps a diary. If we could find that, I believe we'd find out what the young scamp is up to."

Sir Humphrey spoke almost jocularly. He seemed to have thrown

off the anger which marked his earlier disclosures. Many people—
once more the Duke of Munster has been most conspicuous—have
called me "lick-spittle spy," "cringing toad" and similar opprobrious
nicknames, which only serve to betray their singular lack of taste and
ignorance of manners, without in the least affecting my reputation.
I agree that I might have declined to accept the task offered to
me. It is not part of a tutor's duties to discover what his pupil
writes, or where he keeps his diary; but it is, I conceive, a tutor's
duty to do all he can to clear up a misunderstanding between his
pupil and the boy's guardian. None of my critics have shown how
I could have done better:* I, at least, did not, like my predecessors,
forsake my position directly its difficulties were apparent. No: I
told Sir Humphrey I should need a short time for consideration
and prayer; and then I was guided to accept the charge, and pledge
myself to discover where Terence Burke kept his diary; and to hand
the book over, when found, to the boy's uncle.

V

Extract from Terence Burke's Diary.

"Mr. Conyng—it's funny I should write him always as 'Mr.'—
has been here four days now. I found him in my room this afternoon.
He'd come in to leave me a book—something about bees by a man
called Maeterlinck, which was rather decent of him. I wish I liked
him more: but he's so frightfully pally with Uncle. I can't make him

*I dismiss as puerile the Duke of Munster's inept suggestion that I had
no duties but to call in the police, or an Inspector of the Society for Prevention
of Cruelty to Children. As a sound Tory, I could not betray a man of my own
class to the officials of a discredited and dishonourable Government, even had I
been satisfied that Sir Humphrey had exceeded the rights of his position. Nor,
of course could I encourage any society that habitually disregards the sacred
claims of the family.

out. Unless he's an awful duffer, he must have found out about the floggings: and most of them did something when they did. Poor old Fellowes would have left straight away and fetched a bobby, I believe; but Uncle made him frightfully tipsy at dinner—and then buzzed him for being boozed. Somehow Uncle has always got the better of them: I suppose he always will. But I do get so tired of it. Please, Mary, help me. Mary, help of Christians, pray for me.

"Jesus, by Thy Stripes, help me to bear it. Amen."

*   *   *   *   *   *

"She was awfully good to me last night. But she won't talk about Mr. Conyng. Except she says 'Oh! he'll help, Terry, I think.' and *I* think he's much the unlikeliest. She says they are never allowed to explain ways to us, or else she'd love to tell me. But I am certain to get to the Other End before Sunday. It's Thursday now. I don't know what will happen at the Other End; but she says it is more beautiful than anything ever thought of. And that nothing will ever hurt again."

VI

Mr. Conyng's Story.

As I have determined to be perfectly candid in this narrative, I will here say frankly that I had qualms, not about the propriety, but about the necessity of finding Terence Burke's diary. Clever as the boy was in certain ways, he was also childishly simple. I discovered that he "believed" in fairies; that he had stuffed his mind with a great deal of foolish folk lore, and that he was sensitive to a degree almost indecent in a civilised person. He possessed also that curious quality of charm which, in my opinion, is always more suitably found in a woman. A man should be rugged, not tender; stern and hard, not soft and sensitive. Terence had a vein of obstinacy which might pass for character; and he certainly had "pluck" to an unusual extent. But that pluck can subsist along with great weakness we know from the fact that not a few women have been capable of that quality. What most distracted me, however, in my search for Terence's private papers was his straightforward attitude to myself. He might, I can see, have embarrassed me by appeals about the flogging. He might have put me in the awkward position of an arbiter between his uncle and himself; and even though, as it appears from his diary, he refrained from doing this not through generosity, but from a misconception of my character, I was at the time grateful to him.

I have been asked why I did not directly question Terence about his diary, and demand its production. The truth is, I was sceptical as the the existence of any document except perhaps a boyish scrawl of daily event, diversified with boyish comments. And I should have felt foolishly embarrassed if Terence had calmly given me some little note-book with innocent and inane remarks in it. Still, I admit to a feeling of unpleasantness when Terence found me in his room one day. I had, of course, provided myself with an excuse, and he seemed to be genuinely glad to be lent a foolish book about bees. I had scarcely had time to look diligently through his things, but I had searched his desk, and a locker behind his bed. There I found an improvised rosary which I suppose I ought to have taken; but I remembered that to do so would inevitably show him that some one had been through his things; so, sorely against my conscience, I left it.

On Thursday, Sir Humphrey flogged Terence again. He asked me to be present, and I rashly consented. I say "rashly," for, when the time came, I found an excuse to be away. The reason was one I could scarcely explain to Sir Humphrey. I was in his smoking room, and, remembering how cunning people are at hiding things, I was struck with the possibility that Terence might have hidden his diary in the smoking room. So I began a search there. I found a good many interesting things. There was a series of French novels of the type known as "facetious"; and a very curious book called "Nero" with ugly plates of men being flogged. There was also some stories by a man with the odd name of Masoch. These I glanced at hurriedly, and with a certain surprise at Sir Humphrey's taste in literature. But what decided me against being present at the flogging was my discovery of the instrument used. I have already described it: the little cords, of which it was composed, were covered with coagulated blood. Now, from childhood, I have been susceptible to the sight of blood, and it had not occurred to me till then that whipping a boy actually drew blood. So on the plea of a headache I excused myself from the distasteful duty of seeing Terence whipped.

He was evidently a boy of considerable strength, for he seemed little the worse the next morning. Still, I felt that it would be better for the whippings to cease, so I made up my mind to discover the diary. With this end I gave Terence a holiday after 11.0 on Friday. His Popish training was not sufficient to prevent him accepting it with considerable glee, and I took precautions to have an uninterrupted search. I have been blamed for this. On this point I did not expect understanding from the coarse-minded of my critics. But I should have expected those who have some claim to gentility, to realise that I "got Terence out of the way," as they put it, not only to facilitate my search, but in order to spare his feelings. My search, as all who are interested in the case know, was successful; but I must delay the story while I interpolate another extract from the diary itself.

VII

From Terence Burke's Diary.

"Mr. Conyng gave me a day off to-day. I wonder why. I hate being so suspicious, but things seem upset in this room somehow. I went off, of course, to Little Gap, and She was there, and we had a gorgeous time. It was ripping. She told me why they chose oaks: the Other End is much better than with ordinary trees, and lasts longer. And the oak seems to be more hospitable than other trees: and more of them came in when Jesus was born. It is funny that trees and things and They should have known all about Jesus and Mary before human beings. She says it is because of the difference in time. Their time is vertical, while ours is horizontal; and some things, like the Olympians, have their time just abrupt.

"There were a lot of Them there to-day, and they all seemed glad to see me—but I love Her more than any of the rest. She knows more about us than most of them do.

"And She promised me again that I should get to the Other End before Sunday. And this is Friday. I wonder——"

Here the diary ends.

VIII

Mr. Conyng's Story.

When I told Sir Humphrey that I had found the diary he was inordinately pleased. He had expected me to take it away; but I told him that I could not consent to that. I thought he had better ask Terence for it, or else remove it himself. It was hidden below a loose board underneath the bed, and the state of the floor showed that the housemaid had taken her duties very lightly. I complained of this to Mrs. Hansford, and I regret to say that she merely replied

"She likes a man to be a man, and not to go mucking round looking for mistakes in the work of poor hard working gels, which wasn't their business."

Sir Humphrey determined on a plan which I thought unnecessarily elaborate.

"Look here, Conyng. That young imp thinks he's rid of us after we've gone down to dinner. I expect it's then he writes in the diary. Well, I'll put dinner back to-night. I'll give him half an hour, and at quarter past eight when he thinks we are safe in the dining-room, we'll go up and, dam-me, I believe we shall find him at his book."

Nothing would persuade him to take a less theatrical course. He was annoyed at not having thought before that Terence must write in the evening. I believe he felt it was impossible for the boy to do anything after the flogging. I pointed out to him that we should probably have a scene—but he declared his indifference to scenes. So at about 8.25 we went up. The scene was most unpleasant. Terence seemed completely taken aback: he did and said nothing, until Sir Humphrey seized the diary in which he was writing. Then the boy became furious. He rushed at his uncle. He kicked, he struggled and wrestled. He threatened his uncle and me with horrible penalties if we ever read a bit of the book. None of this bad behaviour, of course, had any effect; but I could not help regretting that Terence had been given the excuse for displaying it. I have sometimes allowed myself to think that Sir Humphrey was not sufficiently careful to avoid giving cause of offence. No doubt we cannot take quite literally the injunction and the warning in the Gospels about "causing one of these little ones to stumble"; but there seems no doubt, strange as it appears to us, that the Founder of our Religion expected His followers to be particularly careful in their relations to children. Still, it was evidently impossible to yield to passion, and Sir Humphrey and I left Terence, and went away with the diary. I returned a few minutes afterwards, and found the boy prone on his bed still in a storm of emotion which, I pointed out, could only be injurious to his health and annoying to his elders. I am sorry to say he did not appreciate my attention, and so far forgot himself as to exclaim that he now saw I was the sneakiest of the lot. Seeing it was useless to attempt reasonable remonstrances I left him, and joined Sir Humphrey in the dining-room. Owing to this unfortunate policy of taking Terence "in the act" the entrée, I remember, was dreadfully over-cooked. That Sir Humphrey was greatly disturbed is sufficiently shown by the fact that he omitted to comment on this, although he was a man who was generally quite plain-spoken about the details of his dinner.

After dinner Sir Humphrey began the serious reading of the diary. The character of that work can be judged by the extracts I have given. It was almost entirely occupied with the affairs of the mysterious being whom Terence invariably referred to as "She." Sir Humphrey saw in this preoccupation evidence of his worst suspicions. I, with an acumen for which no one has given me credit, saw that Terence was not wicked but either a maker of fairy tales or a sufferer from mental weakness. Still, I could not deny that, unless the whole diary was a farrago of rather feeble fiction, it contained evidences that Terence believed himself to be in the habit of keeping assignations with some one feminine. The place of the assignation was kept singularly obscure. There were many references to the Great Tree, to Little Gap, to the Kind Hedge, to Silver Pool. But there was no indication where these fancifully named things were. I tried to assure Sir Humphrey that this fantastic nomenclature was almost proof that Terence had simply been romancing like a school-girl—but he would have none of it. He summoned Mrs.

Hansford, and without disclosing his reasons, asked her if she had ever heard of a place called Little Gap.

"Of course, Sir Humphrey. Fancy you not knowing Little Gap. Why, you go 'bout quarter of a mile on the road to Broadwindsor, and then turn off by the big elm, and about five hundred yards on is Little Gap. It's close to the Great Tree—one of the oaks King Charles hid in, or summat."

"Thank you, Mrs. Hansford. And do you know of a pond or anything called 'Silver Pool'?"

"No, Sir Humphrey. That's not near here."

"Ah! thank you. That's all, Mrs. Hansford."

I should like to mention here that Sir Humphrey's kindness and politeness to his menials prove him to be a man of good heart.

When Mrs. Hansford had gone, Sir Humphrey turned to me.

"Well, Conyng, we'll catch him. Catch him with the woman. He's in trouble now: he'll bolt as soon as he can to his Little Gap. I shouldn't be surprised if he went to-night. And we must follow."

*   *   *   *   *   *

I now come to the part of my story which I had much sooner leave unwritten. I know of course that the common, supernatural explanation of what we saw and underwent is false, because there are no such beings as She claimed to be. But who played tricks with us, and why, I cannot conjecture or discover. I am not surprised at the police's failure to find the woman; but I regret extremely that the Duke of Munster refused to have down a private detective. It is a monstrous thing that a man of Sir Humphrey's position (I do not mention myself) should be the victim of a woman whose character can be none of the best, as she was out unattended in the wilds of Dorset in the early hours of the morning.

Sir Humphrey was, to my surprise, perfectly correct in his surmise that Terence would go out that night. We sat up in my bedroom (which adjoined the boy's) and we heard him go out of his room shortly after midnight. We did not follow until he was out of the house, and then we kept at a distance which made it impossible for him to hear our footsteps. Sir Humphrey, whose establishment was singularly complete, had several pair of rubber-soled shoes, and we had donned these for our midnight excursion.

Terence seemed particularly light-hearted that night. He went fast and gaily down the road, and he whistled an odd tune which Sir Humphrey informed me was a Nationalist air. He followed the Broadwindsor Road, as Mrs. Hansford had said, and turned off by a large elm, a tree I had noticed before, as it overhung the road at a dangerous angle. Quite suddenly, it seemed to me, he stopped. He was standing near a large oak with the moonlight full upon him, and I heard him give a sigh—a sigh of relief. He was perfectly alone; of this I am positive. His first words were "At last," and then he stood with his face up, and I heard a sound which certainly seemed like that of an embrace. I turned to Sir Humphrey.

He was puzzled and I'm afraid, angry.

"I believe you're right after all, Conyng, and the boy's just a natural.[9] But he seems quick-witted, doesn't he?"

"He does; but of course he may be defective in one direction only."

"H'sh—he's talking."

Terence was speaking, with his face still up, and his arms in the position of one holding some one else round the body.

"Oh! It was horrible to-day. They've taken my book, and they're reading it. It's beastly, and I don't know what I shall do."

---

[9] A person with a profound intellectual disability.

Then came the greatest shock I have ever had.

A voice of very deep quality distinctly said:

"To-night, darling, you shall come to the Other End. And you may stay there. I obtained permission from Them all."

"Oh you dearest—may I? For always?"

"For always—for our always—and then we will all go together."

"And is it far to the Other End?"

"Not to-night, Terry, nor for you. You see how high this end is——"

Terence looked upward and nodded.

"Well, Other End is twice as far as from the ground to the top-most leaf. Shall we go now?"

"Please, dearest. Carry me!"

Then a singular thing happened. Although Terence was still alone, his body rose in the air and lay in a position which would have been natural had he been in the crook of some one's arm. Nothing visible supported him.

Sir Humphrey spoke again, and his voice sounded a little frightened.

"Conyng, I'm going to stop him. Come on!"

He rushed forward—and I tried to follow. But something stopped us both. A great force pressed against my body. I put my hand up to ward it off, and felt something shaped like a finger, which I could not move. Then as I wrestled, there was a huge clap of thunder, though the sky was perfectly cloudless, and Sir Humphrey who had been struggling wildly to get forward, fell flat on the ground. The clap was followed by a dazzling brightness which blinded me for a moment. In the actual moment, while my vision swam, I seemed to see the outline of a tall woman, one of whose arms was stretched towards us, while the other encircled Terence.

The brightness lasted but a minute, and, when my eyes were used to the night again, the figure had disappeared.

Terence was lying at the foot of the oak, smiling, and Sir Humphrey lay where he fell, with his face unpleasantly distorted and his right leg drawn up in an ugly fashion.

That is the true account of Terence Burke's death and Sir Humphrey Burke's paralytic stroke.

The jury at the inquest insisted that Terence died of exhaustion following the floggings given him by his uncle, against whom no proceedings were taken owing to his state of health.

No one else that night heard the clap of thunder or saw the lightning; but no one has explained why there is a pattern of oak leaves all down Sir Humphrey's paralysed arm and leg; or how I acquired on my chest a red mark, in shape like the two fingers of a woman's hand. I believe myself that the whole affair was a gruesome practical joke, worked by some one with an uncanny knowledge of electricity. The country-side, of course, takes the most superstitious view of the matter, and some of the more ignorant and profane even dare to call this deplorable affair a judgment of God.

THE MINOTAUR

I

"IT'S all very well, my dear, but I cannot bring myself to like a man who killed my old friend Damastes."

Minos said this with an air of finality, as he took the last olive from the silver dish on the table. Before he ate his olive, a further remark occurred to him, and he hastened to express it, anxious to anticipate his daughter's retort—"No, depend on it, nothing good ever came out of Athens—except olives, Ariadne."

"Really, papa, you might remember that Theseus is not Athenian. His father is, I admit; but a man born in a stable—" Ariadne checked herself in time. She had a grievous tendency to fall back on proverbs, and was rather proud of her competence in finding suitable ones; but she perceived that this one was a little lacking in tact at the moment, and she was anxious not to anger Minos before she had secured from him Theseus's address. So she abandoned her proverb, and went on, "Anyway, papa, why you should mind about Procrustes, I can't think. You never really got on with him, when you did meet. Besides, the man was a terrible nuisance. You know, with a landlord like that, no neighbourhood has a chance of improving. When I think of the poor people who took the trouble to go to that dull Eleusis, and develop the property, and make it fit for civilised folk—and how they . . . they ended— why I don't feel a bit sorry that Theseus *did* kill Procrustes."

Minos, who had motioned to leave the table, sat down again, frowning.

"Really, Ariadne, this is the rankest Socialism. Damastes—and

I wish you would not adopt that detestable modern fad of using nicknames—Damastes had a perfect right to do as he liked with his own. He was far more generous than most landlords. He not only supplied the fixtures; but, as you know, in many cases, the furniture."

"Yes, and in too many cases, carved his tenants about to fit the furniture.'

"My dear child, you have been reading *The Athenian News*. All that gossip about the bedstead was a gross exaggeration of the facts. I remember dear old Damastes telling me about the one incident which has been the basis of so much misrepresentation . . . . 'If you believe me, Minos, there came two dam' fellows—brothers they said they were—one about six foot ten and the other about three foot eight. They grumbled at pretty near every dam' thing in the villa—they were only taking it furnished for six months—and they just talked to me about the bedstead as if I were a dog. First the giant lay down in it, and pushed his great ugly feet through the bars at the bottom and twiddled his bloody toes at me'—I beg your pardon, my dear, but you recollect Damastes's honest, straightforward speech—'then the dwarf squatted down beside him, and showed me he couldn't reach beyond the bolster. Well, Minos, I'm a good-tempered fellow, but no one could expect a man to stand that sort of thing, could they? So I whipped out my sword and took off the giant's feet very neatly at the ankle; and set a couple of sturdy slave-masters on to the dwarf till he was stretched out a bit. I've had nobody since throwing my bedsteads in my teeth.' Poor Damastes! how he used to laugh when he told the story! And now that young prig Theseus has killed him."

Ariadne had yawned discreetly once or twice as her father told the story of his old friend. When he had finished, she said:

"Well, papa, I never cared for Pro—for Damastes. He was

a coarse, drunken person with very little manner and no real refinement. No one in our set would dream of mutilating a tenant. It was a thoroughly *bourgeois* thing to do."

"Great Zeus, girl, what would you have the poor man do? Alter his furniture? It's all very well for you and your friends with your shoddy furniture from the Athenian Stores, stuff that falls to pieces when you touch it—you've no feelings for things, no sense of the beauty of——"

"But we have for the beauty of the human body, papa."

"Pah, sentimental gush! A couple of cretinous mattoids!"[10]

"Really, papa, with poor dear Taury making that hideous noise every night, I don't think we are the family to talk about deformities."

Minos rose, with a certain dignity, in spite of his huge bulk; as he stood at the table, glaring down at his daughter, his flushed, angry countenance still showed sufficient signs of past nobility to make her wonder whether even Theseus was finer than her father must have been as a youth. She knew she had gone too far in her reference to her unfortunate brother; but it had slipped out before she could stop herself. Minos, after swallowing emotionally once or twice, ejaculated in low, grieved tones:

"For shame, Ariadne!" and left the dining-hall.

Ariadne sat for a moment in silence. She was a graceful enough figure in her saffron skirt, with its wide under-trousers, and her decorated, purple blouse. Rather too tightly corseted for our modern idea of feminine beauty, the slim lines of her body had a charm which even her dressmaker had been powerless to destroy. Her hair was arranged in distracting little ringlets over her forehead, while down the back of her neck it fell in waves which did the

---

[10] One who exhibits symptoms of mental degeneration.

utmost credit to the court hairdresser. Her black eyes, their petulant appeal heightened skilfully by a courageous use of paint, were at the moment clouded with the most unwonted thought. It was a long time since Ariadne had wanted anything as much as she wanted the address of the Lord Duke Theseus; and this was the first occasion for years that she had failed to get any desire of hers accomplished as soon as was practicable. Her father's opposition only confirmed her in the view that Theseus was evidently supremely worth knowing, and she was determined that he should meet no other marriageable and royal maiden before he met her. There was Athens, of course; but much as Ariadne admired that city's go-ahead spirit, and frequently as she copied its fashions in dress and aped its prejudices in art and letters, she was far too much her father's daughter to believe that a man of Theseus's evident capacity would not be anxious for an alliance with the oldest and most respected of the European families. Though she did not believe the nonsense—which Minos encouraged—about her grandfather being a god, still there was no doubt that Zeus was a remarkable person and had very considerable psychic power. She remembered a certain thunderstorm . . . but there, she must stop dreaming and get to business.

As she got up from the table and summoned two slaves with a soft clap of her hands, a strange low moan of immense but suppressed volume echoed weirdly through the great alabaster corridors. The slaves visibly quailed; but Ariadne merely shrugged with a faint annoyance as she stepped into the carrying-chair which the slaves were holding. She settled herself comfortably into the cushions, and murmured to herself:

"Brother . . . . I wish I had not mentioned Taury to dad; it always sets him off. I wonder if Theseus will mind—, but there, he won't be marrying the family."

II

The bright Cretan sun was streaming down on Daedalus as he stood, rashly indifferent to a stroke, in his garden at noon; and watched through a highly-polished emerald of enormous size a speck on the blue horizon. As he stood there gazing, his figure, for all its eighty years and his manifold disasters and discouragements, seemed brisk and full of nervous activity. Suddenly he stopped looking through the glass, took up a whistle, and blew several piercing notes over the sea. The speck, at which he had been gazing, rapidly came nearer, and in five or six minutes a rock-blue pigeon, with quiet whirr of resting wings, settled on his shoulder. Daedalus took from under its wing a piece of thin and carefully folded papyrus; dismissed the bird with a light tap on its head, and walked slowly to a seat in the shade where he could examine the message. Its contents appeared to cause him some surprise and not a little anxiety. He sat back in his chair, with a frown on his handsome brow; rose suddenly and went towards the house, still peering at the papyrus.

Daedalus, taking advantage of the universal Cretan custom of the siesta, had long been in the habit of receiving his pigeon-post at noon, or thereabouts; so his reputation for acquiring information in semi-miraculous ways survived even the sceptical spirit which had grown so strong since the amazing career of Theseus. When that Duke had first commenced hero, both Minos and Daedalus thought that he would prove to be simply an athenian Heracles; one of those strong, stupid heroes who are a perfect godsend to the cunning. Up to now, however, Theseus showed a very disturbing combination of muscle and intellect, and no sort of inclination to be diverted from his purpose by any particularly foolish adventures—

whereas Heracles was like a child and would wander miles away to clean a dirty stable or drain some poisonous fen. That neither Minos nor Daedalus had the slightest idea what Theseus was after made them no easier; still less were their fears calmed by the maddening and idiotic laughter of old Zeus, whose villa-temple, The Cave, had been visited by them several times in the hope of acquiring some hint as to the action which would be wisest to take against this upstart son of Poseidon. Knowing the shaky condition of Athenian finance, Minos fully expected Theseus to make difficulties about the tribute which he had for the past three years successfully screwed out of the old king Aegeus. And now comes the very distracting news that the tribute had already left Athens, accompanied as usual with the seven youths and seven maidens for the Minotaur . . . and with, as the wretched scribe put it, His Imperial and Royal Highness, the Sublime Lord Theseus, Duke of Athens, Prince of Attica, Conduct of Innocence, Sole and Supreme Sovran of the Ægean Seas, Turannoctonos, Poseidoniades . . . in command of the frigate.

It was certainly very annoying. As Daedalus was trying to decide exactly how annoying it was, the curtains of the room were slowly parted, and a huge eunuch sidled deprecatingly towards his master. "I cannot be disturbed now by any one," said Daedalus.

"But, my lord, it is the Lady Ariadne."

"Oh . . . ."

Since that unfortunate affair with Icarus, when Ariadne had encouraged the young aviator to go up at midday, while the sun was far too hot and poor Icarus had had a bad stroke, while executing a particularly daring volplane, and fallen ignominiously into the sea . . . well, since that incident, some two years ago, Ariadne and Daedalus had not spoken to one another. He wondered what Ariadne wanted.

"Admit the Princess, Sogden"; and the fat eunuch bowed and disappeared. A moment later the great yellow curtains parted again, and Ariadne entered. She was wearing a curious slashed skirt of saffron and blue, and a thin, almost diaphanous, blouse cut low in the neck. On her head was a rather tall hat of straw. It was shaped like a funnel and the crown was flattened; three wide ribbons of white silk were passed across the front of the hat, carried round to the back, and there crossed and held in position by a golden grasshopper, whose long, trembling antennæ were of a bright emerald green metal. The princess was accompanied by four maids of honour—the slaves had been left outside with the umbrellas and the carrying-chairs—whose clothes, though less fine than hers, resembled them closely in their general effect. Ariadne indicated a bench near the entrance of the room to the four ladies and went forward herself to accost Daedalus, who had stood on her appearance, but made no motion to receive his guest.

"it is good of you, my lord, to receive me at this rather untimely hour . . ." Ariadne faltered a little as if expecting Daedalus to make some response; he remained, however, silent, merely acknowledging her remark by a slight bow. The Princess went on, not quite so cheerfully . . . . "The matter on which I wish your help is of some importance . . . . to me. My lord," this with just a shade of imperiousness, "I trust I have your attention."

"That the Lady Ariadne secures from every one. If she tell her business, I will do anything I can to assist her."

Ariadne approached nearer to the old man and looked appealingly up at his face: then she whispered, rather hurriedly:

"My lord, can you give me the Duke Theseus's address?"

Daedalus looked quizzingly at Minos's daughter. He had heard rumours as to the interest Theseus had created in the Princess; but this was his first intimation that Minos disapproved of that interest. He parried the eager question.

"I hope the High King is well?"

"Thank you, my lord, my father was in excellent health when I left him: but why do you ask?"

"I wondered how it was that you had not sought information from him." Ariadne bit her lip. "My lord, I will be frank. You remember the affair of Procrustes?" Daedalus nodded. "Well, father cannot—or pretends he cannot—get over that. I think it's absurd. Procrustes may have come from an old stock—but he was quite *démodé*.[11] Indeed, the man was frankly *impayable*:[12] and I'm glad Theseus put him out of the way. What I believe is that father is really a little—well, shall we say, jealous for our house's honour and glory? The Lord Duke Theseus is certainly a remarkable man, and has done remarkable things, hasn't he?"

"He has. Not the least is the way in which he has intrigued the Lady Ariadne."

"Oh! my interest is not merely . . . merely personal. You see, father will not ask Theseus here: and I thought it would be nice if I could drop him a line and ask him to propose himself . . . ."

"H'm. You think that would be tactful of him?"

"I'm sure he could be trusted to do it with tact. I shouldn't trust a Cretan, but an Athenian——!"

"Theseus is not altogether Athenian."

"No-o-o-o. But I'm sure he's a perfect gentleman. Do you know where he is, Daedalus?"

"Well, at the moment I do *not*. But two days ago he left Athens."

---

[11] Out of fashion.

[12] Priceless (drôle).

"Left Athens!"

"I suppose you hadn't remembered, my lady, that Crete and Athens have a certain connection?"

"You mean in art—in—Oh! you mean that stupid tribute. No. I had forgotten all about that. I don't know why father doesn't stop it. I'm sure Taury has had enough by now."

"It's not Minotaur who worries us. It's the need for money."

"Oh, that's so vulgar. Or why don't we take it from somewhere else? But, anyway, what has all this—high Zeus! you don't say——"

"Yes. Theseus is in command of the frigate which will bring the tribute and the—er—companions for Minotaur. He is one of them."

Ariadne almost forgot her manners in the excitement of the news. She called to her women, bade Daedalus a hasty farewell, and ordered her litter to take her back to the palace.

III

In the heart of the labyrinth, Minotaur sighed deeply. He did not understand. That had really been his perpetual difficulty. He never understood. Nothing had more distressed and grieved Minos than the stupidity of his "heir." It was not as if poor Minotaur was ordinarily stupid. He had not even got the low cunning of the aborigines of the mainland. Why, when young Icarus had taken his toys away, Minotaur, instead of beating him, had asked him if he'd like some more. "That lad's a perfect moon-calf," exclaimed Pasiphae; and then slowly, bred from a taste we can only deplore as rococo, sprang the absurd and disgusting fable of his begetting by a bull. Still, it was evident that Minotaur could not be allowed to remain about the palace. He was really too much of a fool. He gave things away to the courtiers, and he had no sense at all of the respect due to his birth. Pasiphae in vain tried to threaten him by hinting at a summer holiday with Zeus; but Minotaur only said he thought that Grandfather must be lonely and he'd be glad to go to him. Even had he been less stupid, his physical appearance made it difficult for the family. He was of huge bulk, and he had an odd malformation of the feet, which lent colour to the fantastic story of the bull. In addition, his voice was one of such enormous volume that Daedalus had to invent an instrument through which he might engage in ordinary conversation. Otherwise, his interlocutors would have been deafened. He took no interest in war or in money-making; and while he despised the culture of the Minoan Court, he listened avidly to the stupid songs of the indolent peasantry. It was his tendency to wander about among the lower classes which compelled Minos to take steps for secluding him. So, at last, on Daedalus's suggestion (the contract was worth at least £10,000 to that skilled architect) the Labyrinth was built; and Athens was forced to send companions for Minotaur.

The question of companionship had worried Minos considerably, for he was a kind-hearted man, and could not bear the thought of his son, however stupid, living in complete solitude. On the other hand, it was evident he must not associate with Cretans, who would certainly conspire against the dynasty if they thought Minotaur was in the succession; and the same reason made it impossible to allow any Athenians to return home with stories of the heir's extreme incompetence. Then Daedalus came to his rescue with the idea of the Labyrinth—a structure from which it was almost impossible to effect an exit. It was very cunningly built. If you ventured any distance from the main building, you came upon doors upon which was painted in bright characters "No Exit"; and each lintel was guarded by the Holy Peacock to prevent any aggressor attempting to force his way out. Thus, you roused at once the sceptical spirit and the ordinary human instinct of the imprisoned Athenian, who pushed against the door and was promptly soused by a douche of cold water, while a mechanical voice sang, in rather metallic tones:—

In ye have come, and out ye may not go.

Do ye prefer swift death to life however slow?

This put off all but the boldest. If any one ventured further he had a surprisingly swift passage for another hundred yards or so, and then he stepped on a secret spring which flung him violently up, while a voice chanted:—

If go you must, go up, you sill ass!

Beyond the portals you may never pass!

Few ever went on after that. But to render everything secure, besides various other devices to scare or discourage the adventurous, the great gates of the Labyrinth were kept securely locked with a patent lock, whose secret none knew but Minos, Daedalus, and, I regret to say, Ariadne.

Well, in the innermost chamber of this building, Minotaur sighed deeply. He was very bored. The most tragic thing about his fate was that he had a strong sense of duty. He liked nothing less than entertaining guests: but here they were, and strangers at that, and he felt bound to make them comfortable. On their first arrival, each batch of Athenian visitors was a trifle nervous. The simplest of them—and it was becoming difficult to get any of the *intelligenzia* to consent to the exile—almost credited the absurd fables as to Minotaur's origin and habits. But they were soon reassured. When they saw his great round face, his huge spectacles made of pebbles mounted in horn, his hesitating smile, and limp, deprecating hand, they felt their owner could not be really dangerous. Minotaur had really become the manager of a monstrous hotel. He did not know how many guests he had—for, besides the regular arrivals from Athens, there were always servants from the country; and also, as most of the Athenians formed what they called Labyrinthine alliances, there was a fairly steady arrival of babies.

Minotaur sighed again. Minos in his palace heard him, and grunted with displeasure. He little knew what was disturbing his son. Poor Minotaur was sitting in his big stone chair, on which were carved in coloured relief fennel, borage, and cowslips, with a frown on his broad, amiable brow. In front of him stood a fat little eunuch in a puce-coloured, sleeveless tunic, girt about the middle with a girdle of green cord. Minotaur leant sideways in his chair, so that the eunuch should not meet the direct power of his sighs. Heavily he spoke:

"They complain, Belisarius, of rabbit stew?"

"Sire, they flung the last pot in my face."

Minotaur sighed again.

"It is very difficult to satisfy them, Belisarius. Can you suggest anything?"

"Well, Sire, braised goat——"

"The very thing: get some goats and—er—braise them. And do you mind bringing me my nasturtium salad, and a little cream? My breakfast was forgotten this morning."

"Certainly, Sire. I was going to remark that as we shall have visitors to-morrow——"

"Visitors?"

"Yes, Sire. Surely you have not forgotten? The new guests from Athens will be here, and Theseus, it is said, is among them."

"Theseus? Theseus? I seem to know the name. Is that the scholar who produced that enlightening book on the reasons of poverty and how the rich avoid it?"

"What a fool the Prince is," thought the eunuch scornfully.

"No, Sire," he said, "this is *the* Theseus, Duke of Athens, Poseidoniades, the Sublime Governor of the Outer and the Inner Seas."

"Oh! I remember. The chap who put old Damastes out of the way—. Rather hasty, but, on the whole, a good thing. But how on earth have they induced him to come here?"

"I believe His Highness comes from a strict sense of religion, Sire."

"Really—well, I shall be glad to see him."

"And may I make suitable preparations for the banquet, Sire?"

"Yes—yes—don't bother me more than you can help."

Minotaur at this turned towards the eunuch and sighed gently: the little man was caught in the gust and floated gently and safely down the flight of porphyry steps on to the lower hall.

IV

It was the day of Theseus's arrival. Hitherto, the disembarkation of the Athenian captives had been accompanied by a mixed ceremony. The Court herald, Snake King at Arms, had carefully devised a solemnity which symbolised the legendary fate of the victims, represented the hospitality of Crete, and was just tinged with a note of triumph at the reception of so important a gift. This year, however, at Ariadne's request, the ceremony was profoundly modified. She wished everyone's thoughts to be occupied with the arrival of Theseus, to the exclusion of his lesser companions and the sordid question of money. When the frigate arrived, a series of detonators, one for every year of the Duke's age, was exploded by Daedalus from his terrace. When the bark was actually in the harbour and against the pier, a long procession of men and maidens was formed, reaching for miles from the Palace gates to the pier. On a large car, supported by outriders, and drawn by huge black bulls, Ariadne herself sat, symbolising Crete. Beneath her throne there was a smaller chair. To this the Duke Theseus was conducted by twelve Ethiopian slaves of gigantic stature. Each slave carried a great flambeau, which flared palely against the setting sun, and burnt with the sweet, strong scent of aromatic herbs. The Duke's companions were convoyed in less splendour to double carrying-chairs. When Theseus approached the great car, Ariadne placed her hands on her forehead, and made him an exquisite little nod. The Duke was ravished at the impudent archness of her expression, and dumbfounded at the wonderful fashion of her clothes. For this occasion Ariadne wore a new costume, designed by Arachne. Her trousers, of cool green, were fastened just above the ankle-bone by slim, silver-grey cords, which looked like slow-worms. Her ankles were bare. Her feet were shod in slippers of shagreen, hard and bright. A brilliant yellow jacket covered her to just below the knees in front, and flowed in a train at the back. She could not avoid the traditional low corsage of the Cretan women; and her breasts were visible. Between them were three great black roses. Her head, to the great scandal of the suburbs, was bare; except that over the left ear she had fastened another black rose. Four slim boys, each dressed in a long white toga, held over her a huge umbrella, painted outside in alternate stripes of black and green, and inside a deep rose madder. In response to her greeting, Theseus shaded his eyes with his hand.

He bowed low. "Lady, the sun has done well to set."

Ariadne smiled her pleasure: but she would not miss her retort.

"*Our* lords say the sun never *does* set in Crete, your Grace. But come, will you be seated."

Theseus went to his chair.

"Athens is proud for once to sit at the feet of Crete."

Ariadne had arranged for this compliment as carefully as her maid had done her hair; and she was obviously pleased Theseus had known his cue.

"Shall we proceed, Lord Duke?"

"With you, any whither, Lady!"

On the rather tiresome journey home—for black bulls are not to be hurried easily—Ariadne told Theseus how desolated her father was that a touch of gout had forced him to stay indoors. The truth was that, when Ariadne told her father of her determination to receive the Duke worthily, Minos had growled that she might do as she pleased, and have what damn'd flummery she liked—but he would wait for the fellow in the Palace. "And mind, my girl, no tricks. I'll just say 'good-evening' to him, and then off he goes to Minotaur. You're not to encourage him to get above himself, even if he is a Duke. He's chosen to come here as a companion, and a companion he shall be."

Ariadne had consented at the time, but had no intention of allowing Theseus to be mewed up in the Labyrinth. His obvious admiration had encouraged her light affection for him, and she proceeded to make with him a plan of action.

"I'm afraid, my Lord, my father will be vexed if you don't visit Minotaur."

"But, Lady, of course, it is what I have come for. By the way," Theseus added, and in a less consequential tone, "how bad is he exactly?"

"How bad, my Lord? I don't understand you. My brother is very retiring——"

"Your brother, dear Lady!——"

"Great Chronos, Duke, you do not believe those vulgar legends about Minotaur? You mean to say that a man of your education and experience——"

"Oh—of course not—though some of my poor companions are fully expecting to be eaten. But I thought His Royal Highness must be—well, hang it all, dearest Lady, one does not usually keep the heir to the greatest throne in Europe penned up in a puzzle-box, does one? Be frank with me."

"No—of course, Minotaur is not *ordinary*. You see, he has no inclination to kingship. He doesn't care about power. Daedalus has a hard phrase about it—now what was it?—After the last examination he diagnosed the complaint definitely—I remember. Minotaur is a scientific philosopher!"

"Is he, by Pallas!"

"Yes, or a philosophic scientist. Do you know what it means, Duke?"

"Thank Heavens, no. But I know those who might. They're beginning to breed them in Athens—but *not* in the royal family, what?" Ariadne laughed gaily.

"I'll tell you later, Duke—but there are stories about you, you know!"

"Hush—but then no one can hide the mark of Olympus."

"Well, Duke, what I wanted to say was that there is an old tradition that no one who enters the Labyrinth must come out. And, indeed, no one ever has, I believe."

"That will not suit me, Lady."

"No: so I'm going to tell you the way. After you have had your interview with Minotaur—tell him some of your stories, won't you—you'll be conducted to a special apartment in the Labyrinth. When lights are out—the last flambeau is put out somewhere about 1.0, leave your room and go to the right, down a passage. Have you a glow-worm torch?"

"Yes, I brought mine from Athens. I wasn't sure——"

"Oh! we've had them for months. Well, you'll need it down the passage. You'll see a great many doors with 'No Exit' written over them. Don't try to get out that way, as there are traps and things. But there is one door on which is simply written 'Way Out.' Conquer your natural repugnance, and open that. There may be a shower over it—but I don't think so. Then you will find on the right wall a rope, distant from the ground about four feet. Follow that, and it will bring you to the great door. It will be padlocked. Here, Duke, is the key, and here," ended Ariadne, as she pressed the slim key into his hand, "are Papa and the Palace!"

V

"I haven't enjoyed an evening so for years," said Minotaur through his speaking tube, glowing with admiration and affection at Theseus, who, with a complacent but kindly look on his face, was sitting near his host in the Minotaur's private den.

Ariadne, although she had secured a polite reception from Minos, had not been able to prevent the Duke being dispatched to the Labyrinth at sundown.

There had been a magnificent banquet. Belisarius had excelled himself. Apart from the *pièce de résistance*, a lamb stuffed with quails, which were stuffed with olives, themselves farced with larks' tongues, there was an astonishing array of side-dishes. There was a wonderful salad of nasturtium, apple, and poppy seeds. There was a sweet— raspberries pounded to a juice covered with whipped cream, in which had been melted six pounds of sugar; this was covered with whole raspberries, whose stalks had been taken out, and replaced by an artificial stalk made of pineapple. There was a duck stuffed with green figs and damsons, and served with a sauce of orange juice and peacocks' brains. There was a monstrous venison pasty, on whose top little pigs, compounded of spices, held truffles in their mouths. There were tongues cooked in old Minoan wine, and then smeared with honey and milk. There were pineapples whose cores had been cunningly removed; and in their place peaches, soaked in maraschino, had been introduced. There were great gilt cakes, from which sprang wonderful drinks hidden in the centre of each.

Minotaur made a hearty meal of two apples and a lettuce; and Theseus, after admiring everything, ate nothing but a duck, a dozen goose-eggs poached in cream, and a small plum tart.

After dinner the two had adjourned to Minotaur's room, and had continued their conversation about Theseus. It was well after midnight when Minotaur expressed his pleasure in his evening, and Theseus thought it was time to retire—especially if he were going to leave that night. Somehow he felt mean in sneaking away from this big, ugly, unsuspicious, good-humoured creature, with his mis-shapen feet and head, and bellow of a voice. Also the Minoan wine is strong and Theseus had drunk freely. Anyway, whether we put it down to the generosity of his character or of the wine, Theseus blurted out:

"Look here, Minotaur, do you know why I came?"

" 'Pon my soul, I don't: but I'm heartily glad of it."

"Well, I really came to stop this stupid business of the tribute and—and——"

Theseus felt he could not say "kill you": besides, he had never seriously thought it would be necessary.

"To see me—ah! to rid the people of Athens from the plague, etc.—eh, Theseus?"

"Something of that sort, old man. I'm sorry, but, but, of course, I had the merest gossip to go on."

"Of course—but you don't want to put me out of the way?"

"Great Pallas, no. But the tribute must stop, we really can't afford the cash: the men and girls don't matter—Zeus! I have it. Look here, Minotaur, I'm leaving here to-night——"

"You can't—it can't be done——"

"I can, I tell you. I'll tell you how later. But why not come too? Come to Athens with me. There are a lot of—of—jolly fellows there whom you can talk to. Lots of—you know—philosophic chaps. And if you are in Athens, your Governor can't go asking us to send you the companions: and we won't send him the money."

Theseus looked anxiously at Minotaur. The big creature sat and smiled. Then he nodded.

"I will. I must just collect my things, and I'm with you. But how are we going to get out? I don't know the way, and though, of course, I could find it in the daytime, I can't in the dark. And I should make such a noise. I'm a clumsy fellow."

"Oh! that's all right. Ariadne gave me the key, and told me the way."

Minotaur, who had got up, sat down again heavily. He shook his head.

"That's bad. I'm sorry for you, Theseus. I am really."

And although the Duke followed him about, begging him to explain, Minotaur refused to say more than:

"Poor fellow. Ariadne after him. Poor old fellow," which nearly drove Theseus frantic. Only as they went along the little passage which led to the Great Gate, Minotaur boomed cautiously to his guest:

"I say, Theseus, when we are outside, I'll slip down to the harbour and get aboard. You won't want me about."

VI

The *Bird of Athens* danced gaily over the waves.

Ariadne was lying in a hammock on the upper deck.

She was very cross. She was already a little tired of Theseus; but this did not annoy her. She was bored with having Minotaur on board; but that was not the cause of her anger. She was furious because he had perceived that Theseus was tired of her. So as Theseus approached her, Ariadne frowned. Before he could speak, she asked him:

"When shall we reach Athens, Theseus?"

"It is a little difficult to be certain—the wind is so variable. That"—and he pointed eagerly at a dim shadow on the horizon—"is Naxos."

"Really," said Ariadne. As a matter of fact, she was excited, for Naxos had the reputation of being the smartest watering-place in the Ægean. It was the only one left now with a casino.

"Yes—jolly little island."

"I daresay, Theseus. I notice you always change the subject now. I want to know when we shall reach Athens, because I am thinking we had better get married on board ship."

"Get married!"

"Yes."

"But, really, dearest. I hadn't thought of it. I mean—well, I can't. I *am* married."

"Liar!"

"Very well, Ariadne, if you take that line, rational discussion becomes impossible." And Theseus turned to go.

"Stop. Even if it were true, as *I* am willing to overlook it, I don't think it very delicate of you to mention it. Still, what can one expect from an Athenian?" She tapped her foot impatiently on the deck, while Theseus stood by, resolutely dumb.

"Are you determined not to marry me?"

"That's not the right way to put it. I can't marry you, as things are."

"Very well, Theseus. Then I cannot stay any longer on your ship. It would not be *convenable*. You must put out of your course, and land me at Naxos."

Theseus attempted to disguise his joy.

"Well, my dear, perhaps it would be wisest. These few days will always be precious memory to me. We have loved, Ariadne."

Her beautiful eyes filled with tears. She had practised that habit for hours on end.

"Ah! Theseus, *I* have loved. Leave me now."

VII

In her first floor suite at the Megadomos, Naxos, Ariadne sat. She had writing materials in front of her, and had just finished a note. She hastily dusted the ink, and folded it. Then she turned to her maid.

"You are sure he is stopping at Vine Villa?"

"Yes, my Lady."

Ariadne wrote carefully on the note:

"To the HIGH LORD DIONYSOS IACCHOS."

She dusted the words, her head prettily on one side. Then she handed the note to the maid.

"Take that round yourself, Eustochion, but first give me the glass."

And as Eustochion left, Ariadne began to heighten the pallor of her cheeks.

"I'm glad I landed," she murmured, "I was never born to be a sailor's mistress."

* * * * * *

About the same time Minotaur, leaning on the poop of the *Bird of Athens*, gazed eagerly at the City of the Violet Crown. Theseus clapped him affectionately on the shoulder. He had got really fond of this quiet, kindly philosopher.

"There, Taury, there she is. And you can philosophise there at your heart's content."

"And they'll let me into their house? I can discuss in houses?"

"My dear soul, in the market place, if you like. We're not afraid of talk."

Minotaur sighed with a sort of solemn joy, and gripped the Duke's hand.

III

VISION

Who wills may see; who sees must take
The risk of blindness. Since the snake
Wisdom brings sorrow: sorrow knows
A beauty happiness foregoes.
Only the child's heart sees without
The blinding tragedy of doubt.

THE NARROW WAY

I

ALT his confirmation he had annoyed the Bishop of London (at that time it was Frederick Temple) by insisting on taking the additional names of Alfonso Mary Alexander. He had surprised him by the resolute manner in which he had answered his questions about the origin of taking names at confirmation; and enraged him by his explanation that he desired to be called Alexander in memory of that great Pope, the Lord Alexander VI, who had put the whole Christian world under an obligation by his discovery of the devotion of the Angelus. "This devotion," the boy murmured to the astounded Bishop, "as your Lordship no doubt knows, has been from eternity the privilege of the Holy Angel, and was not entrusted to men until the proximity of the horrible heresies of the German deformation rendered the patronage of Mary necessary for the protection of her son." The Bishop's chaplain had tried to prevent Frank Lascelles' indiscretion; but Temple's abrupt gesture had hindered his efforts. When Lascelles finished the Bishop gazed at him in silence for a minute.

"Well, I hope you'll live to grow out of this foolery. But you know your rights and you shall have 'em."

Temple, was, as his old foes had discovered years before, eminently just.

More than twenty years had passed since that confirmation. Frank Alfonso Mary Alexander Lascelles had gone to Oxford and to Ely, and had been ordained to a small country parish in that diocese. After two years of his curacy, an injudicious layman presented him to the living of S. Uny and S. Petroc in the north of Cornwall.

He had been there now for over nineteen years. When he had come he found his church empty; now it was full. It was full of children and boys. Occasionally a few mothers, and, when he was sober, the village drunkard, and, when she was penitent, the prostitute from the Church Town, came to Mass as well; but generally the Church of S. Uny, down by the beach, was filled only by children and boys.

This result Frank Lascelles had been long in attaining. The parish he served was predominantly Methodist. He had found a congregation of three—the publican, the ostler of the hotel, and an old maiden lady who rang the bell, and called herself the pew-opener. Lascelles soon shocked the respectability of the publican and the Protestantism of the ostler: but the old lady remained faithful to him. She did not stir when he had the three-decker cut down, and a new altar reared at the East end. She seemed to welcome the great images, Our Lady of the Immaculate Conception, The Sacred Heart, S. Joseph and S. Anthony which Lascelles put up in his church. She did not care whether he said Mass in Latin or English; and incense and holy water both left her tranquil. It was otherwise with the village. Though the Methodists never entered the church, except for a wedding or a funeral, they thought they had a right to control its services and its priest. There were stormy Easter vestries; there was a Protestant churchwarden. One horrible day the fishermen broke into the church and took out the images and threw them down the cliff: by next week new ones were in their places. Lascelles was boycotted by his parishioners, except a few would-be bold spirits; and was outlawed, in the genial English way, by his Bishop; but he stuck at his job, went on saying offices to an empty church, and singing Mass to his pew opener and an occasional visitor. Then after five years or so the change began.

It was not along the usual lines of such changes. Generally priests of Lascelles religion are eager, masculine people who soon win over the more turbulent elements in the parish, and put them, too, in search of the great adventure of Christianity. But Lascelles, though he had grown up, still remained the boy who had chosen Liguori and Alexander for his patrons. He was obsessed with the reality of the spiritual world, of good and evil. His pillow was wet with the tears he shed for the sins of his parish. He was horrified at the evil of the world, and yet constitutionally unable to defy it in any active way. He had only one strong human affection—and that was a great love for children.

At first this was not reciprocated. His odd figure, his shuffling walk, his stoop and his occasional outbursts of anger produced ridicule and fear rather than love. Then one child somehow found how large the heart of him was; and then another, and then another. He had won the children. But this would have availed him little had it not been for the arrival at S. Uny of the Rev. Paul Trengrowse. Mr. Trengrowse came to minister to the Primitives about three years after Lascelles' appointment to the parish. He was young, keen, and sincere. He had not been long in the village when the leading members of his congregation told him of the sins of the Parish Priest, and horrors of the parish church. Trengrowse prayed for light. He disliked interfering with the affairs of an alien church; but, if half he was told was true, Lascelles must be fought. So he paid a visit to the church, which was always open, and was duly distressed at the idols he saw there.

As he was gazing at the smirking fatuity of S. Anthony, he heard a footstep. It was Lascelles who was coming from the sacristy to the altar. Fortunately, before he began Mass, Lascelles looked down the church and saw "a congregation" so he said Mass in English.

Now Trengrowse was no ordinary minister. He was a man of personal holiness, and of real devotion; and that in his spirit which was sincere and mystical recognised in the Popish-seeming priest, muttering his Mass, a kindred soul. Lascelles' absorption in his work, his grave, yet joyful solemnity, his keen sense of the other world made an immense effect on Trengrowse. The Mass proceeded, and when Trengrowse heard "Therefore with Angels and Archangels and all the Company of Heaven," he felt that he had had the answer to his prayer. This man was a Christian, however erroneous he might be in details.

So the next Sunday the Primitives who were hoping for a strong sermon against the Scarlet Woman, were disagreeably surprised. "Mr. Lascelles may be wrong. I think he is wrong, sadly wrong, in many things: but he du love the Lord, and he du worship Him. And, brethren, no man calls Jesus Lord save by the Holy Ghost. Let us pray for Mr. Lascelles and the church people of S. Uny; and that we may all be led along the narrow way to everlasting life."

Had Trengrowse been a man of less character he might have failed in his defence of Lascelles. But he was an acceptable preacher, and a man whose plain love of his religion it was impossible to doubt. So, first with grumbling, later with a ready acquiescence, the villagers of S. Uny followed his lead.

The result was odd. Lascelles attracted the children more and more; and his services attracted them. This worried Trengrowse not a little; but when one of his congregation said scornfully, "Those bit games to the church be only fit for babes," he looked gravely at him and replied, "Ah! Eli, but the book says 'Unless ye become as little children.' " This silenced Eli, but it did not silence Trengrowse's own heart. How was it Lascelles could do anything with children, a good deal with boys up to fifteen or so, and nothing with men and women, and little with girls? Lascelles' own explanation was simple. His Bishop would not confirm his children until they were thirteen. Lascelles presented them year after year when they were six or seven. He preached an amazing sermon on the three great aids to the Devil in the parish of S. Uny—and the three heads of his sermon were: Lust, Hypocrisy and the Lord Bishop. The more respectable of the neighbouring clergy were furious, but the Bishop, who was a simple, humble-minded man (quite unlike the ex-head-master who had inducted Lascelles) refused to take any notice of the attack; but also refused to relax his rule about the age of confirmation candidates. The Archdeacon told Lascelles that his parish was the plague-spot of the diocese, and Lascelles retorted that in a mass of corruption any sign of health looks ominous and unusual. But, although he kept up a brave front to the disapprovers, his failure with his people galled him. He would not have minded if they had still been actively hostile. But that had long ceased. They were now fond of their priest. They liked and shared in his notoriety. They supported him against the officials; and when a malicious Protestant from London attempted to stir up a revolt against Lascelles, he was promptly put into the harbour; and Trengrowse started a petition to the Bishop, expressing the affection "all we, whether church people or Methodists, feel for Mr. Lascelles."

Lascelles' philosophy refused to permit him to see in his failure evidences of his incapacity for his work. He had the proud humility of the perfect priest. Regarding himself as a mere channel for divine grace, he forgot that his personality was so distinctive that it affected the way in which grace reached his people. Once an old friend had tried to make him see this; but the task was hopeless.

"My dear fellow," said Lascelles, "I don't see what you mean. All they want is the Gospel. And that I give them. I say Mass for them. I will hear their confessions. I instruct them. I lead their devotions. All beside is mere human embellishment. No doubt a more competent man would be more pleasing to them, but he could not do more than give them the Gospel, could he?"

On All Souls' Day, in 1912, Lascelles was depressed. Early that morning he had gone up to the cemetery, and said a Requiem in the little chapel. Then there had been the early Mass at 8.30 in the church. The church had been full. Not only were all his children there, but there were a good many fathers and mothers: for the services on the day of the dead appealed to a deep human instinct with a power which not even Lascelles could spoil. The Dies Iræ,[13] sung in Latin, had sounded oddly from a congregation so predominantly childish: and Lascelles had preached a short sermon on the "Significance of Death."

"We exaggerate the importance of death. It is to us death matters, not to the dead. For them it is a release, for us it is a warning. Death of the body is only a symbol. It is death of the soul we must fear. Believe me, it would be worth while for every one of you in this church to die, if by dying, you could bring a soul to Jesus. God knows, I would die for you, if that would bring you. There are those here to-day—you, Penberthy, and you, Trevose—who have not been to Mass since you were boys. Make a new resolution to-day, and ask the Holy Souls to help you keep it. Come to your duties, and return to your church."

Lascelles felt at the time that his appeal lacked force. He knew that after Mass, Penberthy would say to Trevose:

"Bootivul service, bean't it, Tom?"

"Iss—it be that. I du like it for once or twice. But for usual give

---

[13] Lit. 'Day of Wrath', it describes the Last Judgment and is used in the Roman Requiem Mass (Funeral Mass).

me the chapel. It be more nat'ral like."

"Iss—it be. Poor Mr. Lascelles, I did think he would have a slap at us."

"Iss—it be his way. My gosh! I don't mind."

So Lascelles was depressed. He sat among his books, reading a Renascence treatise on "Death." He thought a great deal about death. Sometimes he feared it horribly. It seemed that great enemy of faith. It was so disconcerting a thing, so heartless, so unregarding. At other times he felt defiant. But never did he reach the spirit of S. Francis about death. He was too remote from natural life and the events of animal birth and death to understand death as an ordinary thing, something not less usual than the sunset.

"It may be"—he read, "that there be more deaths than one. For it is evident that some are so hardened in sin that the death of the body comes long after the man has been really dead. Such men are commonly gay and cheerful: for with the death of their soul, has died all godly fear, all apprehension of judgment, all hope of salvation. They become but as brutes. Wherefore the church has always held that heretics, if they be obstinate and beyond recall, may be handed over to the secular arm for the death of the body. It should not trouble us that they display ordinary human virtues: for these be common in the unregenerate, and are but devices of the devil who would persuade men that religion matters naught. They are his children, and may be lawfully treated as such by any godly prince. The church herself kills not: though the Lord Pope, being a Temporal King, has the power of the sword, and may exercise the same."

Lascelles put the book down and stared at the fire. The words roused a train of thought that almost frightened him. But he was not the man to dismiss any idea because it was terrifying. He believed in giving the devil his due, and always insisted that all temptations should be met boldly, not evaded. He left his chair, and knelt at his prie-dieu,[14] looking at the wounds of the great Crucifix which hung above it.

Half an hour later he rose with a look of resolution on his face.

II

The first case of the plague, as the villagers insisted on calling it, happened just before Epiphany. It attacked Penberthy, who was never ill before; and in four days he was dead. His disease puzzled the doctor from the market-town, but he put it down as a curious case of infantile paralysis. His colleague from Truro, whom he consulted after the third case had occurred, insisted that the symptoms did not disclose anything more definite than shock following on *status lymphaticus*.[15] The most serious thing was, however, not their incapacity to name, but their inability to cure the mysterious disease which was spreading in S. Uny. Except for a general weariness, a disinclination to move, and a curious "wambling in the innards," there were no definite symptoms at all to go on. After the second case they had an inquest, but it yielded no results at all, and Dr. Marlowe began to talk of getting an expert from London.

It was not until February, however, that any one came. Then by a fortunate chance Sir Joshua Tomlinson came down to S. Ives for a holiday. The "plague" at S. Uny had got into the London paper. There had been ten deaths, and two women, the first to be attacked,

---

[14] A piece of furniture, consisting of a kneeling surface and a rest for the elbows, that is used during prayer.

[15] Hyperplasia of the lymphatic tissue once thought to be the cause of sudden death in infants and children.

were lying seriously ill. Dr. Marlowe called on Sir Joshua, and the great physician said he would come over and see the patients. Marlowe was glad that chance had sent him a great general physician rather than a surgeon or a specialist. Although he was willing to defy any specialist to find his pet disease in the mysterious sickness that had killed the ten fishermen, he was relieved that no specialist was to be given the opportunity.

"You see, Lascelles," he said to the priest, "it's not as if we were in the fifteenth century. We may be in theology, but I'm hanged if we are in medicine. These men are dying like savages: but the savage makes up his mind he has got to die, and dies through sheer hysteria. These fellows want to live. They lust for life."

"You are right, Marlowe. Their desire for life is a lust. It is scarcely decent in a Christian to cling so to this existence. But there—it's not my business to judge. You know, Marlowe, I have sometimes thought this last month that this mysterious disease is a judgment on S. Uny. It is God's hand held out over our village. Let us pray for those who are dead, and those who are dying, and most of all, dear God, for those who are not yet to die."

Marlowe, though friendly with Lascelles, was more than a little afraid of him. The vicar had worked like two men during this distress. He had nursed the sick, he had consoled the mourners, he had said Masses and had a service of general humiliation. Somehow he had identified himself with his parish to a degree he had never reached before, and S. Uny was grateful to him. But the little doctor was rather afraid. Lacelles was strained and odd in manner. He spent too long a time in prayer, and not long enough at meals or in bed.

"No, Lascelles. I don't agree with you there. Oh! I'm a good Catholic, I hope, and I know God could intervene; but I don't see why He should."

"No: you don't see why. No one does, Marlowe, until He speaks, and then they are forced to."

On the Saturday Sir Joshua came over. He saw Mr. Pentreath and Mrs. Whichelo, and he shook his head over both of them. He asked them questions about their diet, and about their way of living, while Marlowe stood by, silent and impatient. Then he said a few kindly, cheerful words, and left them in the big room, which the vicar had fitted up as a hospital ward; for Marlowe thought the cases were better isolated.

"Well, sir, what do you think?"

"What sort of man is your vicar? He seems liked."

"Yes—he is. He's an odd chap—a bit mad, I think. A very keen Catholic, and very depressed at his failure to keep the people."

"Ah! they don't go to church."

"Well, they *do* now. They have done since this damned illness. He's been awfully good to them. And the children have always gone."

"It's a funny thing, Dr. Marlowe, that no child has been ill."

"Isn't it? That's what I say to young Jones of Truro. He will insist on his shock theory, following on *status lymphaticus*. I keep on pointing out to him that most of the patients are men who have had shocks every week of their lives since they were twelve. They'd have all been dead long since."

"Yes. I am sure Jones is wrong. But I don't know what this disease is, Dr. Marlowe. I suspect, but I don't know."

"Here is the vicar coming, Sir Joshua. Shall I introduce you?"

"Please do."

Lascelles was walking rapidly towards them. He looked ill but eager. His eyes were full of a frantic pleasure, a kind of holy rapture that appeared to make him even taller than he actually was. He acknowledged the introduction with a bow, and would have passed on, but Sir Joshua stopped him with a question.

"You have come from your sick people, Mr. Lascelles?"

"Yes. They are no longer sick. I was just in time to hear their confessions, and give them the viaticum."

"Good God!" Sir Joshua was evidently shocked. "It's not ten minutes since we left them."

"No? The end has always been very sudden, hasn't it, Marlow?"

"Yes. But this is quicker than usual. Do you think, Sir Joshua"—and he lowered his voice—"a post-mortem?"

"No. It would be useless. At least it would be no help to me. By the way, Marlowe, how have you entered the cause of death?"

"Well, sir—I've frankly put 'heart failure, cause unknown.' There seemed to be nothing between that and 'Act of God.' "

"Ah! Marlowe, that's what you should have put," intervened Lascelles. "It is the hand of God—the hand of God." Then, with a bow to Sir Joshua, he hurried away.

"So your vicar thinks it is the hand of God. He may be right. God works through human agents. He is an interesting man, Dr. Marlowe."

"Yes: he is. But this trouble has worried him frightfully. I'm rather nervous for him. Have you got any theory, sir. You talked of suspicion."

"Well, Dr. Marlowe, I'll tell you what I think. Your patients have been murdered."

Marlowe looked at the great physician, as if he was afraid for his sanity.

"No, Dr. Marlowe, I'm not mad, though I have no proof of my assertion. All I ask is this, that I may be allowed the see the next patient within at least half an hour of the beginning of the illness. By the way, can they give me a bed here, do you think? Where do you put up?"

155

"Oh! I'm staying at the vicar's. I expect he'd be charmed to have you."

"No. I don't think I will stay with Father Lascelles. I would rather not. I'll find a room somewhere. I think there will be another case to-morrow night."

III

That Sunday morning Lascelles preached on the "Hand of Judgment." The church was packed. Trengrowse had his service at nine and brought all his congregation to the Mass at eleven. Lascelles seemed wonderfully better. His eye was clearer, his step gayer and his whole figure more buoyant. His tone as he gave out his text was exultant.

"They pierced his hands.

"The symbolism of the Divine Body is strangely arresting. The Jews thought of God as an eye watching, caring for them from heaven. We Christians watch God—here in the Tabernacle, or in the arms of Mary. His care for us we typify by his Hand—the Hand we pierced. This last month God has been with us very wonderfully. He is always with us in the holy Sacrament: but lately He has been with us in the Sacrament of Death. His Hand of Judgment has been over, and under us; it has clasped us—and some of us it has not let go.

"Our natural feeling is one of fear. We are not used to such immediate handling as this of our God's. We have most of us tried to apply religion to our life, now we have to try to apply our life to religion. God will have us think of nothing but Him, speak to none save Him, hope for none save Him. His Hand is still with us. It will bear yet more away from S. Uny before we learn our lesson. Let me help you to learn that lesson right. Let us all take care that we renew our trust in God, that we recognise His Hand, that we answer His Love."

Sir Joshua had listened attentively to Lascelles' sermon. He seemed vaguely disappointed, and he was unwilling to discuss it with Marlowe afterwards. There was no doubt that Lascelles' almost fatalist attitude, while it annoyed the doctor, had a strange welcome from the villagers. They turned in a childlike way to the words of this man who spoke as one who knew the ways and the meaning of the Almighty. Never had Lascelles so much real devotion from his people as he secured during the "plague." It was not that they shared his feeling of complete abandonment to the Will of God; but the fact that he had such a feeling made their fate seem more tolerable.

On Sunday evening there was a new case, as Sir Joshua had expected. The disease attacked Mrs. Bodilly, the wife of the chief grocer in S. Uny. Marlowe was summoned immediately, but he found Sir Joshua already at the poor woman's bedside.

She was frankly terrified; in this her case differed from previous ones, in which the sufferers, though generally resentful, had been not the least afraid. Mrs. Bodilly had been at Mass that morning. She had got back and prepared the dinner. At tea-time she had "felt queer," but after tea she was better. Then as she was getting ready to go to the special service of Exposition, she fell down and had to be carried up to her room by her husband and sons.

She was, unlike most of the tradesmen's wives, a nominal church woman, but she had never been confirmed and rarely went to church. The fit of external piety roused in her by the "plague," was frankly based on nervous alarm. She felt that God was taking it out of S. Uny in this way; and she was anxious to escape.

Her illness found her divided between anger and fear. She

was angry that efforts to placate Divine wrath had not been more successful—she was terrified of dying, terrified still more of death as a punishment. In the most desolate way she sought reassurances from Marlowe and Sir Joshua; but neither could give her any certain consolation. The disease presented no different aspects. It indeed presented no aspect at all, except extreme weakness, astonishing slowness of the pulse, and irregular beating of the heart. Although Sir Joshua was there within five minutes of the seizure, he admitted to Marlowe that he could discover nothing of what he suspected.

"I'll be frank, Dr. Marlowe, I suspected poison. I still suspect it. I believe all these people have been poisoned in an extremely subtle way by a man so fanatical as to be almost mad. But I can find no trace of the poison. In this case, I will, if you will permit me, conduct a post-mortem, but I expect I shall fail. If I do, I must take my own line, if you wish me to help you."

"Really, Sir Joshua, you talk more like a detective than a physician."

"This is a detective's business, Dr. Marlowe. I wish it were not."

Before they left Lascelles arrived. He had been summoned by Mr. Bodilly, and he came prepared to give Mrs. Bodilly the last rites. As the boy with the light and bell approached the stairs, Sir Joshua whispered to Marlowe:

"Your vicar seems very certain of her death."

Marlowe shrugged his shoulders. "We haven't saved a case, you know."

The post-mortem yielded no result. That evening Marlowe dined with Sir Joshua at the village inn, and after dinner the great physician told him of his suspicions. Marlowe listened at first angrily, then with an incredulous horror.

"It can't be. The man lives for his parish, I tell you. Why, he would die for it."

"Yes: I believe he would. Had I found what I looked for, he certainly would."

"But, my dear sir, there isn't a trace of any known drug. There's no trace of anything."

"No. I had expected to find—but never mind. I have a great deal of experience, Dr. Marlowe, and I am convinced that your vicar has been murdering his parishioners. And to-night I am coming to tell him so. I will walk home with you. You may be present or not, as you please."

IV

Lascelles looked up a little wearily when Sir Joshua had finished speaking.

"Is that all?"

Marlowe intervened.

"Look here, old man—I only came because—you'll forgive me, Sir Joshua—I didn't want you to be alone under this monstrous, this fantastic accusation of Sir Joshua's. You've only got to contradict him, and we'll go."

Lascelles looked gratefully at his friend.

"Thank you, Marlowe. But Sir Joshua is right in telling me his suspicions. You have finished, Sir Joshua?"

"Yes. I should like your explanation if you have one, or your admission of my charge, and your promise that this—this—plague shall cease."

"You use strange words, sir, for a man who has no evidence for what he says."

"Yes,"—ejaculated Marlowe, "yes, by Jove, you do——"

"Please, Marlowe. You will not be content with having relieved your mind, Sir Joshua. You wish me to answer you?"

"I do. I require it."

"You know, sir, you great doctors have one failing. It is one priests have too. You cannot avoid talking to me as if I were your patient—a mental, a nervous case. You can't help believing that your firm tone, your almost—may I say it—discourteous manner will impress me. Well, it doesn't."

Sir Joshua got red. Lascelles' words too entirely diagnosed his method. He was annoyed that he should seem so transparent to a man whom he regarded as at least half-crazy."

"I beg your pardon. There is something in what you say. Men in all professions have their—ah! tricks."

"Thank you."

Lascelles got up and stood by the fireplace looking down on his visitor. In the last month he had changed. He seemed bigger and more masculine—more as if he now had personal responsibilities: he looked less of an official, more of a man. He spoke rather slowly.

"You have accused me of murder, Sir Joshua. You ask me to admit my crime, and to promise to cease. Well, I expected your visit. I have long been familiar with your Treatise on Renascence Toxicology: it is as complete as any published book. And I am glad you and Marlowe came to-night. I have my answer ready. I admit nothing and I promise nothing."

Sir Joshua looked with a puzzled air at the priest. For a moment his accusation seemed a monstrous thing to himself. Then his common sense surged back.

"Father Lascelles, your answer does not satisfy me. I must take other steps."

"They will not lead anywhere, Sir Joshua. If *you* find no evidence, no other man can. You say my poor people were poisoned.

Well, find the poison. Ah—you know you cannot. It is foolish to threaten me. But I will tell you what I had determined to tell Marlowe to-night. First, I do not expect there will be any more deaths from this plague for a long time.

"Secondly, I have a confession to make. Last All Hallows I was depressed. The work here has not gone as it should. I had the children, but not the parents. I thought much of Death and the Departed at that season of all the dead—and at last I prayed to God that if nothing else would move these people, he would send Death. Send Death mysterious as a judgment. Death has come, and my people have learnt their lesson. All of those who died were reconciled to Holy Church before death. Of those who remain nearly all have adhered to the Church. This afternoon, Mr. Trengrowse came and asked to be prepared for Confirmation——"

"Trengrowse, the minister——" cried Marlowe.

"And this evening I had notice that all who are competent intend to make their Communion next Sunday. This parish has been won for God, Sir Joshua, and at the cost of thirteen deaths. Isn't it worth it?"

"Father Lascelles, I cannot regard you as sane. You are not only practically admitting your crime, you are disclosing your motives."

"I beg your pardon, I admit nothing. I acknowledged I prayed to God to visit the people, if necessary, by his secret Death. That is not a crime. Next Sunday I shall tell my people."

"And have you *prayed* that the deaths shall cease?" asked Sir Joshua ironically.

"I was doing so when you entered," replied Lascelles quietly.

"Good God, man, your hypocrisy sickens me. You prate of God's intervention, and all the time you've been sending man after man to death by some foul poison of your own."

"Sir Joshua—do you believe God commonly works without human intervention?"

"Bah! That is sophistry."

"You condemn the machinery of justice, the compromise of war, our human evasion of rope and guillotine?"

"Surely, Marlowe," exclaimed Sir Joshua, "you can't sit and listen quietly to this damnable nonsense?"

Marlowe had been siting dazed, looking at Lascelles as if he were fascinated. He replied in a remote voice.

"I don't know. I'm wondering"—he gave a nervous laugh—"wondering if Lascelles is a saint or a devil."

Lascelles went on imperturbably.

"You don't answer me. You can't. Why should you think I, an anointed priest, am less fit to be the door-keeper of death than Lord Chief Justice Ommaney? At least I use no case-law. I am the slave of no precedent. I know my people. I know them individually. I love them as persons. And as persons I judge them."

The tall figure of the man seemed to glow. His face was lit with an unnatural beauty as he stood looking down on the other two, and dared them to answer him.

Sir Joshua rose. He had lost his somewhat pompous judicial air. He was deeply, humanly moved; and he spoke with an anxiety far more impressive than his previous authoritative tone.

"Father Lascelles, I have nothing more to say. I believe you have done a very horrible, a very wicked thing. I have heard how you would defend yourself if you were legally brought to book for such an offence. Your defence has, as you are aware, no legal force. I think it has no moral force. You are deceiving yourself strangely. One day you will have a great loneliness of heart. You will realise how terrible a responsibility you have taken. Without

162

the sanction of society, without the approval of your church, you have decided, alone, the fate of your fellow-creatures. I am sorry for you. Good-night."

The light left Lascelles' face. He looked suddenly ill and careworn. Then with a high, frantic gesture he flung his hand towards the Crucifix.

"He, too—He, too—was made sin."

THE CAGE

I

SHE was not in. Tom Barnes sank into a chair by the hearth, and looked gloomily into the fire. He was a big, well made man, with a face of curious refinement. None of his features was especially noticeable; but something in the balance of his head, the lines of his mouth, and the withdrawn expression of his eyes combined to give him an air which sat somewhat oddly on a thatcher. Thatching is still a skilled art in Dorset, and still in demand; but in 1745 it was one of the most desired of country occupations. The men of the Barnes family had been thatchers for some generations, and had lived in the neighbourhood of Morecambe for as long as any one remembered. Tom lived in a cottage which had a garden running down to the coach-road from Morecambe to Charmouth. The road did not run as it does now. Instead of going down hill almost the whole way from the Ship Inn, it turned towards the coast and followed a line well above the track of the present road. There is still a good cart-track, grass-covered and pleasant for riding and walking, which keeps the lines of the old road; but no coach has run, no horse been ridden along the old road since Tom Barnes' death. And even now, when the memory of his story is vague, there are many who will not pass the place of his death, except in the daylight.

On this winter evening in November, 1745, Tom, as he sat, could hear the cries of a postillion urging his horses up the hill from Charmouth, and from the great valley bellow there came the slow, comfortable sounds of farm-life, the heavy movements of men and horses, the scurrying, busy delight of dogs, and the occasional solemn interference of a child, helping his father, and playing, with astonishing efficiency, at the work of the grown-ups.

Tom shivered slightly, and stretched his hands to the fire. Things were going bad between Mary and him. He didn't know why, and he didn't see how to stop it. He had wanted children as passionately as she. He thought, with an anxious, grasping affection of the nephews and nieces who lived at the Great Farm in the Vale. He had wished to adopt one: his brother had been willing, and his wife, gentle little Susan Charteris of Beaminster, had almost pressed the child on Mary. But Mary had refused bitterly.

"I'll have no children at my bosom that hasn't come out of my body. If I can't bear children, I suppose I bean't fit to rear 'em. Thank 'ee all the same, Susan."

Tom had been grieved, and had yielded. How often since had he been grieved, and how invariably had he yielded. The neighbours' sympathy was frankly with his wife. They didn't understand Tom's gentleness. Indeed, one man hinted that Tom was responsible for there being no children, that one so "soft" was likely to be impotent; and his sneering insult had waked the rare, fierce anger of the Barnes'. Tom had almost killed the fellow in a sudden wrath. And there was no further talk in Morecambe about Tom's lack of virility. But still Mary had people's sympathy. She had turned to the gaiety of life, when she missed happiness. She was thick cronies with old Mrs. Wilson and her sons, the greatest smugglers down at St. Gabriel's. She was always going into Bridport, and getting what excitement she could out of the little market town, and she would go and watch the gentry at Lyme Regis and take the attention of the raffish bachelors who lounged along the Cobb.

All of this Tom bore with, patiently and with a heartfelt kindness which his wife misunderstood. She, too, thought he was weak. She could not comprehend a pity so strong and so deep that it grasped the meaning for her of desires and ways of escape which she herself cherished but never understood. Although he could not express his feelings, Tom had a keen perception of the uneasy desire which drove his wife out of the home and the house, plunged her into alien excitements, and forced her to find release and relief in pleasures which had but little place in the simple life of the country. Yet his sympathy was getting strained. His wife's neglect was tinged now with contempt. He saw she neither understood nor appreciated his forbearance. She took his kindness for silliness. At times he wondered himself; but dismissed the devil of doubt as a temptation.

Still, his tenderness was sorely tried. He had always detested drunkenness. It was not so common a vice in the country as in London, but there was a good deal of over-drinking of cider and mead. But women, except smugglers like Mr. Wilson, and a few would-be fashionables at Bridport, were sober. His wife, he began to realise, was rarely that. Thrice he had found her drunk on his return from work. More often, as to-night, he returned to find nothing ready, and his wife still away. Sometimes she stayed away the night, sending a message by some youth who cadged between Mrs. Wilson and the "Ship," or who fetched for the gentry in the Vale who were glad to get cheap cognac.

Even here, however, the village sympathised with his wife. Tom's piety, unostentatious but sincere, revolted a population which had not yet been roused by Methodism. The rich folk at the chapel disliked and despised the few who clung to the parish church; and Tom was suspected of being little better than a Papist.

This accusation in a country where more than one Barnes had been killed by a Kirk or died for Monmouth, was equivalent to a charge of treachery. Tom, whose friends were the animals and the little children—Tom, who had been found once on his knees near the shrine of S. Candida, was condemned as a "fool," and only escaped violence because he was a "Barnes." Himself, he would scarcely have noticed his neighbours' unfriendliness, had it not been displayed in sympathy for Mary. He was a man singularly indifferent to his fellows. His intense, narrow nature, combined with wide sympathy and small gift of expression, found little help or companionship in his neighbours. He had a passionate love for nature; and he had learnt from the old vicar a kind of traditional Catholicism which sufficed for his spiritual needs. He was the only man in Whitechurch parish, perhaps, certainly the only man in Morecambe village who took an interest in the past of his countryside. He loved to remember that Alfred mentioned Whitechurch in his will. He liked to explain to the occasional sojourner at the "Ship" what "Canonicorum" meant.[16] He boasted in his quiet way of the antiquity of Marshwood Castle and Whitechurch Church, compared to the more celebrated Lyme Regis or Beaminster. He had tried on various occasions to interest Mary in these things. He was aware, in a dumb kind of way, that his own interest in them was really his way of escape and was akin to her excited gaiety and continued lust for pleasure; and he hoped he might divert her into his paths. But it was useless. And she made no effort to keep him. She did some of her duty. She kept the house spotlessly clean—at least, until she took to drinking. After that, there was a certain relaxation of vigour; and Tom had noticed sadly the gradual slackening of his wife's standards.

To-night, however, he looked on an orderly kitchen. Everything

[16] Meaning 'of the canons', from the fact that the village and the living from the land around it were at one time appropriated by the canons of the cathedrals of both Sarum and Wells.

was there, except his wife. In another minute a hand fumbled at the door. At last it stuttered open, and Mary stood, blinking slightly at the glare of the fire.

Tom got up to greet her—then he paused, seeing beyond his wife a dim figure whom he seemed to recognise.

Mary came into the room, grinning, and as she advanced, she turned and threw over her shoulder, in a voice still beautiful though husky with drink, "Come in, lad, I tell 'ee."

There shambled in, making a pitiful effort to look bold, young Tom. It was his nephew—the boy, whom eighteen years ago Susan had offered her for her own. He was obviously intoxicated, and he smiled sleepily and stupidly at his uncle. The latter stepped forward. "Hullo! Tommy, it was good of 'ee to see thy aunt hoam—"; then he stopped, silenced by an unpleasant giggle from Mary; and the unfading grin on his nephew's face. Tom stooped towards his wife.

" 'Tes a shame, Mary, to meake the lad drunken. It's disgusting of 'ee." Mary glowered at him, and said nothing.

Tom stood, perplexed. Then young Tom broke the silence.

"Good evening, uncle. I be come—"; then his voice faltered away, and he resumed his silly grin, and shifted his feet uneasily on the paved floor.

His stupidity roused his aunt.

"Well, Tom, ain't you glad to have Tommy here at last? You'm always wanted him."

Tom looked at her in his long, slow way. She stared defiantly back, and then continued:

"I brought 'en up—but he was ready enough to come, weren't thee, Tommy?"

Tommy made an affectionate gesture—"Yes, Aunt Mary, I be glad to go anywhere with 'ee—very glad——"

Tom had stiffened during this conversation. He stepped back to his wife who had sunk in the chair by the fire, and asked her quietly yet with a strange vigour,

"What do 'ee mean, Mary? What do all this mean? Why isn't Tommy to home? Why have 'ee made 'un drunken?"

His anger—for his wife recognised the signs of his rarely-roused passion—seemed to anger her. She leapt from her chair and fronted him.

"You wanted 'en once, Thomas Barnes, wanted 'en when 'e were a poor pulling brat. *I* want 'en now. He be grown up. Happen he may get me a child—happen he may be a better man than his uncle."

In the dark silence which followed, the logs in the hearth twitched uneasily, and one lurched forwards out of the fire. Tom pushed it back with his foot, and then spoke in a low voice.

"Go hoam, Tommy."

"Nay, uncle—" the boy blustered with a tipsy effort at gaiety— "Nay, Aunt Mary be right. I be willing. I be a man now."

His uncle took him fiercely by the shoulder. His taut anger pierced through the boy's stupidity.

"Go hoam, I tell 'ee—before I kill 'ee. Happen thee would be dead now, if it were not for Susan."

As Tommy, frightened, turned to go, Mary screeched at her husband, "Ay—it was always Susan thou didst care for. Well, she've borne enough, surelie."

As the door slammed. Tom turned back to his wife.

She was still standing, swaying in the fire-light, one hand on the broad mantel-shelf, the other on her hip.

"Where did you meet Tommy?"

"Oh! that be all right—all right. No one knows. I didn't say aught at the inn. 'Twas in the wood at S. Gabriel's I made him love me. He be a brave boy——"

"Stop, Mary, stop——"

But the unhappy woman went on.

"He be proper and fierce, when he has some drink in him, I can tell 'ee. He got rare and saucy. But I told him he should come hoam with me. He did come with me. Thee canst go, Tom. He can kiss—that boy——"

Tom had been restraining himself, with a difficulty. His breath came in uneasy gasps. Mary looked at him, half-terrified, half-pleased at the agitation she had roused.

"He ca-a-n kiss——" she repeated.

Her husband rushed at her, and put one hand over her mouth, the other rested on her neck, threateningly.

"Stop it, Mary. Stop thy filth, I tell 'ee."

She gasped back at him through his muffling fingers. "Ah! 'ee can't squeeze like young Tom——"

Then a sudden frenzy came over Tom Barnes. He felt that, at all costs, he must stop his wife from speaking—his wife, Mary. He pressed his left hand over her mouth—harder and harder. With the other he drew her fair head, with its shock of golden hair, back and back. Suddenly there was a ghastly sound—a kind of lurching noise; and then Mary's body hung limp in his arms. With a cry the man dropped his burden; and as she fell, Mary's head hit the great iron dog at the side of the fireplace.

Tom stood and looked at her. The blood began to trickle slowly out of a wound in the head; and it stained the white hearth-stone. He felt sure she was dead. Dully he thought, "Her neck went; I've broken her neck." He made no motion to touch the body; but stood, just gazing. He found himself thinking how cross his wife would have been, for the mess on her hearth-stone. She had been very particular about the house. She would not suffer dirt. It was odd—very odd.

Tom gave a great sigh—then went out into the darkness, shutting the door behind him very quietly.

II

"I tell 'ee, he was always a dry, maggoty sort of a man: temper—yes, he could get up into a temper—but there was no honest, decent blood in him at all. He fair crazed poor Mary—doithered her into dullness—and now he just kills the poor woman—for why—tell me that, neighbours?"

Nobody in the Ship Inn seemed inclined to answer Herbert Taylor. They had scarcely yet got over the shock of Mary Barnes' death, or the news that Tom had gone to Bridport and delivered himself up. Most feeling in the village had always been against Tom; because the general opinion favoured a laxer married life, a more cheerful and less urgent view of matrimony than Tom's. They could not understand his "softness." Still less could they understand his apparent want of spirit. He had never—to their knowledge—taken any active measures against Mary's indiscretions; he had certainly never ventured to take his revenge by indulging in the usual infidelities of the injured husband. Nay, he had even, with a delicacy slightly ridiculous to the peasant mind, refused to discuss his wife: he had been downright unneighbourly at times, when folk had proffered him advice.

This was indeed the chief reason why Mary had had so many more supporters than her husband. She had always talked about him. Quite early in their married life, she could chaff him openly about his ridiculous piety, his affection for the church, his absurd tendency to sentimentalism. Tom could not bear to kill animals, except in the quickest and speediest way. He seemed to have none of the natural man's liking for tortures or enjoyment of the death-agony. He would never go to see a cock-fight, and he made himself ridiculous once by interfering with Farmer Melcombe, when the farmer thrashed his bitch till the pups came. True, he had shown pluck enough then; he had flogged Melcombe himself, and fought three of his men, single-handed; and wasn't overcome till Mrs. Melcombe had come from behind and thrown a hot towel over his head. Still, where was the good of a man having pluck, if he had so little sense as Tom Barnes? And now he had murdered his wife. Well, it wasn't surprising—that was the general view. Mary had been a gay, joy-loving creature; and there was something sour in Tom which turned him against her. Still, the gossips of the "Ship" would have loved to find out the reason for Tom's attack on his wife. And that they never would.

When young Tom, dismissed by his uncle, had stumbled home, he was still sufficiently tipsy to blurt out the truth to his father. Robert Barnes, though not in all things understanding his brother, respected him enormously. He listened to Tommy's ugly, drunken story with set eyes. Tommy realised something was wrong as he told it. "Of course—dad—it was—a joke, you know: Aunt Mary's a frolicsome woman. It was a joke. You'm not angry, Dad?" Robert Barnes did not answer his son; he strode to the door, and ordered Jack Davies to saddle his horse. Then he mounted, after one brief message to Susan his wife, and rode furiously to his brother's. When he came there, he found nothing but Mary's body, already growing cold, lying beside the glowing embers. Robert, knowing his brother, mounted once more and rode into Bridport.

That was a week ago: and since then nothing had happened except the legal preliminaries to the trial of Thomas Barnes, of

Morecambe in the parish of Whitechurch Canonicorum in the County of Dorset, thatcher, for the wilful murder of his wife, Mary Barnes. The coroner's inquest had brought in a verdict of wilful murder: and Robert Barnes had told a few people that, in spite of his endeavours, his brother would plead "Guilty" at the Dorchester Assizes. Poor Robert had been through a time of horrible doubt. He felt that, in his son's confession, he had a key which might unlock his brother's prison doors. He was a just man, and would have used the key. But Tom declared that if he did, he himself would swear falsely. "The lad was drunk, Bob: and he was made drunken. It was no fault of his. And God forbid that in addition to my sorrow, you and Susan should have the shame and grief. No one knows of it. She said so, and she always spoke the truth—except you and me, no one must know. Tommy must not suffer for me—nor must Susan, nor you, Bob. And after all they can but hang me."

And Tom had his way.

III

Whether he would have had it, if Robert could have guessed the fate of his brother, is doubtful. The administrative law of England was then still liable to sudden bursts of fury: and Thomas Barnes was not sentenced to be hanged. Instead, after he had been found guilty, a horrible and malignant sentence was passed. His house was to be razed to the ground: and on its site was to be built a huge scaffold. On it was to be hung a cage, and therein the said Thomas Barnes was to be imprisoned with a gallon jug of water and four loaves of bread. And none was to bring him any succour, or any food or comfort, bodily or spiritual: he was to be left there until he was dead.

No doubt the judge expected that, in this novel pillory, Tom Barnes would meet with a swift death from the enraged villagers. One of the disadvantages of Assize judgments is that they never take sufficient account of local circumstances. Although the people of Morecambe preferred Mary to Tom, they didn't hate Tom. The more callous and brutal despised him, the generality pretended to despise and really went a little in awe of him. The children and young people unaffectedly loved him. Even had it been otherwise, Robert Barnes was prepared to break the head of any one who offered an insult to his brother. So the officers of the court who were appointed to stand beside the cage, and take heed that none rendered Thomas Barnes any carnal or spiritual consolation were cheated of their expected business. They had looked forward to making a feeble show of resistance to an infuriated mob, intent on killing Thomas Barnes. Instead they had to stand at dreary sentry duty, through cold days and colder nights, listening to the grim creaking of the cage as it swung uneasily with the movements of their prisoner. It was a difficult position. Old Mr. Armitage, the Lord of the Manor, said the whole thing was illegal; and no doubt had the Assize Court known the result of its sentence, it would have devised some other means of punishment. But there was no person in Dorsetshire capable of setting aside the sentence. It is true that Mr. Francis Palmer, Vicar of Whitechurch, persisted in ignoring the guard, and came and read the morning and evening service with Thomas barnes; and Susan Barnes once succeeded in slipping through the lines and pouring out her gratitude to Tom for saving her son's good name. Otherwise the village rarely came at all near the great cage; and indeed many of the men were occupied in cutting a new road, so that travellers to Lyme Regis should not have to pass by Thomas Barnes' hanging tomb.

IV

It was not until the fourth day that the guards fled. They could never give any coherent account of why they fled; nor reason about their refusal to return. But they did flee, and refused to go back. And on the fifth day Thomas Barnes died. Had he not, it was likely that his brother would have rescued him, and had him down to Broadlands to live.

It was a raw night—in February—that the landlord of the "Ship" was roused by a great battering on the door. He peeked out of the upper window and saw four men with staves hammering at his posts and shutters. They were plainly in a great fright. The light from his candle fell on their sweaty faces, and he heard a ring of unusual terror in their voices, and of an unreasonable awe in their accents.

"Quiet there—can't ye. I be coming down"—for old Thicknesse thought he glimpsed on one, at least, of the knockers-up the silver buttons of the Court. In five minutes or so he had the bars withdrawn, and the men inside his bar-parlour. They were, as he had guessed, the guardians of the cage; and they came in still dizzy with fear, casting sudden looks over their shoulders and jumping at the scamper of a mouse in the larder. They called for cider, and drank heavily.

"You be relieved then, Master Humphrey," Thicknesse said to the senior officer.

Humphrey took another drink before he replied, and then he looked askance at the landlord, and gave a sly grin to his companions.

"Aye, we be relieved—we've had long enough of watching that maggot crawl into fire everlasting. It be others' turns, now. Let's to bed, mates."

"Aye—aye," and they bustled out after their landlord.

*   *   *   *   *   *

Of the true story of the relieving we shall never have a full account. Susan insists that you can find an account in the Bible; that the guard was smitten down, like the Roman soldiers; but Susan always favoured her brother-in-law, even to the point of blasphemy, as old Westly of Charmouth said. Still it is only from her and from her husband that we have any account of the events of the 7th February, and the early hours of the 8th.

All at Broadlands had gone to bed at the usual time—shortly after seven. About ten o'clock Susan woke suddenly. As she said, she felt thrust awake by a great pain at her heart, and a thick catch in her throat. She woke as one may from a nightmare, very sudden and frighteningly, pursued by panic of a quite indefinite kind. But in those days she hitched anything fearsome on to her thoughts about poor Tom. She felt impelled to go to him. So she slipped on her things, not rousing her husband, went to the stable, threw a horse cloth over Bessie the mare, and rode out to Morecambe. Although there was no moon, the night seemed bright. This Susan hardly noticed, till afterwards; but she did see that the old church, especially the north aisle, seemed brilliantly lit up; and she wondered whether any one could be there. As her mare took slowly the steep hill to Morecambe, the sky grew less bright, and by the time she had reached the little gap where one can see into Charmouth Bay, and out towards Lyme, what light there was seemed concentrated and ahead of her. When she got to the main road by the "Ship," she was once more in the circle of light; and she could see quite plainly all her way to the cage.

When she got there she was surprised to see that no one was about. She had approached cautiously, coming up by the side of the hedge in order that she might have a chance of avoiding the guards. But as she came, she perceived that their little huts—improvised sentry-boxes—were empty; and that no figures crouched over the charcoal fire which burnt for their warmth.

She had not then, she said, considered why the night was so light; but she was surprised to see that the cage itself was, as it were, illuminated. It glowed with a quiet radiance like bright moon-light; and she saw Tom Barnes kneeling in the middle of the cage, his eyes shut, and his hands stretched out in supplication. She ran hastily to the cage. When she was near it, she could only just peer in, for it was swung more than five feet off the ground. She stood tip-toe, and called to the captive.

"Tom, it is I—Susan—do 'ee hear me, Tom?"

Tom made no reply. She called again, but not loudly, for fear that the guards were in hiding near. It was a criminal offence to speak to the captive; and she had promised her husband to be careful. It was at her second calling that Robert appeared on the scene; and for the rest of the story we have his word as well as Susan's.

He had wakened soon after his wife; and, impelled by a similar necessity, had ridden up to Morecambe. His experience was almost precisely the same as Susan's, except that he saw the White Lady before she did, and apparently saw her more vividly. Whether this was because he was nearer in blood to Tom Barnes; or because he and his brother were more sensitive to visions, cannot be decided. The important thing is that Susan saw the White Lady before Bob mentioned her. He says that he said nothing about her presence, because he never imagined any one could fail to see her. For him the figure, clothed in white silk, was visible from the bottom of the first field, and he saw that she was the source of the light which bathed the surrounding country.

The White Lady was standing—but standing right off the ground—so declared both Bob and Susan.

"You mean she was floating," suggested Parson Palmer.

"No, sir. She was standing quite firm and solid. Just as if the air were good ground.

The vision was near the cage, and seemed to be speaking to Tom.

Neither of the watchers, however, could hear anything she said. But as they stood there, Susan grasping her husband's hand, they heard Tom's voice.

"It was thin—and clear," said Susan, "more like a flower speaking than a man."

"Shall I have peace, Lady?"

The White Lady bowed a grave assent.

Then as they watched, Tom Barnes fell forward on his face. As he fell, a thick darkness came down over the cage, and a great wind blew towards the sea.

Bob and Susan stumbled on to the "Ship," where they found the guards in bed. They refused to stir till dawn; and at dawn they all went to the cage together. In the middle was lying the body of Thomas Barnes; but not as he fell in the early morning. He was lying on his back, clothed in a long white silk garment. His hands were crossed on his breast, and his eyes closed; and the floor of the cage was strewn with roses, lilies and violets. This everybody vouches for; and a note as to the finding of the body and of the mysterious flowers was made by the vicar, who, in spite of the not very energetic warning of the officers, insisted on burying his parishioner in the churchyard.

He was quite clear as to what had happened. S. Candida, whose body was still in the north aisle of his old church, in the old shrine, had come to console a poor sinner whose punishment had been more than unjust. Francis Palmer was one of those rare eighteenth century priests who refused to submit to the prevailing Erastian rationalism, and he saw nothing impossible in this visitation from heaven. The common people were strangely stirred, and very perplexed. The men of substance there had long been Independents; and they were ill-pleased at this amazing history which they could not explain. It is true that their minister, the Rev. Ebenezer Hold-the-Fort, proved to his own satisfaction that the whole thing was a device of the Devil's. Once more the Evil One had appeared as an Angel of Light. But why should the Devil bother about a man who was already his? argued the shrewd farmers in his congregation: and they got no answer.

From the time of the vision, the people began to go back to their parish church; and the grand chapel was only half full. That was one result of the fantastic punishment of Thomas Barnes. The other was that the old main road became entirely deserted. At first a few bold spirits used it in the daytime; but there were so many stories of wayfarers being tripped up—of being held fast, nay, of being buffeted, that gradually all abandoned it, and were put to considerable inconvenience until the new road was finished. The last echo of the case was heard some six years later when, as the result of some protracted law-case, a stern reprimand was issued against the person or persons unknown who, in disobedience to the order of the Court, had entered the cage of Thomas Barnes, and clothed the body of said Thomas Barnes in a winding-sheet; and such person or persons were ordered to deliver himself or themselves up to be held at the discretion of the nearest Justice of the Peace. But, as Francis Palmer said, there is no tradition that S. Candida has ever called on his old neighbour, Giles Fitzpaine.

ROBIN

I

THERE was no doubt that Jane's death had made a great difference to her. The two sisters had been devoted to each other; and Isabella had always contentedly remained second to Jane. Most people at St. Uny had assumed that the difference between Jane and Isabella FitzGerald was one of intellectual capacity. Jane talked more dogmatically, more widely and more frequently than her sister: Isabella generally agreed with Jane: and therefore—the conclusion was natural—Jane was the stronger character. After the great change, a few people were found to insist that they had always suspected—"after all, Jane was so self-assertive that one was bound to take more notice of her; but of course, by Jove, there was obviously more *in* Isabella." When pressed by others who pretended to no such insight, the cunning ones would admit that they had never divulged their belief in Isabella's strong character.

"Hang it all," said fat Mr. Billson who was most emphatic in his claims, "hang it all, Jane didn't give Isabella a chance. Of course I saw—we saw," he corrected, with a hasty glance at his fluffy wife, "that Isabella had more in her: but it was—it was——"

"Latent, Octavius—" murmured Mrs. Billson.

"Quite so—latent. After Jane's death, Isabella had her chance; and we are not a bit surprised at her—her——"

"Experiences," cooed Mrs. Billson.

"Quite, quite; her experiences."

Well, I had known both the FitzGeralds since they came to live in St. Uny: and I was very surprised at Isabella's "experiences," and at the startling development in her character; and I may say that, alone among the people at St. Uny, I had some chance of noticing the change in her, before the arrival of Robin. I alone, of all her old friends, was welcomed to the house in the first week after Jane's funeral; and I noticed very soon that Isabella had changed both in her method of self-expression, and, I thought, in her actual mental make-up. She was as courteous, as deferential, as tolerant as of old; but she was no longer in the least dependent. She seemed careless of external opinion in so far as it effected her own ideas; though she was still affectionately careful not to wound or distress her friends. So I am in a position to say that the change in Isabella was not due entirely, nor even to any large extent, to the arrival of Robin.

And the part played by Katie has been exaggerated. It is at Isabella's own request that I now make the story public. "Not," as she says in the letter I had this morning from San Miniato—"not that either Robin or I care very much what St. Uny thinks; but because, Nancy dear, we both have an odd little prejudice in favour of the truth." There, that last sentence shows how real the change was: the Isabella of Jane's time could never have expressed herself like that—yet she would have felt it. So the Billsons are not so completely wrong, after all.

II

The FitzGeralds' house was about half a mile out of St. Uny. At the time of Isabella's "experience," St. Uny had not become the crowded seaside resort which we now know. Whistler had chosen it, as later he chose Lyme Regis, to paint in: and made himself offensive to the fisher-people in his own peculiar fashion. There were a good few painters at St. Uny, but no great "colony" as there was later. The FitzGeralds—their mother was a Smith O'Brien, so they united two very different and very "good" Irish families—had chosen St. Uny out of caprice. That was Jane's admission. She was tired of hearing people boast of having discovered the artistic possibilities of the place, or having been struck by the quaint houses or the odd people: the FitzGeralds just happened there. And instead of either building or buying a house on either of the two hills which overlooked the bay, they had bought an old farm-house way out along the coast to Hayle. It stood on the cliff-edge, and it had a private path down to the Little St. Uny beach, a beach more tempting to the luxurious bather than that of St. Uny proper. In fact a few of the more energetic St. Uny folk came before breakfast to Little St. Uny beach: neither there nor (at this time) at St. Uny itself was the nuisance of tent or of an "Oxford costume." You just stripped and got into the sea: and if the fisher folk saw you they were not shocked at the absence of bathing suits. Their difficulty was to understand why you got in the water at all. I must except the boys from this charge, however.

It is true both Jane and Isabella—who painted in a rather attractively Umbrian manner—encouraged the boys to come and bathe on their beach: and any time in the summer you could see slim brown bodies dart along the sand, or pose for odd quarters of an hour in the hot sun. Indeed this was one reason why Robin's arrival seemed less startling than it was. Naked youths were common enough on the beach, even if they were a little unusual in the garden. So Isabella was not very alarmed—it was a month after Jane's funeral—when Anna Maria rushed up to her, most unnecessarily excited, and exclaimed:

"Ma'm—there be a stark-naked man in the arbour."

"It's one of the boys, you mean, Anna Maria: he oughtn't to come up here without anything on, but it is very hot."

"No—It bean't none of them young worms, ma'm. He be a stranger, and he won't go away."

"Dear—dear—well, ask him what he wants, Anna Maria. Explain that this garden is private, and that he mustn't stay here."

"Please, ma'm—I be feared. I can't go nigh him again. There he is sitting as cool as cool and asked me if the cream had 'come!'"

"If the cream had 'come!'"

"Iss, ma'm. And by the same token it did 'come' this morning, quicker than usual."

Isabella saw that her maid was thoroughly "dithered"; and so she must go herself to expel the intruder. She found him in the arbour. He obviously was not one of the St. Uny fisher-lads. He was far too tall, he was not brown enough, and he carried himself in a way they could never achieve. He looked gravely at Isabella as she approached, and then said:

"Welcome—I want shelter."

Isabella was struck with the odd inconsistency of his address. But something in his look, combined with his extremely matter-of-fact air, prevented her from asking him even the simplest questions.

"Certainly," she replied. "Come with me." And she led him straight into the house.

*　　*　　*　　*　　*　　*

Anna Maria insists that as he entered, the stranger made a mark on the door-post, and stooped and made another on the inside of the top step: and thus with a grave, comprehensive gesture he seemed to bless the whole of the house. But Isabella noticed nothing. She took the stranger up to her big room—and motioned him to sit down. Then her more ordinary self returned, and she asked:

"Who are you?"

"I am Robin," replied the guest. "Who are you?"

183

The point of the question—the retort—dazed Isabella for a moment. Then she was suddenly struck with the humorous side of the affair. To have a naked stranger sitting in your drawing room calmly asking who his hostess was!—the idea overcame her, and she burst into hopeless laughter. For a minute, as she watched him through her tears, she was afraid the stranger would be offended; but only for a minute. He looked at her gravely, then his eyes twinkled, and he joined her laughter unrestrainedly and gladly. Still, as she explained afterwards, he wasn't quite a "man." When he stopped laughing, he stopped altogether, suddenly; and said abruptly:

"That was good. Why are you covered in so many places?"

"Why am I——?"

"You—you have your own face, your own hands, your own ankles" (Isabella had a pleasant habit of not wearing stockings)—"Why do you not have your own body? It must be more beautiful than those"—and he pointed accusingly at her black dress.

"Well—you see it is not the custom. And—" she hurried on, thinking this was an admirable moment to explain—"you see, you startled my maid rather——"

"Your maid—you mean the woman who fluttered at me?"

"Yes. I daresay she might. You know—of course I don't know where you came from—but one must wear some clothes here, unless one is bathing."

"Who makes you?"

"Oh! I don't know that anyone makes us—but everybody does—you know. In winter it is cold."

"This is not winter," the stranger remarked rather severely: "and it is hot."

"Yes—it is—isn't it?"

Isabella felt things were getting rather hopeless; and she didn't know whether her surprise or relief was greater when Robin stood up and said:

"Well—then I must have things to cover me: for I shall stay here. I like you."

*   *   *   *   *   *

"I'm afraid," Isabella said, in telling me this first part of her story—"I'm afraid you'll think I was stupid: but I really couldn't say anything but 'Will you, that will be very delightful. Then I'll go and see Father Kelly about some things for you. Will you be all right here?' "

"I will sleep," answered Robin. "I have never slept under such a short sky." And he looked uneasily at the ceiling. "I suppose it will not fall." And he just went to the couch, my dear—gave me a beautiful smile, and was asleep before I left the room."

III

If Father Kelly had been a different kind of priest, it is possible that Isabella's adventures would have ended there. There are rectors who would have insisted upon calling in the police, or the doctor, or having Robin removed. But Kelly was Irish and Catholic, and he had that sound curiosity which prevents a man slamming the gate on the least field-path that seems to promise a way to new country. He had been rector of St. Uny for some years, and had always been very friendly with the FitzGeralds. So he listened attentively to Isabella's story, interrupting her with occasional and sensible remarks.

"He does not seem a foreigner?"

"Well, he's not Cornish, I fancy. He speaks English well enough, but occasionally he uses words in a way he shouldn't. Really, Father Kelly, he seems as if he had been lost for some time—unused to society."

"Yes—certainly his costume—by the way, where are his clothes? He can't have come to St. Uny without any?"

"That's what's so odd. I came along the beach in the hope of seeing something. One doesn't like to be suspicious—but of course he might be a poor person who had chosen this eccentric way of getting rid of his clothes. But there were no rags lying about on our beach."

"H'm: and there's certainly been no shipwreck. Besides, he didn't hint that he had been in any disaster?"

"Oh! no. He didn't hint anything. He took things in the quietest way. He didn't suggest that I should lend him anything—except clothes. Not that he really asked for those: he just said he must have some, because he was going to stay. And I shall certainly not send him away. He obviously would be very easily imposed upon, and I'm glad he happened to get to my garden." And Isabella drew up all her sixty-three inches, and tried to look her full thirty-one years old.

"Well, my dear, I must see what I can do. I'll certainly bring some clothes up now: if I may come with you."

"Please do."

Miss FitzGerald left Father Kelly to have his interview with Robin alone. She just took the rector to the door. As they entered the room, Robin woke up; she murmured Father Kelly's name and went out of the room.

Robin sat on the sofa and smiled at his visitor.

Father Kelly was a little taken aback.

"May I ask where you came from—I understand from Miss FitzGerald——"

"Miss FitzGerald?"

"Yes, Miss Isabella FitzGerald, the lady whose house you are in."

"Isa-bella—I like that. I shall call her Bella."

And he always did, to the scandal of some of Miss FitzGerald's oldest friends.

Robin then sank into a reverie, gazing at the rector's face. Kelly attacked him once more. "I don't think you told us how you got here———"

"Got here? I am here. I am always here."

"You mean you are a native of St. Uny."

"Yes: I am Robin." The stranger looked suddenly wistful. "I may not say more. I thought you would know. You are a holy man. The holy men of old here—they knew. They knew that if we appear thus, we may not tell. We must be known first. I am always here—but I have never appeared before. I liked Bella—and I shall stay. Do you understand?"

"I'm not sure that I do: but I daresay we shall get to know you better. Then perhaps I may."

"You see I have crossed the line. When I am on the other side, I can tell any one who I am, as you say. I can even tell the woman who fluttered at me. But when I have crossed the line, I must not tell."

"Who stops you?"

"It is the law. You must not take the things of one life and use them in living another. Now I wish to try this life of yours. I have been on the other side for so long. But I may always tell my name. I am Robin."

No doubt it was a little stupid of Kelly not to guess who the stranger was claiming to be. It seems stupid to me now. But there was nothing about him to suggest that he was not an ordinary man, except his extreme self-possession, his simplicity, and his odd manner of talking.

As Kelly saw him, he was a tall, slim boyish-looking figure. His legs were long, especially from the knee to the ankle. His skin was a golden colour with the faintest touch of red in it. His hair was dark—Isabella always insists it was blue-plum coloured; his eyes were dark blue, and he had strong, capable looking hands. His features were not regular—but extremely winning and affectionate. His mouth was beautiful in movement, but a thought stern while he was silent. Both Father Kelly and Miss FitzGerald insist that his body had a curious radiance about it—as it if were insulated in some incandescent mist.

Acting on impulse, at the end of Robin's last speech, the rector stepped to him, and shook him by his hand. To his great surprise, Robin, after pressing his hand, bent over him and gave him, with grave courtesy, the ceremonial kiss of peace, as it is given at High Mass.

"That is right, is it not? I have seen that. Now let me be covered."

The rector had brought in a suit case some old clothes of his own. There were flannels and some Norfolk jackets; many old ties, and a suitable selection of vests and shirts and socks. Robin, once he had begun, took a great deal of pleasure in trying the things on and looking at himself in the glass. He was best pleased with a suit of tussore silk—and as he stood gravely surveying himself, he turned to Kelly and said:

"This throws up the uncovered places, doesn't it? I suppose that is why you do it."

And I regret to say that instead of pleading modesty, or even climate, Kelly hastily assented to this theory of the origin of clothes.

In his brown suit, Robin looked a youth of twenty or so. There was no sign of hair on his face; and Kelly, wondering at not having done it before, asked him:

"How old are you, Robin?"

Robin put his hand on his shoulder and pointed out of the

window. The window looked over the bay towards Godrevy and St. Agnes Head.

Robin waved his hand at the distant view.

"I am so old," he said.

IV

So began Isabella's life with Robin. From the first her attitude towards him was protective and sisterly. She had almost ceased to wonder who he was, where he had come from or by what accident one so gifted had such curious mental lapses. It was very soon apparent that he was quite unused to practising the ordinary habits of civilised life: but he seemed very familiar with those habits. He knew for instance immediately what everything on a table was for—from a soup-spoon to a finger-glass—but he showed a singular lack of practice in their use. Then he had heard of little domestic customs which are usually only persisted in by the women of a house. He offered to top-dust one morning, and did it, most effectively, by opening the window and blowing all the dust out. The first morning at breakfast after Bella had given Bismarck his morning's milk, Robin picked up the saucer——

"Oh! Robin, I always——"

"You wash this three times. Anything the animals touch. That is right. We do that too. It is more reverent."

He not only displayed a great interest in Bella's painting, but no little skill of his own; and soon they both started regularly to work of a morning. He was frankly puzzled with money and its uses. He knew you gave it away—but he didn't understand that you gave your butcher half a sovereign, and your milkman two half-crowns, and your beggar twopence. So on the morning that Robin was helping Anna Maria in the kitchen, and the beggar happened to come before the tradespeople, Peter Penberthy went on his road to Bodmin with great speed and joyfulness spreading the news of the "noo loonatic at old FitzGerald's cottage." But Robin never repeated his mistakes. Bella insisted that he never repeated any mistake; and he certainly was very quick at picking things up, and entirely free from that self conceit which does not permit a man to ask questions.

Of course St. Uny was very puzzled about him. How had he come? Who was he? What connection of Miss FitzGerald? Was he quite—well, quite normal, dear Father Kelly? Wasn't it a little odd that he should live in the house with their old friend—quite alone? Kelly grunted out that his idea of loneliness did not include Anna Maria, Deaf Ellen the cook, and Tom Trenoweth the gardener. "Still, there is no one of her own class," murmured Mrs. Billson— "no discreet friend." She didn't say "chaperon," because it was an understood thing that the artistic society of St. Uny did without chaperons: but it was chaperon Mrs. Billson meant. She had never been quite happy over the fact that both the FitzGeralds painted naked boys. Billson painted nothing but seascapes—"and they," his wife insinuated to the rare summer visitor—"are always so pure, don't you think?"

Not even Mrs. Billson, however, thought anything really scandalous of Robin's presence at The Cottage. The majority of Miss FitzGerald's friends thought she had been taken in by a smart and plausible adventurer—probably a foreigner, and then bothered themselves no more about the matter. Except for an occasional startlingly naive remark, Robin was extremely "possible" in society; and St. Uny was glad of a new young man, who was not quite as other young men. He was, it is true, very athletic. He could out-run and out-jump any of the youths in the town; and his swimming was declared by Commander Atkinson to be the best he had ever seen. Anna Maria believed he was a merman: but, at the request of her mistress, she kept the strange story of Robin's arrival perfectly secret, and no one else but Father Kelly knew that the stranger had simply been found in Mis FitzGerald's garden.

Isabella asked the rector whether she ought to attack Robin on the matter of religion, or whether he would. Kelly was dubious. Finally, after a good deal of meditating, he said:

"On the whole, I think not. I should wait and see what he does—see if he is used to the idea of worship. He may say something on Sunday when you are starting to Mass. After all, he is a guest: and I think I should treat him as you would any guest."

"Yes, Father—but he's such a boy—such a child somehow. I can't help feeling responsible."

"Ah! my dear, that's good of you; but it would be bad for him, if it were really so. We all ought to feel responsible; and we all ought to thank God that none of us are."

When the first Sunday came, Robin said quite naturally after breakfast:

"You go to Mass to-day, don't you?"

"Yes, Robin."

"I will come. I know my way in it."

And he went with her, and behaved quite naturally.

Dr. Pettigrew's theory was of course that the poor simpleton had lost his memory. It was before the days of dissociate personality or else he would have called in the famous Miss Beauchamp to solve the mystery of Robin.[17] It is true that Robin annoyed him rather. It

---

[17] Miss Sally Beauchamp (pseudonym) was one of the first people to be diagnosed as having multiple personalities.

was at the famous tea-party at Mrs. Billson's—the first big party which Robin attended. The elder Miss Blackstone fainted, and Dr. Pettigrew was very busy, bringing her to, and murmuring polysyllables over her prostrate body. Robin looked at him for a little time, and then said in a rather loud voce:

"She should be made to run. She has eaten too much. Then the stomach invades the heart, and she faints. It is not serious."

"Really, sir," said the doctor, with a little fat sneer, "are you a medical man?"

"I—oh! you mean have I tubes, and do I go so"—and then he gave a fair imitation of Dr. Pettigrew using a stethoscope. "No: but I know about health. You, doctor, have an enlarged liver: and your digestion is bad. Am I not right?"

"I must protest——"

But while he was protesting Robin was scurried away by Bella and Father Kelly; but the rector found it difficult to keep his countenance, as he looked at Dr. Pettigrew's rotund and disgusted figure—a figure quite forgetful of his patient, who was hastily reviving to see why she was so neglected.

The only other untoward incident at the party was Robin's remark about Mrs. Billson's figure. That lady dressed fashionably— I will not describe the fashion, for it would seem ridiculous now, but it demanded a good Parisian corset.

At her special request that dear Robin FitzGerald—a fiction of remote cousinship had got about, and Isabella didn't think it worth while to contradict it—was conducted to the seat on her right hand. He was engaged in talk about art, and life, and his sweet cousin; and he replied very courteously and adequately to all Mrs. Billson's questions. But his attention seemed elsewhere. Kelly, who was watching from a little distance, saw Mrs. Billson turn very, very red suddenly, and, with a rather indignant shrug, get up and go. The rector came up.

"Robin, what have you been saying to annoy Mrs. Billson?"

"Nothing, really, Father, nothing. She went away just as I was going to ask her. I was touching her."

"You were what?"

"I was touching her. She is so in at some places, and so out in others; and I was wondering why: so I felt. As you know, Father, from here to here"—he indicated the position on the priest's body—"she is quite hard, and from here she is soft again. I do not like the hard pieces."

"Oh! dear," thought Kelly, as he impressed on Robin that he must never "touch" any one except at their special request. "Oh! dear, how can one explain the wearing of stays to any one of Robin's simplicity."

Of course the real tragedy of the incident was that Mrs. Billson could not mention it to any one, except, in the most guarded way, to Isabella. Fortunately she had been warned by Father Kelly, and so was suitably apologetic and promised amendment for her disgraceful protégé.

There were no more incidents of this kind; for, as has been said, Robin was remarkably quick; and he obviously preferred the society of Bella and Father Kelly to that of any one else in St. Uny. And I suppose he would have settled down, as a sort of favourite nephew, if it had not been for the coming of Katie. Yet I don't know—for, as Kelly said, there is no doubt Bella got younger every day he stopped in the house, and as she got younger, she got even more charming.

Katie Wallace arrived in September. She called Bella FitzGerald aunt: really her mother was sister to Terence FitzGerald's wife. Anyhow it would have been impossible to believe there was any blood relationship between the two.

Katie's fair complexion, soft, feminine ways, exact little mind and hard little will were all as unlike a FitzGerald as could be. Yet she was fond of her aunt, I feel sure. Like so many ultra-feminine women, she was very modern. I write of the days before the "Suffragette" movement; but Katie would have been in the van of it.[18] She was keen for women's rights, keen on political emancipation, took a broad view of social problems, held theories on child nurture and education, was a rigid agnostic, twenty-two years old, and extremely pretty.

Father Kelly said, "The chief difference between Bella and that little cat of a niece of hers, is that Miss Wallace talks about women's right—while Bella takes them—just as Jane, with all her stiffness, did before her."

Katie came to St. Uny rather suddenly. In fact a telegram arrived at ten-thirty, "Can you have me arrive 6.10," and by the 6.10 she arrived.

Her two brothers, with whom she lived, had suddenly developed scarlet fever. "So I packed them off to hospital, Auntie, and thought I'd come to you. I'm thoroughly disinfected. Are you glad to see me?"

"Certainly, my dear," said Miss FitzGerald, "you know I'm always glad to have you here. By the way, I must introduce you to my friend. Mr. Robin FitzGerald—my niece Miss Wallace."

So in the little room on the ground floor Robin and Katie met.

Robin, as Isabella had noticed, was always susceptible to feminine beauty of the flowerlike kind. It was, as he explained afterwards, because in his world appearances were not deceitful. "If a thing looks soft, it is soft. The appearance of beauty means the presence of beauty. I didn't understand. After all, I was right about you Bella."

---

[18] In the van (as in vanguard): leading the change.

And Robin fell immediately, if at first unconsciously, in love with Katie.

Even Kelly admits that the young woman had a charm of manner—with young men—he would add. And she was of course immensely intrigued about Robin. Bella evaded her questions with considerable adroitness; for Katie was no fool, and even apart from Robin's occasional solecisms and the general unusualness of his manner, must have perceived he was no ordinary guest. What he thought about her, it is difficult to say. None of us had then guessed the extent of his simplicity. It is not easy even now to realise that his mind was actually simpler than his manner. He did not comprehend how things could pretend to be other than they were. He had no perception of the uses of deceit; he had no idea of the convenience of the lie, he had never himself spoken or done anything false, and he had not conceived the possibility of even unintentional misrepresentation. Afterwards Kelly got some idea of the thing into his head by pointing out that he himself, by his very simplicity, had beguiled some people—Katie among them; but then, Robin fairly retorted, it was not his fault, they should have believed him.

So it never occurred to him to take Katie at anything but her face value. When she said "she'd love a thing," he took it at that. A great deal of conversation—for she plagued him about rights and wrongs—must have passed over his head; but this would not distress him much, because he had the same difficulty with everyone except Bella and Father Kelly. Their first serious difference arose on the Sunday after Katie's arrival. She had got on very good terms with him by then, and called out about ten-thirty:

"Robin, come along and let us talk about evolution while Aunt Bella is at her superstitions."

"But, Katie, I must go to Mass."

Katie turned indignantly on him.

"You don't mean to say you share Aunt Bella's absurd creed. I did think you would be a freethinker."

Robin even then had not got accustomed to our slang use of plain words, so he answered plumply enough.

"But of course I am a freethinker. How is it that thought can be anything but free? No one can imprison your thoughts."

"Oh! I mean an agnostic."

"Agnostic? I do not know what that means."

"No? It means—oh! well, you don't really mean to say you believe in God?"

"Katie"—the boy seemed really shocked—"of course I do. I know God."

His seriousness prevented a flippant reply. And as Katie paused he went on:

"So do you. Else Whom do you thank for this?" and he fingered a tress of her honey-coloured hair, smiling the while.

"Robin, I can't scold you now, you're too much of a dear. Go to your church, and we'll fight it out afterwards."

I don't think they ever did have it out. Katie could have argued with a theologian; but she had no weapons against devotion. Nor indeed has anyone, except the Devil.

Whether she was even in love with Robin I'm not sure. Kelly insists that she was, as far as she could be, in love with her idea of him. She thought him something of the Renascence. His love of form, of colour, of sunlight and naturalness, all struck her as splendidly pagan. She was one of those difficult young women who are thrillingly aware, in a most æsthetic way, of the body. She could not help being rebellious in her love of it. She thought it was a

Protest against Something when she admired the boys bathing from the beach below; and she rejoiced in the absence of bathing-dresses not because it delighted the artist in her but because it shocked the Puritan. So she took Robin in hand and flattered him not a little. He liked it, and he thought it was all far more personal than it was, at any rate at the beginning. The two soon became inseparable; and Mrs. Billson only just escaped congratulating Isabella on the understanding between the two young friends.

Isabella was frankly miserable. She had not suspected herself of being so fond of Robin; and she had not realised she could be jealous, angrily jealous of her niece. Yet afterwards she was glad of the affair between Robin and Katie; for, had it not been for that, she might never have discovered who Robin was.

She saw practically nothing of him except of an evening; and then as often as not, he and Katie would sit chattering about her interests, and any efforts she made to intervene were greeted patronisingly by Katie and courteously but absent-mindedly by Robin. So Bella took to playing Patience and watching Robin. She had never given up wondering about him, whether he was English or foreign; whether he was really slightly deficient, or whether he had had some shock, some breakdown and lost his memory. As she watched him during that fortnight she became more and more struck with the fact that most of his habits seemed familiar. This was the more curious, because she and Father Kelly had agreed that they had never known anyone with so distinctive a personality. His every action was personal, was peculiarly his own; yet she seemed to recognise them. The way he did things—put coal on the fire, fetched the letters, made their coffee of an evening—all awoke in her a fantastic sense of something remembered. She would sit of an evening and muse about him, comparing him to her brother, to some remote cousins, to casual acquaintances; but she never succeeded in recollecting anyone like him; and yet she never lost her sense that once she had met the exact image of him.

The awakening came one morning. She was awake rather early—and she heard a voice downstairs. It was not yet six—and she knew Anna Maria rarely got down before half-past. So she slipped on her dressing-gown and came out with the idea of calling Trenoweth. Then she thought she wouldn't, and went softly downstairs herself. The kitchen door was open, and beyond that the scullery. In the scullery was Robin, busily washing up plates and whistling: with no idea of spying, Bella stood and watched him. He had just finished the job. He was at the glasses, and his young face was bent seriously over them in the glow of the lamp. Bella admired the firm lines of his neck, and the curl of plum coloured hair at the nape—feeling a little ashamed at having caught him unaware. He finished his polishing—emptied out the water, and put the pan neatly below the sink. Then he turned and walked into the kitchen. He looked round, and picked off the dresser the large blue pitcher. Bella, as he took it, thought "Anna Maria had no business to leave the milk-pitcher there. It is one of her old country superstitions." As the word flashed into her mind, Robin was lifting the pitcher to his lips. Suddenly it came to Bella.

"You're Robin Goodfellow," she cried.

And they stood looking at each other—she feeling vaguely uneasy and frightened, he looking frankly pleased and happy.

V

Robin wanted to have it out then. But for once Isabella lost her head, and didn't feel equal to explanations. So she went back to her room, with her brain in a whirl, and her mind divided between the odd irrational certainty that Robin was a—fairy, a myth, and her intellectual prejudice that he could not be anything of the kind. Yet there he was, He was extraordinarily unlike a human being in precisely the ways in which the fairies traditionally did differ: but he was far kinder, and pleasanter and "gooder" than the book fairies. It was a very worried and childish-feeling Isabella who fell into a disturbed sleep, and came down to a late breakfast at nine o'clock. Robin was the same as ever, except that he had a cunning twinkle in his eyes, and surprised Katie by telling her that he'd join her on the beach later on; but that he wanted a chat with Aunt Bella first.

As he put it, it sounded simple enough. There they were, the community of elves and fairies, real enough, generally invisible, immortal, occupied much as poets have represented them to be. "Of course we are not so fussy, not so malicious as some men have made us. But, I suppose, that mistake comes from the odd human pretending. Observers have not been able to believe what they have been told."

"But Robin, I don't understand how you got here———"

"I just *was*. Any of us have the right to enter human life once; then if we stay we become human. But if we like we can return to our old state. Of course, if we become human, we miss something— and we gain a great deal."

Then Robin signed, and seemed rather impatient.

Bella perceived this, and said gently,

"Well, Robin, go to Katie now: I'm afraid I'm rather slow and stupid; but if I have time to think it over, I daresay I shall grasp it."

Robin smiled, and turned to go.

A hasty exclamation from Isabella made him pause.

"Robin, may you tell—now?"

"No—you may; but I must never tell those who do not see.

I knew you would see. And I hope Katie will soon."

When he had gone Isabella went and told Father Kelly. He did not seem so astonished as she had expected; and his readiness to credit what at first struck her as fabulous made Bella slowly realise that Robin's story might be true.

No doubt he would have convinced her more, had not his mind really been with Katie while he was talking to her. Under the arguments of the rector Isabella was prepared to weigh the possibilities of the existence of other beings than human, and to admit that, if there were such beings as fairies, Robin might well be one. Also she and Father Kelly were agreed that Katie must be told. As it happened, however, Robin arranged otherwise.

It was for a short time a matter of surprise to Isabella that Robin went as far as he did with Katie without taking steps to let her know what he was. It seemed unlike his usual easy candour. But as he said to Kelly, "Why should I have delayed? I am what I am: and a name here or there makes no difference to me. Your name for a thing should spring out of your feeling for it; not your feeling out of the name. Am I not right? Besides, I had decided then to accept mortality and humanity. Indeed, I believe, in a way, I had already done so. I felt a change."

Certainly Katie suspected nothing; and when she and Robin returned at dinner time, she seemed more human in her attitude to his affection than she had ever been. Robin was at his gayest, playfully admitting the existence of a confidence between himself and Bella, and evidently prepared to tease Katie about it.

Isabella felt that she could not say anything; and anyhow she thought she would rather Father Kelly was present when she told Katie. It seemed too absurd calmly to announce to a girl of her temperament that she was encouraging the attention of an elf. So they all went to bed that night, each expecting some change the next day.

When Isabella first heard the shriek it was just on midnight. There was no mistaking the scream for any one but Katie's; and Isabella rushed straight to her niece's room. In the hush which her appearance caused, she could hear plainly the church clock at St. Uny strike the hour.

There, by the light of two candles, she saw Katie sitting up in bed, angry, flushed and evidently alarmed; and at the foot stood Robin, looking puzzled, a little petulant and terribly grieved. As Isabella entered, Katie's mouth opened for a fresh scream; but something in her aunt's look stopped her—and she sat there, slightly ludicrous, with her mouth half open. Robin said nothing, but turned and gave Bella a wan, appealing smile. For a moment—not really measurable in time—Bella, as she confessed afterwards, was in doubt. Sudden recollections of evil wrought by plausible spirits flashed to her mind; her head seemed full of strange stories of assaults by evil-minded imps; all the crazy volume of old-wives' fables burst on her—and for a moment she doubted Robin. Then she remembered his invariable kindness, his gaiety, his sweet sanity, his extraordinary honesty, and she deliberately put aside the bugbear of fancy.

She steadied herself to question Katie.

"What is the matter, Katie?"

"Matter! Your—your friend has insulted me. He broke into my room. He has been talking the most disgusting nonsense. He is either mad or drunk." The girl was still slightly hysterical; but through her hysteria showed the ignoble vulgarity, the commonness which Bella had always deplored.

Isabella turned to Robin.

"Robin, why are you here?"

Gravely Robin looked at her: his eyes met hers confidently and truly.

"I love her. I do not understand. I am here. I came to her. And Katie shrieks at me. Is it not so"—with a passionate gesture he flung the question at Bella—"is it not so with you as with us? If one loves another, does he not come to her? You call it marriage."

His simplicity baffled Bella. Then she remembered his constant plea for honesty—and she replied:

"Yes, Robin: the best of us do as you do—but we are more hindered by things than your people. Just as we are more 'covered' in ordinary life."

"Yes, Bella, yes—I understand that. But before love one uncovers, does one not? And when I would, Katie screamed."

Isabella looked at her niece, and inwardly she could not avoid smiling. Katie glowered at her.

"I suppose he's mad, Aunt Bella. I must say you take it very calmly. I don't think you've been quite straight with me. You ought to have warned me that he was not to be trusted. I hoped—in spite of some oddness—he was an English gentleman."

"I'm sorry, Katie, perhaps I have done wrong. But I only knew yesterday that Robin was not quite what he seemed. Before then I knew no more than you."

The three were silent for a moment. Robin was evidently thinking hard; he had followed the conversation painfully, and it seemed to leave him still disconsolate. Isabella spoke to him:

"Robin, why did you come to Katie in the night. People get frightened in the night, you know."

"But Bella—it was midnight, it was morning. It was our hour. Is not midnight the true time for love? And—and," his voice broke, and he looked strangely pitiful, "I was so lonely."

Then something seemed to seize Isabella, and she replied:

"If you were lonely, Robin, why did you not come to me?"

Robin looked at her—with hot, strained eyes. His hands made a pitiful, ineffective gesture; then he burst into tears, and cried in tones more ordinary than any yet heard from him:

"Oh! What a fool I was! What a fool!"

And he rushed out of the room, downstairs and out of the house.

As her door shut, Katie exclaimed to Isabella:

"Well, really—Aunt Bella——!"

VI

Isabella thought she had lost Robin for always. So she never felt sorry for having made that bold declaration. As the front-door banged, she resigned herself to a return to the ordinary hum-drum life she had previously led. Before she left Katie, that young woman had completely recovered her self-possession, and decided to leave St. Uny by the early morning train. So Isabella was sitting listlessly over the remains of a breakfast when Father Kelly and Robin (an old ulster of the rector's hiding his lack of clothes) came up the garden path.

"Robin has told me everything—yes, everything, my dear. And he's going to lie down and sleep, while I talk to you. Run away, Robin."

And Robin reluctantly vanished.

"Where's Miss Wallace?"

"She went to London by the 7.40, Father."

"Thank God for that. I hoped she would. What a plague a prudish, vain woman is."

"Still, Father, it was a difficult situation——"

"To be so honestly and passionately loved? Yes, it's unusual enough. My dear, I have not felt so humbled for years. That good—elf, fairy—whatever he is, has a far better idea of Christian marriage than nine-tenths of the good people who bind themselves in church. It seems, from what he tells me, that marriage is their one natural sacrament. Nothing, he said, with them can take the place of love. And if love comes, marriage comes."

"Then he is still in love."

"No—no—there he admits things are different. He complains that Katie said misleading things, behaved in a misleading way: and he was deceived. But he knows now where he is, and whom he loves. I baptized him before Mass this morning—" Kelly concluded abruptly.

"I'm so glad."

"Yes—and I shall get a special license from Doctors' Commons by next Tuesday, my dear."

"Father!"

"Now, Bella, don't disappoint Robin and me by behaving like Katie. He saw clearly enough where his heart was before he left your house."

Kelly and Isabella looked at each other. It was difficult for her to find words. Yet she felt she must speak.

"But—I'm not sure that had he mentioned a license, Katie would not have—" her voice failed her.

"My dear Bella, you did not wait for the promise of a license. When he heard your question———"

Isabella lifted a hand of protest.

"Well, well, my dear. Believe me, there's no doubt about it. You know you're in love with him; and he knows he's in love with you. He might never have known that, if you had not spoken. So be thankful."

Then Bella made a thoroughly feminine remark.

"But, Father, doesn't the difference in our age make it unsuitable?"

Kelly laughed. "Well, if a husband who saw the Phœnicians buying tin isn't old enough for you—you are hard to satisfy. Besides, he can choose his own age: and he has insisted on being precisely six months older than you. I've just entered it in the register."

So when Mrs. Billson came, rather early, to congratulate her dear Isabella on the understanding between Robin and Katie, she met Father Kelly on the doorstep.

He tried to stop her going in. (In St. Uny we have a pleasant habit of running in and out without bothering maid-servants to answer the doors.) But Mrs. Billson pushed past him and knocked softly at the drawing room door. There was no answer. She went in—and she came out without delivering her message.

"They were on the Chesterfield, my dear"—she told Billson afterwards—"and somehow there was something unrestrained in their attitude. They did not seem to hear me, so I slipped out again."

She found Father Kelly waiting on the doorstep.

He looked quizzingly at her blank countenance, and somewhat startled eyes:

"H'm, I told you not to go in. Still, perhaps it's as well women like you should see love for once."

THE SAMARITAN

"I AM afraid, sirs, the best room is already occupied." The landlord was ill at ease. Issachar ben Israel and Gamaliel ben Isaac were good customers; and he was afraid he was offending them. He stood there, a fat little figure, anxiety peeping from every crease in his face, and evident in each quivering of his capacious paunch. Hi interlocutors, a Priest and a Levite, stood in the shelter of the porch, themselves tanned by the hot sun that beat down upon the Jerusalem Road.

"Perhaps, sirs, the gentleman might be persuaded to share———"

"Dog," broke in Gamaliel, "think you we can sit at meat with any Samaritan spawn you admit to the inn? Why———"

"Nay, pardon, sir; my guest is a true Jew. I am not sure he is not a personage of some importance; though he has no money. He gives his name as Solomon ben Jonah. And in truth———"

But he got no further

"Dolt! Ass!" exclaimed Gamaliel, "has ben Jonah's fame never penetrated your uncircumcised ears? And you keep us here, when the Master of all the Pharisees is staying upstairs; and we might be drinking from the well of his incomparable wisdom. And how did the shadow of Solomon ben Jonah condescend to darken your inn, you miserable little Greekling?"

"He was brought here sick and wounded by one whose name I know not," answered Timaeus. "He had been set upon by robbers as he was proceeding to Jericho. And your excellency knows that you miscall me is saying 'uncircumcised'; I was a proselyte before———"

"A plague on your circumcision! When did Solomon ben Jonah—when was he brought here? And was he naked as well as wounded and sick?"

"It was about seven days ago, sir. And indeed he was naked save for a rich cloak which his friend had cast over him for a covering; and it was on his friend's mule he was riding. A fine upstanding man was his friend, and generous with his money. He paid me for two days, and promised to discharge all debts when he returned. As to the matter of my circumcision, it is not right that my servants——"

"Silence!" interposed Issachar. "We would be alone. Where would you put us?"

"There is the dining-room, or the small room——"

"No, we will go into the vineyard; and stay within earshot."

Timaeus bowed low and wabbled into the inn.

Issachar and Gamaliel slowly turned and walked towards the back of the house where, in a small arbour among the vines, they could obtain shelter from the sun and converse in private.

They were a prepossessing pair. Issachar, tall and bearded, looked, as he often flattered himself, much as Aaron his great exemplar looked, with his magnificent presence and oiled beard. His countenance had so much of regular beauty and calm gravity that the ordinary observer would not notice its complete lack of intelligence; nor take warning from the eyes set rather closely together or the stern line of the eyebrows. Gamaliel was thinner and slighter than his friend. His quick and intelligent face was clean-shaven; and the girlish petulance of his mouth was an attraction rather than a fault. His deference to Issachar was from policy rather than from respect for the other's greater years had presumed wisdom. He took the lead without allowing Issachar to suspect the truth; and was content to be regarded as an echo of his companion, so long as he was quite sure of giving the note. They were on excellent terms at present, as they had just patched up a quarrel which had separated them on a journey recently undertaken together.

"I am afraid it was he, Issachar."

"I am positive of it, Gamaliel. It remains for us to settle what to do: although he was too near death to recognise us, his servants will not forget either of us, I fear. Of course we might proceed on our journey; but that would look like running away. That pagan Timaeus is certain to babble; and his servants may arrive at any moment."

"My friend," answered Gamaliel, "I think I have a plan which might do. Suppose——"

For some minutes Gamaliel conversed rapidly with his friend, whose face gradually grew lighter as the other's plan was unfolded. When Gamaliel had finished, Issachar arose slowly and said, "Blessed be God! Thou hast a shrewd mind, Gamaliel."

Then, with a dignified gesture, he walked towards the inn door.

As he clapped his hands, Timaeus came running forwards.

"Timaeus," said Issachar, "ask his excellency Solomon ben Jonah whether he will deign to receive two miserable disciples of his learning. Issachar ben Israel and Gamaliel ben Isaac. Quick, dog!"

Timaeus fled.

After some minutes he returned, important with his message.

"If your excellencies will pardon the absence of formalities, his excellency Solomon ben Jonah will receive you immediately, and will be pleased if you will accept his hospitality and join him at dinner. There is an admirable wine that I am recommending to his excellency," he murmured in a confidential tone, "and I have perfected a method of treating olives—" and he smacked his lips.

"We will answer his excellency ourselves," said Issachar. "Show the way."

"Certainly, sirs. And, sirs, I assure you that my circumcision——"

"Will you never cease with your circumcision?" There! I am sure you are a genuine Proselyte and were paid handsomely for your conversion."

"Indeed, no! your honour," asseverated the little Greek. "A beggarly twenty denarii was all I received, though I was promised twenty before and twenty after the operation. But Timarchus, who was my witness—may he rot in Tartarus—swears that I had been paid in full, and was given five denarii for his false witness. Handsomely paid——"

"Peace," exclaimed Gamaliel. "Is this the room?" Without waiting for an answer he knocked at the door and entered, following Issachar. They both bowed low, and then walked forward into the room.

A dignified man, of about forty-five years of age, rose from a couch to greet them. He was shorter than either of his guests, but his keen, grave face and his quiet yet moving manner pronounced him immediately a man of better brain and stronger character. He advanced, and kissed each in turn on the left cheek, and then, with a gesture, requested them to be seated.

Issachar sat down, but Gamaliel remained standing, as if soliciting a favour.

"My son," said Solomon, "be seated; or hast thou any request to make of me?"

Now Gamaliel was an observant man, and also a man with a memory. He had heard fairly often of the brusqueness of Solomon, of his sardonic humour, of his hatred of circumlocution. So he had decided to tell his story as abruptly as possible.

"Rabbi!" he blurted out, "Issachar and I left thee by the roadside naked a Sabbath ago." Then, with seeming disingenuousness, he added: "But indeed we knew not it was thou."

Solomon ben Jonah smiled. He liked a good-looking youth, and Gamaliel's mingled modesty and straightforwardness pleased him.

"Even Solomon ben Jonah,' he said, "cannot proclaim his identity when he is lying stripped and unconscious in a ditch. The robbers took even my phylacteries."

The two companions permitted themselves a furtive smile at the Rabbi's humour.

"But why did you not succour the needy, as the Law enjoins?" Solomon queried.

"Rabbi! it was on the wise. Issachar ben Israel came along the road first. And he saw thee lying there; and he bade his servant look to thee and fetch thee on his beast. But his servant refused, saying there was a band of robbers in the wood hard by; and while Issachar argued with him, his slave beat the beasts and so urged them on to Jericho. And when I came up shortly after I dismounted and went up to thee; and in truth I thought thou were dead. And as I had taken the vow of the Nazarites, Rabbi, I could not defile myself with a dead body, so I went on, intending to tell the first villager I met that they might come and bury thee——"

"I thank thee, Gamaliel ben Isaac, for thy courtesy," chuckled Solomon.

At this Gamaliel stammered and blushed and made as if he would burst into tears. He had expected some such little outburst at this point.

Solomon, highly pleased at his wit, spoke, cheering him.

"Nay, nay! I meant it not. I know thou didst intend good. But—blessed be God!—I was not yet ready for burying. What then, my son?"

"Rabbi, I hurried on my way and by luck I overtook Issachar, who was even still arguing with his servant. Issachar is a better Jew than I, Rabbi; and his heart smote him that he had left a needy man wounded by the roadside. When we had greeted one another he told me he was sure thou wert not dead, and at length the twain of us persuaded—not without many blows—our servants to turn back. But when, Rabbi, we had come to the place we had left thee, thou wert no longer there. And so—and so—" here Gamaliel managed to break down rather effectively. Then, beneath his breath, he murmured: "Praise be God that the golden bowl of true wisdom is not broken!"

Solomon sat for a moment regarding Gamaliel who still stood, with downcast eyes, before him. In spite of his learning in the Law, Solomon was no great judge of character. A good manner and good looks had taken him in before and would do so again. Besides, Gamaliel was a Jew who respected his vow and praised his elders.

"My sons," he said at last, "you acted well and discreetly. My fate was in God's hands and he sent me succour in His time. Blessed be God!"

"Who was it who rescued thee, Rabbi?" asked Issachar.

"I do not know, my son. He poured wine and oil into my wounds and brought me here, and paid the landlord somewhat. To-day I expect moneys from Jerusalem and a new set of phylacteries. I have never been without them before for the last thirty years. My succourer, when he returns, must be repaid manifold. Now let us to dinner!"

As they were eating the olives prepared in Timaeus' particular fashion, there was a knock at the door, and the little landlord stood on the threshold, waiting to be noticed.

"Yes," said Solomon.

"Your excellency, the messenger has returned from Jerusalem with moneys for your excellency."

"Let him come up."

When the messenger was ushered in, Solomon took from him

a small box. Opening this, he drew out the two phylacteries. After kissing each in turn, he bound them solemnly about his forehead and his left wrist; then he took the large bag of money from the slave and dismissed him.

"I was almost beginning to feel like one of the people, or as a Samaritan,: he said, as he turned towards his guests. "But God willed it; blessed be God!"

The two younger men were now quite at their ease with the eminent Rabbi, whom they had not so long ago left stark in a ditch. They had no fear of the truth coming out; that each in turn had refused the prayers of Solomon's servants, who had been scouring the country some half-mile away from their master in search of help. Besides, as these servants had themselves run on sight from the robbers they were not in particular favour with their master, who had no reason for disbelieving Gamaliel's plausible story. Solomon was now indulging in some of the casuistical discussion for which he was so famous; and Issachar and Gamaliel listened eagerly to the minute ratiocinations of the great Pharisee. As they conversed there was another knock at the door.

"Plague on that Greek!" muttered Gamaliel.

Then the door opened, and Timaeus, in a voice shaking with excitement, exclaimed:

"Your excellency's deliverer, to pay his respects to your excellency."

Solomon rose and warmly embraced the young man who stood in the door-way. He had a short thick beard, rather like those of the Assyrian kings, a pleasant open countenance and steadfast grey eyes. He seemed rather embarrassed with the effusiveness of Solomon's welcome.

"Nay, my lord, it was nothing," he murmured. "I am more than repaid by seeing my lord so well. I trust you have quite recovered."

"Thanks to thy speedy remedies, I have. But it is only to-day I have managed to hear from Jerusalem. The servant whom I sent, directly I was conscious, for money and for phylacteries, returned but to-day." Then Solomon gazed at the new-comer curiously.

"Hast thou had an accident, my son?" he continued. "I see thou wearest no phylacteries?"

The other blushed slightly but replied with composure:

"It is not my custom, Rabbi."

"Nay, but surely it should be the custom of every good Jew——"

"Perhaps: I am a Samaritan."

A deeper silence fell over the little room. Issachar and Gamaliel gazed eagerly at Solomon, wondering how he would meet this startling disclosure. The Samaritan sat still, troubled, yet not ill at ease. He seemed rather sorry for the evident discomposure of his host. Just when he began to make some motion to speak, Solomon clapped his hands loudly, three times.

Timaeus entered, after what seemed an interminable delay.

He stood at the door, puzzled at the heavy silence that pervaded the room. Then Solomon spoke.

"Timaeus, will you show this gentleman to another room. He has made a mistake."

He looked steadily at the Samaritan, who had risen and stood with hands clenched, irresolute. His gaze wandered to Issachar and Gamaliel, who with bowed heads smirked approval of the Rabbi's verdict. Then, with a sigh, he turned and followed Timaeus out of the room.

"You were asking me, my sons, concerning defilement of the dead?" said Solomon, calm and unmoved.

"Yes, Master."

And the three continued their discussion.

NON-FICTION

ARTHUR MACHEN

The Bookman, September 1922

I

THERE are authors who are more to us than any individual book of theirs, just as there are authors who seem less than their masterpieces. "Paradise Lost" or "Areopagitica" mean something more magnificent to the mind than John Milton; but Charles Lamb is more than all his essays, and Johnson bigger than his own works or Boswell's biography. It is to the latter class that Mr. Machen belongs. Of living authors he alone, with Mr. Chesterton, furnishes the sensation that much of him, if not most of him, still remains unwritten, and will probably always remain unwritten. His last book, "The Secret Glory," which has beautiful things, does not take his admirers any further than did "The Hill of Dreams," which was published fifteen years ago; but it is, if not so good as a story, full as was the earlier book of the strange beauty which has haunted Mr. Machen all his life, and whose wonder he has endeavoured to convey to a prosaic generation. He has always written of mysteries, and ultimately all his mysteries are the same mystery, are but different forms of the one search, visions of the one unattainable Grail. You can divide his work into the mystery of beauty, the mystery of horror and the mystery of satire—and he has been perhaps most successful with the mystery of horror. The influence of Poe is plain enough in Mr. Machen's early books, "The Four Impostors" and "The Great God Pan." In some ways Poe and Dickens may be called Mr. Machen's masters. His view of the horrible is different from Poe's. He is not so oppressed by it, and in certain episodes he is more successful, to my mind, than Poe in arousing horror in the reader without plunging him into the nethermost pit of despair as Poe does. Mr. Machen believes in horror; but he believes in beauty more. Poe saw the worm at the root of the tree of life: Mr. Machen believes in the permanence of beauty, in the transience of evil, even while he knows that this is the time of the prince of this world.

"The Secret Glory" is the story of how one of the children of the other world tries to fit his life into the routine and convention of ordinary ways, and fails as is necessary. Ambrose Meyrick compromises, and though you may compromise and save your soul, you cannot bow in the House of Rimmon and be as free as the man who has never bowed. In detail "The Secret Glory" is a vehement attack on the public school system. The Celt has never taken kindly to the English public school: he values home and women too much, and is too keenly aware of how degraded the mob can become, especially a mob of youths. It is not that Mr. Machen believes that all boys are bullies or brutalised in obvious ways. The worst evil of the public school is generally proclaimed as a good—the formation of character, the destruction of eccentricity, the repression of individual conscience, the denial of choice.

Here is a boy's description of the process:

"I was a dreamy young fool. My head was stuffed with all sorts of queer fancies, and I expect that if I hadn't come to Lupton I should have turned out an absolute loafer. But I hated it badly that first year. . . . Then, quite suddenly, it all came out bright and clear. . . . One minute I was only a poor little chap that nobody cared for and who didn't matter to anybody, and the next I saw that, in a way, I was as important as the Doctor himself—I was a part of the failure or success of it all. Do you know what

I did, sir? I had a book I thought a lot of—Poems and Tales of Edgar Allan Poe. It was my poor sister's book; she had died a year before when she was only seventeen, and she had written my name in it when she was dying— she knew I was fond of reading it. It was just the sort of thing I used to like—morbid fancies and queer poems, and I was always reading it when the fellows would let me alone. But when I saw what life really was, when the meaning of it all came to me, as I said just now, I took that book and tore it to bits, and it was like tearing myself up. But I knew that writing all that stuff hadn't done that American fellow much good, and I didn't see what good I should get by reading it. I couldn't make out to myself that it would fit in with the Doctor's plans or the spirit of the school, or that I should play up at socker any better for knowing all about 'The Fall of the House of Usher' or whatever it's called."

There are many people who would read that and think it a very sound statement of a sensible point of view; for them Mr. Machen does not write. To him nothing is so important as the supernatural; and he is so possessed with the fellowship of the Catholic Church that he is deeply jealous for its dignity, and he finds in the English worship of the old school, of good form, of *esprit de corps*, the worst kind of idolatry. The hero of "The Secret Glory," Ambrose Meyrick, has the mysteries revealed to him. The more positive part of the book is not free from confusion. It is never quite made clear why Meyrick has been guilty of any profanation of the vision of the holy cup, unless it be in his speaking of the vision to his school-fellows. Nor is his love affair with the little servant girl, though it is delicately, even imaginatively handled, made explicable. Here Mr. Machen's book suffers from an inattention to individuality, to personal character. I feel as if he had been mixing the technique of lyric with the technique of the novel, and the result is incoherent and inconsistent. There is no such inconsistency in the story of "The Hill of Dreams." That too is the tale of a misunderstood youth; it too is a mixture of the mystery of satire and the mystery of wonder, but it is a far more complete book than "The Secret Glory." Lucian Taylor is a more satisfactory if more disastrous figure than Ambrose Meyrick; Lucian who "dived deeper and deeper into his books," who took "all obsolescence to be his province" and "in his disgust at the stupid usual questions, 'Will it pay?' 'What good is it?' and so forth, would only read what was uncouth and useless," this Lucian is one of the most successful strange characters of fiction. He really does excite us, as we might be excited by the presence of some one who lived a life of dreams and was haunted by presences unseen by the rest of us. He is obsessed, if not possessed; and he and he his adventures make the people of such stories as Mr. Blackwood's seem thin and their experiences mechanical. Mr. Machen has the great art of omission, of never shouting when a whisper will carry, of never elaborating when a hint will horrify.

The secret Lucian learns is that the world is a sacrament, either of things holy or things obscene; that all life is a sacrifice, and that it matters supremely, matters more than anything, in whose name the sacrifice is made and on whose altar the gift is offered. And thus is there always more hope for those who, by mockery, profane the mysterious than those who, in dullness, deny them. The man who celebrates the obscene orgies of the Black Mass does, in a terrible way, acknowledge the very validity which he is blaspheming.

220

II

In his earlier stories Mr. Machen revealed the mystery of horror. In a sense all horror appeals most strongly to youth. We get blunted as we get older, and even Poe does not thrill, except at his best, as he thrilled us in boyhood. Except Poe's stories, I know nothing so terrible as "The Three Impostors." In that book Mr. Machen not only achieves some perfectly new thrills of his own; but he was and is reading among the odd books of the Middle Ages to give to his horror a secular air of ancient awe which indescribably heightens the effect. The effect is strengthened too by the commonplace circumstance of much of the book—the scene in Chandos Street when Headley in found in the mummy case; the terrible beginning when Rose Leicester laughs herself into the story. Rose Leicester is indeed one of the most cheerful "bad women" in fiction. Her brightness, her devilish humour, her recondite mirth make the adventures of Walters even more terrible than the horrors which Mr. Machen so ingeniously contrives.

The debt to Stevenson in form is obvious; but Mr. Machen's fancy is as fertile as Stevenson's, and his fancies have an imaginative background which is lacking from "The New Arabian Nights."

There is at the moment a reaction against what its opponents call "fine writing." No one wishes to defend, except in purely artificial prose such as Beardsley's, the use of deliberately external ornament; but it is easy to say too much in denigration of an ornate style. An ornate style can be perfectly natural—Ruskin's style is as natural and normal as Swift's. Mr. Machen does not indulge in the purple episode. He can write a very muscular, sinewy narrative style when he pleases, as he shows both in "The Great God Pan" and in that excellent parable "The Terror"; but he can also enjoy writing a more elaborate descriptive prose. In his fascinating essay "Hieroglyphs" Mr. Machen claims that great literature, great art, is always distinguished by ecstasy; and he agrees with Mrs. Meynell in denying the title of great artist to Jane Austen, because of her deliberate acceptance of the commonplace, her zest to abide in the ordinary and the seen. Art is, in short, not a substitute for, but a form of, religion; and the artist who does not believe in some pattern in the heavens is no artist at all, but a very skilful craftsman. Realism in the old-fashioned sense of the word is impossible; because nothing that is, is what it seems. The whole universe is a gateway to the unseen world, and every sunrise and sunset shows the pathway of imagination and desire. Mr. Machen's own work illustrates his creed. Even in his lightest things, in such an essay as "The Bowmen," he is true to his faith, and that unfortunate satire, "Dr. Stiggins," can only be excused on the ground that Mr. Machen is in it defending, though mistakenly, what he values more than life.

ARTHUR MACHEN

THE MONEY REWARDS OF AUTHORSHIP
"Things Near and Far." By Arthur Machen. Seeker. 7s 6d.
Daily News, 22 February 1923

M R. Machen is a reluctant denizen of our world. He has a
capacity for enjoying certain things in it, and of those he
can write well and forcibly—good drink, the Strand before they
spoiled it with huge buildings, the solace of letters, the good-
fellowship of the stage, the humours and humbug and occasional
wisdom of Cabbalists, the loveliness of nature and the patience of
man. But his heart is elsewhere. He writes best when he is describing
his efforts to pass beyond the visible world, and to achieve the vision
for whose sake his royal namesake formed the noble company of
the Round Table.

This new volume of his recollections treats discursively of his
life from 1884 to 1901. During that time Mr. Machen earned a "living"
in that most unproductive of professions, the career of literature.

I have just been running through a list of my books
from 1881 to 1922, and reckoning how much money I
have made by them. The list contains eighteen titles. Of
these the "Heptameron," "Fantastic Tales," "Casanova"
represent more or less laborious translations. "Casanova"
runs to twelve sizeable volumes. Any my total receipts for
these eighteen volumes, for forty-two years of toil, amount
to the sum of six hundred and thirty-five pounds.

It must be poor consolation, though it must appeal to his ironic
humour, that collectors, especially in America, now seek and pay
large sums for his first editions! In spite of his unease in a world

given over largely to materialism, in spite of the hardships he has suffered, Mr. Machen does not write as though his life had been an unhappy one.

Unfavourable Reviews

He is very entertaining about the unfavourable reviews he receives, and quotes a gem from a notice of "The Three Impostors": "There is scarcely a place for it in the widest utilitarian view"; and even now, except for ardent eulogy from Mr. Masefield, those earlier stories have rarely got their due of praise.

Mr. Machen tells some good tales of his friends. He had a passion for exploring the wilder, more deceased suburbs of North London—adventuring to that other Baker-street, by Lloyd-square (did he know, I wonder, that there was a convent there?), and once he took a friend into "the obscurer byways of Islington."

His London was Piccadilly, the Haymarket, St. James's, and the many polite neighbourhoods where there are flats, and calls are paid and tea is taken, and literary and theatrical and artistic circles meet and gather. But this London was a great wilderness, these streets that went to the beyond and beyond, these squares which nobody that my friend could ever have known could ever inhabit; it was all too much for him. His face darkened with terror and hate, and with a poisonous glance at me he struck his gold-headed cane violently on the pavement, and stopping dead, exclaimed: "I wish to God I could see a hansom!"

Mr. Machen was not always driven to this exploration of grey streets from which he fetched such startling and terrible treasures. He had little legacies, and looked, in Touraine and Provence, for the Castles of Dore (if he saw Tarascon Castle on a moonless night he would have been satisfied), and found peace in the country. Of his birthplace, Caerleon-on-Usk, he writes with tender piety, but I do not feel that even there he was altogether at home, altogether unreluctant. Something urges him to look over the barrier, something persuades him that there is always a greater beauty on the other side. Perhaps one day he will try again to give us a picture of it.

ARTHUR MACHEN*

The Sewanee Review, July 1924

E XCEPT to a small and enthusiastic band of devotees, who missed nothing by the author of *The Great God Pan*, Mr. Arthur Machen's name and merits were little known until the publication of his famous story *The Bowmen*. It has not fallen to many authors, I imagine, to create a legend and watch its many strange metamorphoses; that was Mr. Machen's fate when he wrote the sketch which was ultimately responsible for all the stories about *The Angels of Mons*. In a way the fame he gained thus was not a benefit. With that odd lack of enterprise about authors which I am afraid is noticeable in the English, those who heard of Mr. Machen as a legend-maker never went on to discover the works of Mr. Machen the novelist, the mystic and the essayist. In the United States some years ago Mr. Machen's books began to be marked among the rare and desirable things for the collector of literature. I suspect that it is largely due to American enthusiasm that we owe the present handsome edition of Mr. Machen's works, which contains almost all he has written, and all that the lover of literature needs—for his early book *The Chronicles of Clemendy* is only pastiche, without any glitter, estimated more justly by its author than by some of his friends.

Why is it, I wonder, that English churchmen of to-day are such poor advocates of those authors who are keen church-people? Our parents helped to make the names of such authors as Miss Yonge, Miss Rossetti, Dr. Neale and Mr. Baring-Gould; our brethren of Rome

---

*The Works of Arthur Machen. Caerleon Edition. 9 Vols. London: Martin Secker.

make more than the most of such novelists as Hugh Benson and Mrs. Wilfrid Ward, and such essayists as Father Martindale and Mr. Belloc—but Mr. Machen, who has never made any secret of his devotion to British Catholicism, has been as neglected by church-people as was Mr. Chesterton. I think one reason is the obstinate strain of old-fashioned utilitarianism in the English people. They like their artists to be writers of tracts, propagandists, ecclesiastical politicians—anything but artists. They need to apply that lovely old fable of *Our Lady's Tumbler*, and to remember that the artist normally honors God, not by preaching or teaching, but by practising his art! If they would understand that, they would acclaim Mr. Machen as one of the stoutest defenders of the supernatural we have, in spite of his being no Englishman.

Mr. Machen is Welsh, and obstinately Celtic. In that surprising tale, *The Terror*, he refers casually to a solicitor—"hereditary solicitor to the Morgans of Pentwyn"—as "a new man, an *advena*, certainly; for he was partly of the Conquest, being descended on one side from Sir Payne Tuberville; but he meant to stand by the old stock." It was in some such spirit that an old Welsh herald drew up his prince's pedigree on some huge piece of vellum, and as the reader's eye glanced up the long row of 'Ap's' he noticed midway in the pedigree a careful rubric, "About this time Adam was created." It is a spirit which no doubt seems ridiculous except to other Celts; but it would be foolish to try to understand Mr. Machen's work unless one insisted on his Welsh ancestry. The Celt in him shows over and over again. His delectation—only just saved from morbidity—in the terrible; his hatred of the public-school system; his anger at all who defile or despise beauty; his passion for the country, and his extreme sensitiveness to natural loveliness; his deep religious mysticism; his occasional wild intolerance; his temptation to say not more than he means but more than he thinks—in all of these Mr. Machen is Celt; and I would advise no one to adventure on his writings who is disturbed at any deviations from the world of fact and the world of sense.

In his early fiction Mr. Machen modelled himself on Stevenson; yet I can remember nothing of Stevenson's which gave me quite such a thrill as those two books, *The Great God Pan* and *The Three Impostors*. Since Mr. Machen's alarming reconstruction of panic, many literary tables have been trodden by the goat-foot; and we have become tired of him. But I still am moved by that evocation of Mr. Machen's—I suppose the chief reason for his power, even in work comparatively immature, is that he writes from a deep spiritual conviction. The conviction among artists that evil is persistent and powerful was rare in the early nineties, when men treated sin as a decoration and vice as a degree. I know no artist of the period, except Aubrey Beardsley, who shared Mr. Machen's conviction of the terrible potency of sin.

In his two volumes of autobiography he had told us much of the origin of his books; but I am not sure that he himself knows how consummately he coveys, especially in *The Hill of Dreams*, and in part of *The Secret Glory* and in *The Terror*, a continuous sense of the reality of those other worlds which surround, protect, threaten, and at times invade the world of fact and appearance. I do not know that I could say that any of Mr. Machen's novels or stories is perfect as a work of art. *The Terror* comes near to being so, but I find the end hurried, and the explanation is too scamped in style. In the longer books Mr. Machen's temptation is a kind of digressive journalism. He is a Welshman and loves an argument; and sometimes his sentences take on the appearance of some old enemy, and he smites hard and irrelevantly. It is good fun, and in the pages of

The Secret Glory where he satirizes the head-master, more than good fun, but it upsets the order of the story, and ruins the reader's mood of acceptance. I have the feeling that sometimes Mr. Machen is himself frightened at what he has evoked, and seeks refuge; but you can divert from great horror only by great laughter, and Mr. Machen, although he is a good appreciator, has no gift for high comedy. He can smile, whether lightly or bitterly, but he cannot burst into the vehement guffaws of the sons of Aristophanes.

Yet in what is, perhaps, his best book, *Hieroglyphics*, Mr. Machen shows his great understanding of those same laughter-giving children. Hieroglyphics is an essay on the meaning of literature, an effort to give a rule by which the fine literature of the world can be distinguished from "a product (possibly a very interesting one) which is not fine literature." Such efforts are notoriously dangerous; but I doubt if any critic has made a better rule than Mr. Machen, for his fine literature, real literature, is that in which ecstasy is present. I differ from him often in his application of the test. I agree heartily that ecstasy is present in the *Odyssey*, *Pickwick Papers* and in *Pantagruel* and *Gargantua*; but I can find it, too, in *Vanity Fair*, just as clearly as *Don Quixote*, and I do not think the author of *La Tentation de St. Antoine* kept ecstasy out of *Madame Bovary*.

The important thing in *Hieroglyphics* is not, however, Mr. Machen's application of his rule to particular books and authors; but his noble and glowing defence of that element in art which always distinguishes the real thing from the sham, art from artifice. His theory has been adopted, or very likely rediscovered, by that school of critics who insist that great art is appreciated, is apprehended immediately; there is an act of faith towards art, as towards religion, and an art which does not, in some way, reach the eternal, is little better than *décor*, a background, lovely and delicate no doubt, but irrelevant as a dinner-engagement on the Day of Judgment. There are splendid things in *Hieroglyphics*: the beautiful analysis of *Don Quixote*, the great defence of *Pickwick Papers*, the noble praise of *Huckleberry Finn*; as an example of his method I will quote the defence of Catholicism:—

> Think of it, and you will see from the literary standpoint, Catholic dogma is merely the witness, under a special symbolism, of the enduring facts of human nature and the universe; it is merely the voice which tells us distinctly that man is *not* the creature of the drawing-room and the Stock Exchange, but a lonely, aweful soul, confronted by the Source of all Souls, and you will realize that to make literature it is necessary to be, at all events subconsciously Catholic.

It is not strange, perhaps, than an author who believes that, and for whom that belief has governed his work, should not be extremely popular; but I think it is time that those who agree with him, those who are attached to the modern movement towards Catholicism, should cease to neglect an author who has shared at least one fate of the mighty; many have found Arthur Machen, as many, according to Fuseli, found William Blake, "d—— good to steal from."

R. ELLIS ROBERTS

The Edge, Stroud, England.

STRANGE HAPPENINGS
TO ORDINARY PEOPLE

"The Green Round." By Arthur Machen. Benn. 3s 6d.
Daily News, 13 July 1933

O DD novels, to be successful, must be about ordinary people. There is a place for fairy-stories; but the essence of a fairy-story is that the surprising things which happen in it seem natural and right. In an odd novel the surprising things which happen must seem strange even to the point of ecstasy. You cannot convey any real shock by a story in which not only the incidents but all the people are odd.

Mr. Wells's understanding of that rule was the source of his splendid success in such tales as "The Invisible Man" and "The Food of the Gods."

The stupendous effect of certain scenes in those and other stories of his was produced by the contrast between the ordinary people and the extraordinary things which happen to them. The same rule has always governed Mr. Machen's enthralling expeditions into strangeness; only while Mr. Wells's extravagances have generally been scientific, Mr. Machen allows the supernatural or the non-human to break into the world of every day.

Mischievous Imps

In his new book, "The Green Round" (where in one or two places Arthur Machen the essayist comments on the material of Arthur Machen the novelist), the fairies are at work—the Little People. The powers of "The Green Round" are not the kind people. They belong to that order of spirits of which the poltergeist is the best known, that mischievous imp which suddenly starts on a career of violent furniture removing.

Mr. Hillyer, the story's hero, a quiet student of fairy and folklore, is found, unknown to himself, to be accompanied by An Other. This Other is unpleasant to look at, dangerous in habits and violent in morals. Indeed, a nasty fellow. Hillyer's subsequent misadventures and bewilderments (for he cannot understand the unpopularity he incurs among those who suffer from his companion's misdeeds) are told in that fine, straightforward prose of which Mr. Machen is a past-master.

The story slackens rather towards the end and is not properly resolved; but who will grumble when Mr. Machen gives us so much of his best? The story is a fine mixture of the familiar and the strange; and there is all the old excitement in the disasters to Mrs. Jolly's furniture, and the odd behaviour of the old men on the bench—all the old terror in the moment when Hillyer is aware of "the horrible child" who follows him about—much of the old sardonic humour in Hillyer's efforts to mix with his fellows.

Milton Keynes UK
Ingram Content Group UK Ltd.
UKHW040351070224
437337UK00011BA/322/J